Nazi Cocktail

by Sean Patrick Hazlett

Dedication

To my son Marius, for putting a smile on my face every day.

Table of Contents

Acknowledgements

I want to thank all the teachers and writers that helped me along the way, or, barring that, did not discourage me when they should have. My fifth grade teacher, Mrs. Umile, was instrumental in encouraging me to write my first fantasy stories. I want to thank internationally best-selling novelist David Vann for having patience with my early writing as a Stanford undergraduate. He never discouraged me and always provided productive critiques that helped me improve my work. The late Jeff Carlson inspired me to write fiction after sharing his wisdom and experience. He also graciously took the time to critique one of my first stories, pointing out all my rookie mistakes. I'm also thankful that *Writers of the Future* editor, David Wolverton, discovered and recognized my work. Mike Resnick has also been instrumental in supporting my early writing career by encouraging me and buying my stories. I also want to thank award-winning author and editor, Nick Mamatas, for his unvarnished and relentless critiques of my stories in one of his fiction writing classes. Most people hold back their criticism, but Nick never sugarcoated his feedback. Because of it, he made me a better writer. I doubt I will ever reach Nick's bar for excellence, but he definitely set a high standard. Lastly, I would like to thank my ever-patient wife, Claire, for sacrificing her weekends to edit my stories.

Introduction

I have always been fascinated by the titanic struggle between Germany and the Soviet Union during the Second World War. Surprisingly, most Americans have no idea how critical the Russo-German conflict was in determining that war's ultimate outcome.

This novel takes place following the Battle of Kursk, the largest tank battle in human history. While the more familiar Battle of Stalingrad was a key turning point in the war, it was the Battle of Kursk in July 1943 that finally broke the back of the German war machine.

I first became intrigued with the Russo-German conflict when I was a Stanford undergraduate, where I focused on modern European history. The scale of that struggle dwarfed the size of military operations on the Western front by orders of magnitude. It involved a clash between two regimes that had each engaged in genocidal campaigns against both their own people and their subjugated populations. Both governments pressed good people into service, forcing these individuals into situations where there were few or no good choices. It is in such murky conditions where the ingredients for great stories lie.

When I was a second lieutenant at the Armor Officer Basic Course at Fort Knox, Kentucky, I conducted an in-depth battlefield analysis of the Battle of Kursk. During that exercise, I learned some fascinating facts about the battle. For instance, navigation was difficult at Kursk since the region's high iron deposits generated magnetic fields that rendered compasses unreliable. I also discovered that the Germans favored the distribution of "wonder drugs" like Pervitin to enhance human performance in tough conditions, particularly on the Eastern Front where the Soviets heavily outnumbered the Germans.

I find these small details make a battle seem much more tangible, breathing life into the narrative. Moreover, when a government is willing to distribute methamphetamine to its soldiers to gain an edge, the stakes tend to be existential – and in the Second World War, they were.

Given the willingness of both sides to use any means necessary to win the war, it wasn't hard to imagine what the Soviets might do if they had the opportunity to make a deal with an advanced extraterrestrial civilization. Trading Soviet and German war dead and German POWs to extraterrestrials in exchange for a technological edge would likely have been a small price to pay in Stalin's calculus. Envisioning how such a trade might play out and exploring how it could easily spiral out of control fascinated me. In fact, the premise intrigued me so much that I wrote this novel—my first—based on a short story I penned in late 2013. I finished writing the novel some time in 2015, and it has lingered on my hard drive ever since… until now.

Besides the historical backdrop, this story is a classic case of opposites attracting. Adding to the tension is the fact that Ivanova and Strauss represent two nations that are bitter enemies, which, incidentally, inspired the title of the original short story, "Enemy Allies". Strauss is an introverted and highly competent soldier just trying to survive, while Anna is an extroverted and politically savvy leader in a male-dominated world. They both rightly conclude that the real threat is non-human, and risk their lives and allegiances to confront that challenge.

A shorter version of this story was first published in Episode Three of *Fictionvale Magazine*. An earlier and longer version of this story won an

Honorable Mention in the prestigious Writers of the Future Contest's fourth quarter of 2012.

Lastly, this novel draws from my experience as a cavalry officer and my scholarship on the Second World War's Soviet-German conflict.

I really hope you enjoy it.

Prologue

Tunguska

2230 Hours, 11 November 1927, Moscow, Russia

It wasn't every day that a man had to audition for his life. Stalin did not suffer fools, but it was how Stalin dealt with them that terrified Dr. Leonid Kulik. But a jolt of pain in Kulik's chest reminded him of far greater terrors and harsher masters.

Kulik had rehearsed his speech for hours as his train had barreled along the Trans-Siberian Railway. He'd labored to get every word right. But no matter how much he'd practiced, he couldn't imagine any sane person believing his story, let alone the General Secretary of the Central Committee of the Communist Party.

Shivering in his black woolen greatcoat and sheepskin *papaha*, a bespectacled Kulik huddled before Lenin's wooden mausoleum beneath the crenelated Kremlin Wall. A chill, howling wind whirled thick snowflakes around him while he waited in the dark for his tardy host.

Yuri Golikov approached Red Square from the Senatskaya Gate. His footsteps crunched on the icy snow. His unkempt greatcoat rippled in the cold gale. Golikov's off-kilter *ushanka*, ruddy cheeks and vodka-laced breath gave Kulik a good idea why the lanky Party official was late. Kulik rolled his eyes in silent protest.

Chiding Golikov for his unprofessionalism would be unwise. Kulik suspected the man was an OGPU agent. One could never be sure these days.

One wrong word or ill-considered phrase earned many a bullet in the head and a shallow, unmarked grave.

An unsteady Golikov guided Kulik past the Kremlin Necropolis and through the Senatskaya Tower Gate. From there, he directed Kulik toward the domed Senate Palace's private entrance. Once inside, Golikov ushered Kulik to the Catherine Hall rotunda.

A foul smelling cloud of mundungus hit Kulik's nostrils. He coughed and then entered the chamber. Tobacco smoke stinging his eyes, Kulik struggled to take in the dome-shaped hall's grandeur. Marble colonnades lined the chamber's edge at equal intervals. Between the columns, windows on the dome's far side offered a stunning view of the Senate Palace's inner courtyard. Sculptured bas-reliefs adorned the wall's remaining surfaces. A ring-shaped, polished marble conference table dominated the room's center. At the far end of the rotunda, Stalin puffed on a black iron pipe. He sat pouring over a swollen stack of documents, holding court over his cabal of senior Party and military officials.

Golikov nudged Kulik, rousing the mineralogist out of a scared stupor. Seeing Stalin in person felt so surreal that Kulik had lost his tongue. Stalin's pockmarked skin surprised Kulik, especially in contrast to the man's unblemished images on Soviet propaganda posters.

Stalin glanced up and raised an eyebrow. He removed his pipe. His stern gaze regarded Kulik as if he were gauging the man's worth. Or maybe Stalin was deciding whether to crush an insect. Kulik couldn't tell. But if Stalin only knew what Kulik was, the dictator would destroy him.

Stalin glowered at Golikov.

"Comrade Stalin, this is Dr. Leonid Kulik, chief curator of the Leningrad Museum's meteorite collection," Golikov said, his voice quavering.

Kulik shuddered every time he'd heard his city's new name. He worried he'd infuriate Stalin by slipping and calling the city Petrograd. One had to be vigilant in Soviet Russia. It's been said that OGPU jackals like Vyacheslav Menzhinsky and Artur Artuzov created fictitious "resistance movements" to ensnare their political enemies. Here, in the heart of the Soviet police apparatus, Kulik was acutely aware of his own paranoia. But that paranoia was also a Russian's most vital survival instinct.

Stalin's rheumy eyes shifted from Golikov to Kulik. Kulik pushed his circular bifocals against the bridge of his nose, cleared his voice, and then spoke. "Comrade Stalin, it's an honor to meet you. Thank you for taking time out of your busy schedule to…"

Stalin held up his hand. "Too many words. Why are you here?"

Kulik nearly swallowed his tongue. Adrenaline flooded his system. "Comrade Stalin, I'm here to report the findings of my Tunguska expedition."

Stalin nodded. "Ah, yes. Now I remember. This is the Soviet Academy of Sciences-funded study, no?"

"It is."

"So where's my iron?"

"Excuse me, Comrade Stalin?" Kulik scratched his beard to avoid shaking.

Stalin's eyes widened. He raised his voice. "Iron. From the meteorite."

Now Kulik remembered. Stalin wasn't interested in scientific curiosities; only things that furthered the Revolution. "Unfortunately, we found no iron. But I think my discovery has far greater value for the Soviet people."

Stalin glared at Kulik and crossed his arms over his chest. "Who are you to tell me what holds more significance for the Soviet Union?" he said in an irritated tone.

"My apologies, Comrade Stalin," Kulik stammered. "What I meant to say is that once you hear more about what I found, you'll want to learn more."

Kulik's heart raced. Another adrenaline surge. This wasn't going well. Everything he'd so painstakingly rehearsed had come out all jumbled.

"What can be more important than organizing the proletariat against the capitalist forces gathering on our borders? What can be more ennobling than destroying the very powers that seek to extinguish the smoldering embers of class-consciousness? We are fifty to a hundred years behind the advanced nations. If we don't industrialize within a decade, they'll crush us. To industrialize, we need iron. It's one of the most critical components of our first Five-Year Plan. The aim of your expedition was to recover iron fragments from the Tunguska impact crater. I hope you're not here to report your failure."

Kulik winced. In his next breath he had to convince Stalin that the Tunguska discovery trumped salvaging iron deposits. Otherwise, it was the gulag or worse. "Comrade Stalin, within five months what I found at Tunguska could make the Soviet Union the most powerful nation on Earth."

An unnatural rush of contentment washed over Kulik. As if he'd just fallen in love. Dopamine. The answer pleased his hidden master.

Stalin thrust his pipe in his mouth and puffed. "Tell me more."

Kulik nodded. He barely suppressed a nervous sigh of relief. He took a deep breath and told Stalin his tale.

છ

Earlier this year, my survey team went into the Siberian hinterland to examine the effects of the 1908 Tunguska meteorite strike. We catalogued a swath of destruction covering thousands of *versts*. The impact's energy was so powerful, it had laid waste to over eighty million trees. Amid the destruction, I uncovered a strange artifact – one I believe is of extraterrestrial origin.

The Siberian taiga's rugged conditions forced me to abandon my 1921 expedition. But my second one this past April was more successful, though not without its own unique challenges.

The region's Tungus villagers were reluctant to discuss the 1908 event, much less lead us to the impact zone. Over the years, these superstitious and primitive people have accumulated a fair bit of lore about the site – lore that proved to have some basis in fact. For instance, the Tungus had an irrational fear of a cryptic tribe they called the Valley Men. Because of these superstitions, it was nearly impossible to hire a local guide.

The closer we got to the crater, we discovered increasing numbers of queer metallic shards composed of elements unclassifiable on Mendeleev's periodic table.

The Tungus peasants we encountered nearest the site were listless, pale, and sickly. If I'd believed in a God, I would have described them as soulless. Those some distance from the impact had reported an eerie green fog that drove men mad.

It was difficult to put much stock in these tales. Yet so many eyewitnesses reported the same phenomena that it was impossible to ignore the stories. Most believed the metallic fragments were cursed.

On the night of April thirtieth, I woke to screams. Gasping for air, my assistant, Sergey Malinovsky, rushed into my tent. "Petrukhin, Timoshenko and Shcherbakov haven't returned from the wilderness," he said. "Earlier tonight, they went to investigate odd sounds and electromagnetic phenomena. Others are reporting peculiar yelps and a faint, strobing green light."

A grim mood fell over the camp. Siberia's suffocating isolation, cold, and gloom only heightened the sense of despair.

In that part of the world even late spring is bleak. Mosquitos nipped at our skin, draining every ounce of blood from our bodies in the bog's chill damp. A cloud-covered sky blotted out the stars. For those accustomed to the warm glow of city lights, it's tough to fathom just how absolute darkness is in that forlorn and desolate place.

To calm my men, I dulled their nerves by issuing extra vodka rations. Then Malinovsky and I ventured toward the impact zone's epicenter. We took our rifles, lanterns, and two dogs to sniff out the scent of the missing men. As we closed in on the impact site, we crossed into a silent abyss where even the chirps of crickets and the hum of mosquitos were absent.

Our compass needles began spinning erratically, as if affected by a strange distortion of Earth's magnetic field.

As we descended deeper into the darkness, a ghostly trilling akin to the call of an American whippoorwill resonated in the blackness. Among the deathly silence, the eerie trills unnerved me. Nevertheless, I pressed on. After wandering several hundred meters, I stumbled onto Timoshenko's corpse. His skull had been sliced open like a tin can. His brain was missing. The cuts on his cranium were precise, almost surgical. Several meters away, I found the bodies of Petrukhin and Shcherbakov. Their skullcaps had also been removed.

"We should turn back," Malinovsky said.

But as the expedition's leader, it was my duty to push forward. So we did.

Our dogs refused to go any further. So we dragged them by their leashes. They resisted. Malinovsky's dog savaged his hand. Frustrated, I handed my dog's leash to Malinovsky.

"Head back to the laager site," I said. "If I fail to return, resume the search tomorrow morning."

He was only too happy to oblige.

As I trekked forward, the emerald light pulsated with increasing frequency. The whippoorwill-like trills and the unsettling yelping grew louder.

And I felt more alone than ever.

As I got closer to the source of that ghostly pulsing light, I unearthed much larger fragments of the strange metal. In some cases, chunks as large as human hands. The material had the texture and color of obsidian, but it was harder than tempered steel. Oddly, it also had unprecedented resilience. I could crumple it, but within seconds, it would return to its original state. As a mineralogical specialist, I've seen nothing of its kind on Earth. I gathered samples until I felt nauseated.

It was becoming harder to breathe as a thick miasma, a kind of frothy green fog, increasingly permeated the wilderness like a toxic soup. My breathing became labored. I soon started coughing up bloody phlegm.

I hiked as far as I could, but the miasma's adverse impact on my health thwarted my efforts to push any deeper into the murky morass. So I turned and made my way back toward the laager site. When I passed the place where my comrades had fallen, their bodies were missing. I assumed Malinovsky and the others had retrieved the corpses and buried them.

But I was wrong.

When I returned to the site, the men were in a frenzy. They were loading rifles, lighting lanterns, and donning their greatcoats. It was obvious they had no plan. The dogs were barking wildly, likely sensing their masters' unease.

When I tried to intercede, Malinovsky rested his hand on my shoulder and said, "The bodies are gone."

I knew there was nothing I could do to stop their ill-considered foray. But I could limit the damage. So I addressed the group, urging patience and calm. "Wait until morning," I pleaded.

My efforts failed.

When people are tired and afraid, they can be stubborn and irrational. If I couldn't convince them to wait, I could at least ensure they'd be safe. So against my better judgment, I accompanied them back toward the crater.

Twenty-one armed men ventured into the wilderness and into the blackest night I've ever known. Their lantern light flooded the darkness, scattered by the pervasive green fog.

Given my adverse reaction to the mist, I stayed a few meters behind the group. As they got closer to the site, the men ahead coughed and retched. Not long after, I felt sick again.

Exhausted and ill, I stopped to rest. The group pressed forward into the wispy miasma. The strange trilling echoed from beyond the toxic fog's swirling shroud.

A riot of commotion broke out about fifty meters ahead. A voice shouted, "Timoshenko!" A rifle shot cracked, reverberating in the night. With bloodcurdling screams, the crowd fled, stampeding pell-mell toward the laager site.

Malinovsky ran toward me. His face was twisted in a rictus of terror. He was wheezing. He grabbed my collar and pulled me close. He whispered, "The Valley Men are real and they're coming for us."

Earlier, I had discounted Tungus accounts of their ancestors rising from the earth. But every report on the Valley Men we'd examined had been consistent.

Malinovsky let go of my collar and fled. Others rushed past me. Soon, the only remaining light was from my lantern and the flickering green strobe.

The trills drew closer. Frozen from fear, I stared into the darkness. The steady crescendo of footfalls penetrated the silence. I say "steady" because they didn't sound like the shaky meandering of a man blindly fumbling in the fog. People walk in irregular patterns, especially in rugged terrain. This was different. These footsteps were as precise as a metronome.

Timoshenko emerged from the mist, his body riddled with wounds. His skullcap had been reattached to his cranium. When he saw me, he halted with military precision. His eyes stared through me. He handed me a black cube. It had a circular impression on its upper face. Paralyzed by dread, I could do nothing but accept the offering. Timoshenko headed to the impact zone, never to be seen or heard from again.

When I left Tunguska on the Trans-Siberian Railway, I placed the device in the train's brake van. An armed detail of ten decorated Red Army veterans guarded the van to ensure the device reached Leningrad.

On the third morning of my passage, I couldn't sleep. So I went to the brake van to check on the cube. I glanced at my chronometer the instant I entered the car. It was precisely 3:14 a.m. The guards stood rigidly along the center aisle in two ranks facing inward. Their eyes were transfixed on the floating obsidian cube. The artifact cast rippling green rays of light that connected each veteran's eyes like the nodes of a spider web.

The cube floated toward me. I watched, mesmerized and unsure what to do. The soldiers' eyes rolled back into their heads. The lights vanished. The cube descended to the brake van's corrugated iron floor. The men turned and faced me. Their eyes glowed a dull green. Two veterans marched forward in perfect cadence. One of them spoke. "Return. One year hence. We will be waiting." He frothed at the mouth and shook before collapsing.

The other man spoke. "Gather men of science and men of war. Bring experts on biology, physiology, and botany." Then he crumpled. And on it went, until all ten were dead. Then I blacked out.

When I awoke, I felt violated and unsettled. A notebook I had had in my possession at the time of the incident was filled with strange runes and mathematical equations I do not recall writing.

I ordered the brake van to be quarantined until the train's arrival in Leningrad. There, we ran several tests on the artifact and the shards we recovered from the impact site. Using the Townsend discharge process, we detected latent alpha decay, a clear sign of radioactivity. So we encased them in lead and sealed them in the Mineralogical Museum's vault.

৪১

After Kulik finished relating his tale, Stalin sat in silence as if weighing the options. The party officials were mute. Their dour and downcast faces betrayed an uneasiness that had become all too common in Soviet Russia. Many of them likely thought Stalin was testing their loyalty, forcing them to choose between treason on one hand and a madman who believed in extraterrestrials on the other. Given the OGPU's reputation, only a fool would bet against Stalin.

"Did you open the cube?" Stalin said.

"No. That's a decision for a head of state," Kulik replied.

Stalin chuckled. "You assumed right, Dr. Kulik. What do you intend to do with this artifact?"

"I'll keep it in Leningrad for further study," Kulik said. "I dare not bring the thing here. It's not worth the risk of endangering Moscow's citizens. Not all we found at Tunguska was a positive omen for the Soviet Union or the human race." Kulik's head throbbed with sudden pressure. He'd said too much. He fought through the pain. "There are forces in the universe far older and more advanced than our own."

Kulik let the last bit linger. He was counting on Stalin's paranoia. He needed to scare the man of steel into marshaling the state's resources to protect these secrets. If the rest of the world learned of Tunguska, there'd be chaos.

"What's this artifact's purpose?" Stalin said.

"I don't know. I think it's some kind of biological calculator. I believe it uses electromagnetic fields to control brain tissue and to transfer data like an analytical engine. I'll issue a full report once I have more time to fully examine it."

Stalin puffed on his pipe. "What did this?"

"I don't know, Comrade Stalin." Kulik lied, wanting to say more. But his fear of the thing inside him kept him silent.

Stalin nodded. "What else did the possessed guards say?"

"They provided instructions for what to bring to Tunguska in exchange for technology centuries beyond our own. Here's the list," Kulik said, placing a slip of paper on the table.

A colonel grabbed the document and handed it to Stalin. Stalin examined it. "What do you expect this future expedition to uncover?"

"I don't know," Kulik hedged, "But whatever's there, it's the most powerful thing on Earth."

Stalin raised his index finger. "One moment." The officials huddled around him. A mumbled exchange followed.

Minutes later, Stalin glared at Kulik. "Take your list to Marshal Tukhachevsky. He'll get you what you need. You'll lead a third mission to Tunguska on the appointed date and time. Until then, learn all you can about the device. Dismissed."

Kulik saluted Stalin. The mineralogist left the rotunda. A dark essence clouded his emotions.

He was no longer hopeful about the future. But a wave of exhilaration swept over him as the parasite rewarded him for his efforts in establishing a foothold on this world.

Chapter 1
Citadel

0630 Hours, 4 July 1943, Near Belgorod, Russia

Georg Strauss stood among the over one hundred soldiers and officers bearing the skull and crossbones insignia of the Third SS *Totenkopf Panzergrenadier* Division. The men formed a horseshoe around *SS-Hauptsturmführer* Krüger, commander of Ninth Company, Third SS Panzer Regiment. Strauss's pale blue eyes focused on the blonde woman's gray image in the locket he'd carried with him since his training at Chemnitz Barracks. He'd been through so much since he'd last seen Inge, and it had been over a year since he'd received one of her letters. It wasn't her fault or his; he was just always on the move in this nasty, cold war that seemed to stretch on without end.

Krüger stood before a detailed topographic map of the Kursk salient papered on the wall of a dilapidated and nearly ruined Russian farmhouse. Threshers, reapers, and a four-row tractor lay idle in a nearby wheatfield. The salient on the map marked the west-facing bulge of the German-Soviet front lines around the city of Kursk. To the right of the salient, dozens of red icons dotted the map, each one representing a Soviet Army equivalent. On the left, blue icons designated dozens of German divisions.

"Tomorrow at oh-three-thirty hours, Ninth Company will form in column in its designated assembly area. Simultaneously, Fourth Panzer Army aviation assets and division artillery will pound Soviet strong points, softening 'em up for our assault, which will commence at oh-four-hundred hours," Krüger said, his confident and booming voice overcoming the poor acoustics of the open steppe.

"Our division has the covering mission for the Second SS Panzer Corps' northern flank," Krüger said. "As our company is the division's only heavy Tiger I unit, we will spearhead the attack in an armored wedge. Scouts report multiple, concentric defensive belts ringed with mines, heavy artillery, T-34 tanks, and antitank guns. Our Tigers' superior armor and firepower will draw enemy fire whilst our sister companies breach Red Army defenses.

"The Wehrmacht's objective for Operation Citadel is to cut off upwards of two million Soviet troops, five thousand enemy tanks, and twenty-five thousand guns and mortars in the Kursk salient. As part of the Fourth Panzer Army, we will proceed north, establish a bridgehead across the Psel River, and then advance toward Prokhorovka.

"Take initiative and be aggressive. Don't fall for Ivan's treachery. If he surrenders, be vigilant. Check for grenades. Watch your backs. I will see you on the high ground." Krüger dropped his arms to his side, and kicked his heels together and shouted, "Company! Ach... tung!"

The assembled men snapped to attention.

"My honor is loyalty!" Krüger yelled.

"My honor is loyalty!" the men echoed.

"Dis... missed."

Men scrambled to their tanks, grease guns in hand. They inspected their tracks, knowing from experience that an immobile tank was a fighting coffin. They oiled their machine guns and boresighted their main cannons. They replaced broken gearboxes, fixed damaged idler arms, and fueled their tanks with gasoline. The battalion surgeon distributed Pervitin tablets in anticipation of a week's worth of continuous combat without sleep.

Strauss rubbed the scars on his left arm. He'd suffered third-degree burns in '42—wounds that had saved his life.

Those had been dark days. Fighting block-by-block in the streets and crawling through the sewers, killing Russians with his brother, Heinz. It was an experience he would never forget. Dirty work, that. Ivan would sometimes get close. So close Strauss could smell the borscht and vodka on his breath. Strauss had had to use the bayonet more than once. When you open a man's gut and his intestines spill out, it doesn't smell pretty. The "War of the Rats," the newspapers had called it, because rats were what the soldiers in the sewers had become. Strauss's injury had placed him on the last medical flight out of Stalingrad before the weather turned sour, and the Soviets had encircled the Sixth Army.

Heinz hadn't made it. Neither did anyone else from Strauss's tiny Bavarian town. Strauss was the lone survivor. The Wehrmacht didn't have an individual replacement system like the well-supplied Yanks. That was why German soldiers formed stronger bonds with one another. It was why they fought better and harder than any other military on Earth. At least that was how the High Command justified a recruitment policy that left entire towns devoid of German manhood.

Strauss felt out of place among the Waffen SS. Most had volunteered for this insanity. He felt hopelessly surrounded by stiff and fanatical Prussians who strutted about as if they actually believed the master race garbage Hitler fed them. Strauss had made it into the elite unit's ranks not because he was particularly loyal or zealous, but because he had an unusual talent for killing Ivan. His actions in the Stalingrad sewers were legendary, even more so since he was a trained *Panzergrendier*, and not an infantryman.

Only two things caught the Waffen SS's eye – impeccable loyalty or battlefield competence. Soldiers rarely possessed both. Strauss exemplified the latter.

Officers were the rare exception, displaying both tactical prowess and fanaticism. Every SS officer had to pass an intense combat course where he engaged in death-defying feats like digging foxholes in front of advancing tanks. Those who failed died.

Soldiers with time and paper often spent their final minutes before sleep writing letters home. For Strauss, it was all a farce. The SS censored most correspondence, and he hadn't received a letter from Inge in over a year, so what was the point? No one could possibly understand this hyper-Darwinian nightmare, so why bother attempting to describe it? Few soldiers would return home alive, anyway. The last thing he wanted was for Inge to waste the best years of her life waiting for him to return. She deserved better than that.

As dusk approached, dark gray, swollen rain clouds gathered on the horizon, threatening to burst. As twilight dovetailed into night, a sliver of lightning tore across the sky, illuminating the bleak landscape's hopeless infinity. The heavens opened up, inundating the expectant combatants with lukewarm summer rain as thunder roared in the distance.

Soon another kind of thunder erupted. Hundreds of Stuka dive-bombers, sirens whining, unloaded their deadly ordnance on the Soviets. Dozens of explosions rippled across the barren skyline. Minutes later, the division ground batteries opened up, blasting Soviet positions with tons of heavy artillery.

&

0830 Hours, 12 July 1943, Outside Prokhorovka, Russia

Strauss's company had suffered through over a week of hellish combat, fighting through two concentric Soviet defensive belts. Now it prepared to penetrate a third ring on the outskirts of Prokhorovka.

The advance coincided with the Luftwaffe's bombing of Soviet positions. As Strauss's unit maneuvered in a tight wedge formation, the Soviets responded to the aerial bombardment with a surprise of their own, launching the blistering fire of *Katyusha* rockets and heavy artillery.

Strauss wiped the sweat dripping from his brow and into his eyes as he surveyed the battlefield through the gunner's primary sight. He felt claustrophobic in the cramped gunner's station.

"*Unterscharführer* Meier," Strauss said to his tank commander. "We should stop and scan for enemy tanks. This ground favors the defender. Ivan's probably got something waiting for us ahead. We could be stumbling into an ambush."

Meier scoffed. "You heard our orders, Strauss. We are to stop for nothing, even if Ivan immobilizes one of our own tanks. We must maintain our momentum."

"Yes, *Unterscharführer.*" Strauss knew from experience not to challenge Meier. The SS had obviously selected him for loyalty, not skill or tactical proficiency.

The tense moments before an engagement pumped Strauss full of adrenaline and helped distract him from his extreme exhaustion and thoughts of Inge. He had only eight Pervitin tablets left, so he had to make them count.

"Driver! Stop! Now!" Meier exclaimed. "Ivan's counterattacking. T-34s are advancing toward our position."

The tank ground to a halt after Bauer, the tank's driver, slammed on the brakes. Once the tank was stationary, Strauss scanned for targets. "They're moving too fast for me to get a good read on them. It seems like they're trying to close in to reduce our range and armor advantages. That's what I'd do. Ivan learns fast."

Meier was not amused. "I don't want to hear excuses or expressions of adoration for these sub-humans. Focus on knocking out their tanks."

"Two Tanks! Eight hundred meters! Right tank!" Meier barked.

The crew spun into action.

"Identified!" Strauss announced as he centered the T-34 in his sights.

Roth, the loader, shoved a round into the main gun's breech, "Up!"

"Fire!" Meier ordered once the loader was out of the main gun's path of recoil.

"On the way!" Strauss pulled the trigger and the armor-piercing round sped toward the T-34, exploding its turret on impact.

"Target! Left tank!" Meier commanded.

"Scanning!" Strauss wheeled the main gun left, and then adjusted its elevation. "Identified!"

"Up!"

"Fire!"

"On the way!"

"Target! Cease fire. Gunner, continue to scan."

Burning T-34 hulks littered the battlefield. Smoke blanketed the low ground, making it difficult for Strauss to identify more targets.

High-pitched whistles heralded the launch of Soviet artillery, and Strauss knew through experience and instinct that the key to survival was a rapid advance through the valley.

On his right flank, Strauss spotted a camouflaged Soviet antitank gun. Breaking chain of command protocol, he yelled, "Driver! Turn right!"

Any second of delay could prove fatal. The Tiger needed to position its front glacis toward the enemy's gun, where the armor was thickest. As the tank reoriented itself, an enemy round slammed against its hull. The impact's vibration deafened the crew and shook loose flakes of interior paint onto the men, but the round barely scratched the Tiger's armor.

The tank destroyed the gun and its crew, and then continued its advance, knocking out several more enemy targets. Yet the Red Army horde seemed to have inexhaustible armor reserves, and the frequency of rounds hitting the Tiger accelerated. It was only a matter of time before the Soviets surrounded the Tigers.

Strauss identified another target, waited for the fire command, and then fired. Nothing.

"Misfire!" Strauss warned as his last round malfunctioned in the breech.

"Abandon tank!" Meier ordered.

Strauss moved by reflex. As he scrambled out of the turret, he saw the Tiger's main gun riddled with coin-sized holes. He knew it was only a matter of time before the unexploded round detonated, blowing them all to oblivion.

As the five men scrambled out of the Tiger, Soviet machine gunners cut down three of them including Meier, Bauer, and Weiss, the radio operator. Bauer never made it out of his driver's hole as a Russian sniper separated the man's head from his body.

Strauss and Roth rushed toward the nearest ditch. A hail of rounds zipped all around the two men, until Strauss heard a dull thud as Roth fell, his wound spraying Strauss with a mist of blood. Strauss leapt for the ditch and regretted his choice the instant he arrived. Blood-soaked bodies littered the field, and the air was thick with flies and other carrion feeders. The stench of death was overwhelming amidst the thick smoke uncoiling from burning metal hulks and engulfing the battlefield. The only Germans near him were dead.

Strauss had no time to process the deaths of his four crewmates. It'd all happened too fast, and he was operating on pure instinct. As he'd learn so bitterly at Stalingrad: survive today, mourn the dead tomorrow.

The ground vibrated as Soviet armor lumbered across the broken plain. The Red Army had launched a counteroffensive with tens of thousands of men, armor, and materiel pouring through the area.

Strauss knew he had three options: surrender, fight until dead, or hide. He judged only one offered him a chance at survival. Crawling into the bloody abattoir of German corpses, Strauss played dead.

He lay there for hours, choking back vomit as the bodies ripened under a sweltering summer sun. Biting horse flies had their way with him. Rats nipped at his limbs and torso. This was the sort of death he had most feared, a slow and painful one.

Toward the evening, echelon after echelon of Soviet regiments passed him by, underscoring a crushing defeat for the Wehrmacht. The advancing Soviets paid no heed to the German dead. They'd likely relegate the burial duties to local civilians, or so Strauss hoped. At nightfall, he planned to make his way back to German lines.

By dusk, smoke still blanketed much of the battlefield, but most of the Soviet formations had advanced farther west. All was quiet, but Strauss knew in his gut that the stillness was nothing but the eye of a storm. Strauss heard scraping sounds ahead. They were barely audible at first, but grew louder as their source drew closer.

Strauss pushed a corpse aside, and lifted his head out of the mire to determine the cause of the commotion.

He noticed the silhouette of a Russian soldier standing one hundred meters away, the man's Soviet helmet juxtaposed against the smoky haze. The soldier was dragging a German corpse out of the ditch and toward a nondescript knoll about two hundred meters distant. Other Soviet soldiers performed the same gruesome task.

Strauss found the soldiers' silence disturbing. Not a whisper passed among them, yet they worked like well-coordinated drones.

Why don't they just bury the bodies in place?

Strauss feared the Soviets would soon discover him in the midst of their macabre undertaking, but curiosity got the better of him, so he decided to investigate.

He crept through the gully, hiding beneath bodies whenever the Soviets returned. In the darkness, he never saw their faces, only a preternatural emerald glow.

The ditch opened up into a vast wheatfield obscuring his vision, yet he could still see the knoll in the distance. A dull green light pulsed from beyond the hill's crest like a homing beacon.

As Strauss stole through the field, he discovered the tracks of a Tiger tank, which he followed. Without stalks of corn to obstruct his path, he'd be less likely to stumble into an ambush.

Strauss realized he was hopelessly lost. The dense iron ore deposits embedded in the region's crust had rendered his compass useless. *"Magnetic interference,"* the High Command had said. The stalks of corn, vast rolling hills and ridges, and thick smoke and fog made map navigation challenging. Everything looked the same.

Aside from thousands of bloated bodies littering the battlefield, the only things distinguishing this specific spot were the peculiar Soviet soldiers he'd observed dragging German corpses up a nearby hill. A dull green light pulsed like a homing beacon from beyond the hill's crest.

The soldiers moved with a stiff walk, like automatons with an unnaturally cadenced gait. Strauss had seen many strange things during his time on the Eastern Front, but never something quite so unnerving.

A waxing moon held vigil over the dark dull gray sky.

Is it any wonder that the Russian soul was so bleak, ever embracing oblivion? Strauss slogged onward.

The air reeked of cordite, burning diesel and gasoline, and charred flesh. Exposure to this toxic stew gave him a headache, while the scent of roasting meat only made him hungrier. Strauss's mouth was dry. Cottonmouth was a side effect of the Pervitin tablets, which had kept him awake for the past three days. But he needed to sleep soon. Otherwise, the hallucinations would start again. Even with methamphetamines, the human body couldn't persist for long without rest.

As Strauss trudged across the loamy earth, he followed deep tread marks that forged a path through a wheatfield. The path widened into low-lying grassland that rose up a gently sloping knoll. To his west rested a disabled fifty-six-ton Tiger tank. Its treads were shredded, but the armor on its hull and turret had suffered no signs of penetration.

Strauss climbed aboard the Tiger to see if there'd been any survivors. When he reached the tank's turret, he saw that one of its two hatches was open. He peered inside, but the crew appeared to have abandoned the tank some time ago.

There was nothing for him here. The answers he sought lay beyond the knoll. Strauss jumped down from the tank, and began his slow ascent up the hill.

The wind swirled around him, carrying the stench of death and burning petrol. The wheatfields had protected him from the worst of it. Now he was in the open. Soon the moisture on the ground would accelerate the decomposition of the corpses surrounding him. Strauss yawned and rubbed his eyes. He needed to take sleep before sleep took him.

Aside from the wind, Strauss found the silence around him eerie. After three years on the Eastern Front, he'd learned to ignore the quiet after a long battle. Firing a Tiger's eighty-eight millimeter cannon degraded hearing after a few days of intense fighting. Maybe it was just his dulled senses, but given the strange figures and lights, maybe it wasn't.

Despair had been a constant companion for so many years, he could barely remember a life without it. Sometimes he asked himself if such a life was worth suffering for. Even if it meant at some point he'd be reunited with Inge. He envied Heinz. An infamous Soviet sniper – a woman, no less – had blown his brother's brains out in Stalingrad. At least Heinz's torment was over. For Strauss, it never ceased.

As Strauss neared the pinnacle, he lowered himself and crawled. The stench of death grew fouler, ripe with decay and putrefaction.

His heart raced as he peeked over the other side, expecting to find the Soviets in a reverse slope defense. Instead, he spied an impact crater about four hundred meters across, with a maximum depth of roughly thirty meters. At its center, a cylindrical structure protruded from a midnight-black disk. An earthen ramp extended from the disk's edge to the south-facing wall.

In the crater scores of German and Soviet soldiers carried dark black minerals from a mine shaft near the east-facing wall to the black structure. Even more disconcerting was that aside from their footfalls, the soldiers made no sound.

As Strauss looked more closely at the men, his apprehension deepened. Some had missing limbs; others, exposed bone. All had the gray-green skin of corpses. Strauss's instinctive terror wrestled with disbelief. *No, this can't be real. I must be hallucinating.*

One of the dead things swiveled its head toward Strauss, its glowing emerald eyes betraying it as something other than human. A rush of panic threatened to overwhelm him. Strauss shivered. With one fluid motion, the walking corpse swung its rifle to its hip and fired.

Strauss hit the ground. A sharp, white-hot pain seared through his left shoulder. He grabbed his shoulder in a futile effort to compress the smoldering wound. Strauss gritted his teeth and grunted. The bullet burned. Below, more Soviet and German soldiers had turned and were approaching his position. All had luminous green eyes. The sight of them shook Strauss to the core.

Strauss's training took over. He rolled away from the crater's edge and sprinted toward the Tiger. He climbed on the tank's turret, opened a hatch, and lowered himself into the commander's cupola. Protected by the tank's thick armor, Strauss closed the hatch and loaded the tank's seven-point-nine-two-millimeter coaxial machine gun.

Scores of German and Soviet soldiers climbed out of the crater. They advanced on his position with calm efficiency. Bullets passed into the tank's tiny gun port, glancing off Strauss's helmet. Strauss's hands shook as he wiped a bead of sweat dripping from his brow. His attackers' uncanny accuracy terrified him.

Keep it together, man. Keep it together.

Strauss unloaded his machine gun in measured three-round bursts. But the corpses kept coming. He struggled to contain an avalanche of doubt and terror. He aimed at their heads. But even when he shattered their skulls, they shambled forward, headless. Strauss wavered. He wanted to flee, but if he did, they'd almost certainly kill him out in the open.

Strauss closed his eyes and took a deep breath. *Think, man. Think.*

He stared through the tank's sights, watching the dead surge inexorably forward. Frantic, he took another deep breath.

He aimed for their legs, hoping to immobilize them. The tactic slowed their progress, but still they crawled forward.

Strauss exhaled. *Progress.*

It took half an hour to disable about forty of them, his machine gun ripping their wriggling limbs to shreds.

He waited desperately, fearing another attack from the crater. None came. Terror kept him vigilant, temporarily pushing away the siren song of sleep.

Perhaps whatever had chased him had calculated that further pursuit wasn't worth wasting any more resources. Either way, Strauss took advantage of the respite. He foraged through the turret for rounds, food, or anything else that might help him survive. In the process, he discovered a map with the knoll circled in red.

After full darkness descended, he left the protection of the turret, and dropped down to the radio operator's compartment on the hull to call for help. Strauss knew he'd be transmitting a message in the clear. Without encryption, the Soviets would most certainly intercept it. But Strauss didn't care. Better the Soviets than some unknown and unnatural threat.

Strauss switched on the wireless. "Any station, any station, this is Georg Strauss, Ninth Company, Third SS Panzer Regiment. Request immediate assistance. Over."

Silence.

"Any station, any station, this is Georg Strauss, Ninth Company, Third SS Panzer Regiment. Request immediate assistance. Over."

A voice with a heavy Russian accent responded in German, "Fascist invader, this is Soviet transmitting station one-zero-three. Relay your coordinates for immediate and unconditional surrender. Over."

Strauss was starting to regret his decision. *Why should I risk my neck to alert the Soviets? I should just sneak back behind friendly lines and leave this problem to the enemy.*

Strauss considered his options.

"Soviet transmitting station, this is Strauss. Unidentified hostiles of neither Wehrmacht nor Soviet designation near current location. Proceed with caution. Grid follows. Prepare to copy. Over."

"Send it."

Strauss pulled out the map he'd found in the turret and relayed the hill's coordinates to the Soviets. Then he returned to the tank's cupola, reloaded the machine gun, and waited for his sworn enemy to arrive.

Chapter 2
The Russians Are Coming

2230 Hours, 12 July 1943, Outside Prokhorovka, Russia

After a tense hour, a diesel engine rumbled in the distance. The squat silhouette of a T-34 emerged from the south, out of the wheatfield. It seemed that the trigger-happy Soviets had deliberately avoided the Tiger's trail. Strauss couldn't blame them. He'd set up some nasty ambushes in the past along similar routes.

Strauss counted twelve soldiers crammed on the tank's rear deck. As they got closer, he noticed one was female. He wasn't surprised. The Soviets had employed women to deadly effect at Stalingrad. He knew from personal experience.

The T-34 squealed to a halt about thirty feet from Strauss's Tiger, the engine still running. The tank commander shouted something in Russian. The squad dismounted. Rifles raised, the troops approached Strauss. The T-34's turret swiveled toward the Tiger. Strauss waved a makeshift grayish-white flag fashioned from his filthy undershirt.

One particular brute with a prominent sloped forehead took no chances. "*Hände hoch!*" he screamed in crude German. Strauss raised his hands above his head in as exaggerated a gesture as possible. Sometimes the Soviets shot first and asked questions afterward.

Rifle still raised, the man's pace accelerated as he closed in on Strauss. When he reached the treads of Strauss's Tiger, he motioned for his squad members to surround the vehicle. The man slung his rifle over his shoulder and climbed aboard the German tank.

His face contorted in a sneering rictus, the man slammed the butt of his rifle into Strauss's face, bloodying his nose. Strauss's eyes watered, his nose throbbing. *Maybe calling the Soviets wasn't such a great idea.* He spit out blood and cupped his nose with his hand.

"*Nyet!*" the woman said. The soldier backed off, but motioned for Strauss to dismount. Dazed from the blow, Strauss had enough sense to comply with the Russian's orders.

The woman wore woodland camouflaged coveralls and carried a Mosin-Nagant rifle. She was short, but shapely with ample bosom and wide hips. Her hair, which she kept in a bun, was flame red. Her high cheekbones betrayed the fusion of European and Asiatic blood, a genetic testament to the thirteenth-century Mongol invasion of Russia. The oval shape of her pale blue eyes reminded Strauss of a wolf's. In some indescribable way, the woman reminded Strauss of Inge.

In heavily accented German, the woman said, "Fascist invader, you are now officially a prisoner of the Red Army. I'm Major Anna Ilyinichna Ivanova, commander of this special detachment. You will answer all questions without hesitation."

Strauss shrugged, and then nodded.

The brute patted Strauss down, confiscating Strauss's old maps, his Luger, and his bottle of Pervitin tablets. The Soviet lifted the Luger above his head and smiled, showing gaps in his rotting teeth. The other men laughed and clapped. A Luger was a highly sought-after war trophy among the Soviets. Strauss couldn't have cared less. Losing the Pervitin worried him more.

The brute then rattled the Pervitin bottle, but seemed unsure what to make of it. He threw it to Anna. She caught it, rotated it in her hand, glared at Strauss and said, "What's this?"

"Please," Strauss pleaded, fighting to keep his voice calm, "I need that. I have a heart condition. Without those pills you might as well bayonet me now. If I don't take them later tonight, I'll collapse."

Anna cast Strauss a dubious glare, then conferred with her men in Russian. After an animated discussion, Anna had the last word. She tossed the bottle back to Strauss, and said, "I don't believe your story. But I'm also not willing to risk your collapsing before we have a chance to interrogate you. Enjoy your pills."

Strauss barely suppressed his joy. "Thank you, Major."

"You can thank me by answering my questions. Who are you, and what is your unit designation?"

"Georg Strauss, Ninth Company, Third SS Panzer Regiment."

"Liar!" She slapped Strauss across the face.

The blow stung.

So this is how it's gonna be.

"Please. There's no time for this. There are walking dead in a crater beyond that knoll." Strauss pointed toward the crater.

Strauss's attempt to take control of the interrogation triggered another slap.

"You see this man here, the one who nearly broke your nose?" She gestured toward the brute. "Fascists raided his village outside of Smolensk in '41. After they killed his parents and razed his home, they raped his sister. He wants to gut you like a chicken. I urge you to cooperate."

"Please, just hear me out," Strauss said.

"Fine. Tell me the truth about your actual unit and I'll listen."

"I'm not lying about my unit."

"Third SS Panzer retreated this afternoon with over seventy-five percent casualties, so you're either a liar or a deserter, and I've never captured a German deserter."

"If you have to put me in the 'deserter' category, so be it."

"Prove you were in that unit."

"Well, my uniform probably won't convince you, because I could've pulled it off a corpse. My outdated company-specific maps likely won't convince you either. It doesn't really matter anyway, since we'll all be dead soon."

That got her attention. "Suppose I believe you. What's on that knoll that has you so scared you're willing to try your luck with the Red Army?"

Strauss told the major his story. Ivanova reacted with a smirk.

"Don't believe me?" Strauss said. "See for yourselves. Be careful though. The things up there have better aim and reflexes than any sniper I've ever seen – Soviet or German. I suggest you drop every piece of ordnance you have on that crater, 'cause what's inside isn't going to go down easily."

Anna smiled and said something to her men in Russian. They erupted in laughter. "I told them about your walking dead and your plan to waste the Motherland's artillery on a harmless hill."

She shouted orders in Russian to a rail-thin soldier. The man rushed forward with a knife and a bottle of vodka. Anna pointed at the soldier. "Not that he can speak German, nor you Russian, but this is Private Dmitry Severinov."

Fearing the worst, Strauss backed away from the knife-wielding soldier.

She waved her hand. "He's here to remove the bullet from your shoulder. If I wanted you dead, you'd be dead."

The skinny man poured vodka on Strauss's wound. Strauss winced. Then Severinov used his knife to extract the bullet. The cold knife stung as

Severinov drove it deeper into Strauss's shoulder and fished for the burning bullet. Strauss howled. A wave of agony and nausea washed over him. His vision turned black and fuzzy at the fringes.

Ignoring the pain, Strauss tried to address a more pressing matter. "So, you'll do it? You'll call in your artillery?"

Ivanova laughed. "We Russians are not so melodramatic. We're not going to shell a hilltop based on some fascist's tall tale, but we did notice both Soviet and German remains scattered around your tank." She pointed at the smoke rising from the corpses. "The bullets are still hot. It's clear you'd killed other Germans. But why?"

"I already told you."

Ivanova turned and issued more commands. The men grinned. Then six of them slung their rifles over their shoulders and marched toward the hilltop.

They disappeared into the smoky haze while Severinov finished stitching Strauss's wound and bandaged his shoulder. Strauss's wound no longer burned, but it still throbbed.

Ivanova regarded Strauss as if he were a wounded bear and said, "Dmitry tells me you are a very lucky man. It seems the bullet in your shoulder missed all three major bones there, and only did minor damage to one of your tendons. If you survive Siberia, your wound should heal quickly."

Strauss just nodded, then fixed his attention on the smoky mist, awaiting the inevitable. "We really should be focused on the hill. If your men stir up whatever's in the crater, it's likely to come down here. We should be ready."

Ivanova huffed and shook her head. "If anything happens to my men, I'll shoot you."

A rifle shot rang out in the distance, followed by sporadic small-arms fire. Blood-curdling screams preceded an ominous silence.

"Call for fire support," Strauss said.

"Again, I'm not going to drop artillery based upon enemy recommendations. The remaining seven of us will investigate what happened. Then I'll decide what to do once I have better intelligence."

"Would you at least ask your headquarters to launch an artillery strike in two hours? You can always cancel it before then."

She considered Strauss's proposal. "I'll put a three-hour delay on the strike." Ivanova walked over to the T-34 and accessed its wireless set. She radioed her headquarters and provided the eight-digit grid coordinates. She returned to the six men and said, "Take us to the crater, fascist."

The seven soldiers stumbled through the smoky miasma. Ivanova had pushed Strauss to the front of the column, but refused to provide him with a weapon for self-defense.

The smell of sulfur flooded Strauss's senses. Besides Pervitin and terror, it helped keep him awake. The last thing he wanted was to collapse from exhaustion minutes after confronting some unknown menace, so he downed half of his eight remaining Pervitin tablets.

The acrid smoke burned Strauss's eyes as he ventured deeper into the haze. As they ascended the hill in near blindness, the sound of metal clanging on rock echoed from the crater. It was faint at first, but grew louder the closer they got to the crater.

A light breeze pushed a bank of smoke past Strauss. He moved carefully to avoid stumbling into whatever was in the mist beyond. He stepped onto something soft, almost tripping over a body. He raised his right hand to signal a halt. Despite their conflicting allegiance, the six Russians complied. He bent down on one knee to examine the corpse.

The body was still hot. Its right shoulder was bloodied. "A wound like that shouldn't kill a man," Strauss said. Then he noticed the man's head.

Its skullcap was cleaved off, and its brain was missing. Horrified, Strauss stumbled backward. *What the hell is going on?*

"Private Bakunin!" Ivanova gasped. She shuddered as she moved forward to view the body. "What did this?"

Strauss ignored her question. "Drop some rounds in the crater and be done with it."

Ivanova shook her head. "No. I must see this through. If I bomb this hill without confirming my soldiers' deaths, the commissar will execute me. We must go on."

Strauss sighed.

The group resumed its trek through the smog. Along the way, they discovered more members of the squad, all of whom had nonfatal gunshot wounds. Their skullcaps and brains were missing. Ivanova tabulated her butcher's bill, collecting each soldier's dog tags to protect herself from execution.

As the seven soldiers neared the hilltop, Ivanova grabbed Strauss's arm. "Stop. This isn't everyone."

A shot rang out. A sharp pain ripped through Strauss's shin. One of Anna's missing soldiers emerged from the haze carrying a rifle and a black cube. The man's face was emotionless, his eyes glowed a dull green and something had sliced off his skullcap with surgical precision.

More shadows pierced the mist's veil, drawing ever closer. Strauss panicked, struggling to breathe. The dead man tossed the cube into the air and it floated as if suspended in water. Greens rays of light emanated from the device and connected with all seven soldiers. Strauss's vision faded to black.

Chapter 3
The Crater

2230 Hours, 12 July 1943, Outside Prokhorovka, Russia

Strauss awoke to a blinding light from above. He lay on a cold metal table. His muscles felt weak and lethargic, as if he'd been drugged with something far stronger than morphine that was only now beginning to wear off. He had a splitting headache coupled with dizziness and nausea.

As Strauss's eyes adjusted to the light, he found himself inside a cylindrical room. The chamber's walls seemed filled with a mustard-colored fluid. Suspended in that fluid were columns of wrinkled gray ellipsoids. Each object had hundreds of folds, and each throbbed in an eerie cadence in synchronicity with the others.

Mein Gott. Human brains!

A man screamed.

The screeching reverberated throughout the chamber, but originated from a table directly across from him. Strauss looked down the length of his body, past his feet, at the chamber's center. Eight tables radiated from an empty three-meter-diameter circular platform at the chamber's center. The tables were spaced at equal intervals like spokes on a wheel. Ivanova lay unconscious two tables over at Strauss's nine o'clock position.

The remaining five tables were empty. Strauss wondered where the other soldiers were. There was a two-meter-wide gap between their heads and the chamber wall. Behind Severinov's head stood the devil incarnate.

A coal-black squid-like being worked behind Severinov with four of its eight tentacles whirling in motion. Each tentacle ended in four opposable fingers. Eight red eyes conveying a deep and menacing intelligence gazed out from its Volkswagen-sized head. A crimson hourglass-shaped mark dominated the crest of its skull. Oily black fluid oozed from its pores. The creature possessed a wide vertical maw lined with rifle-length fangs.

This can't be happening. I must be hallucinating. I have to be. I haven't slept in days.

Beneath Severinov's screams, a faint hissing accompanied a solid shaft of glowing red light boring into Severinov's skull. The screaming abated and a sucking sound followed as one of the creature's tentacles extracted Severinov's gray matter from his open cranium.

The scent of searing human flesh permeated the room and put to rest any doubts Strauss had about what was happening. This nightmare was real. Strauss didn't fear death. But the thought of getting a lobotomy from this squid-thing terrified him.

Throughout the years, Strauss had survived more brushes with death than he could count. He'd hunted and been hunted by people, the most dangerous predators on earth. Strauss was a hardened veteran forged and tempered. But he had never felt as helpless at any moment in his life as he did now in this human abattoir.

Then he remembered Heinz and all the other men from his town who'd served with him and died. He owed it to them to survive.

Strauss racked his brain for a suitable course of action. He realized the squid-thing hadn't bothered removing anyone's clothing or equipment with the exception of the soldiers' rifles and pistols. Severinov still had three grenades on a bandolier strapped across his chest. Perhaps the creature only recognized the weapons people had tried to use against it in the past.

The squid-thing turned its back to Strauss and faced the wall. It lifted Severinov's brain high above its head, then deposited it into a small compartment built into the glassy surface.

This is my chance, Strauss thought, only to realize the chamber had no visible exits.

The grinding sound of operating hydraulics resonated from the floor. A circular platform rose slowly from the craft's center. When it reached the ceiling, the hydraulic noise stopped for a fleeting moment, and then began anew. As the platform descended, a pair of Wehrmacht-issued steel-toed boots came into view.

The thing shifted its hulking black mass and blood-red eyes toward the platform and lumbered forward, propelled by its hind tentacles. The platform reached the floor. A dead German soldier stood facing Strauss in silence, rifle in hand, and emerald eyes aglow.

Strauss feigned unconsciousness; summoning all the lessons he'd internalized from his tour in Stalingrad to avoid attracting unwanted attention.

Keeping his eyes barely open, Strauss saw the creature remove the dead German's helmet. Beneath, the man's skullcap appeared fused back to his lower cranium, judging from the thin scar across his forehead. The creature pressed something on the back of the soldier's head, and his skullcap popped open as if on a hinge. It dipped a tentacle into the man's skull and extracted a swarming mass of lice-like organisms. Another tentacle pressed a floor panel. The platform rose again, carrying the soldier with it. After the platform reached the ceiling, it descended, now empty.

The creature turned and shuffled back to Severinov. Amid all the horror, Strauss had forgotten about the artillery. He surreptitiously checked his watch. *Oh, no. Fifteen more minutes.*

The thing inserted the writhing bugs into Severinov's empty cranium and reattached his skullcap. The creature then moved toward the unconscious Ivanova.

The Pervitin must have been potent enough to revive me before the others.

Strauss had to act now.

He swung off the table. His injured right shin ached. The bleeding had stopped, but the wound hurt like hell. He limped toward Severinov. The creature surged forward, grasping at Strauss with its tentacles. Strauss leapt at Severinov's table and grabbed two grenades, one with each hand.

A tentacle twisted around Strauss's leg, hoisting him upside down. Disoriented and nauseated, Strauss nearly emptied his stomach. The creature pulled him toward its face. Its menacing, fierce red eyes gleamed. Strauss struggled to regain his balance. The squid-thing's maw gaped in a shriek. It was the opening Strauss needed.

He raised his right hand to his mouth, pulled the pin with his teeth, and tossed the live grenade into the creature's jaws. The beast gurgled and flailed its tentacles. The whipping tentacle shook him. Strauss hunched over it, trying to find his center. Helpless, he swayed topsy-turvy. His gut roiled. Dizzy, he closed his eyes to avoid vomiting. Then he curled into a ball and braced for an explosion.

The blast hurled Strauss across the chamber. Time slowed as he sailed through the air. He crashed against the glassy wall. The air burst from his lungs. He labored to suck in oxygen, wheezing and on the verge of panic. His ears rang from the explosion, assigning false distance to close sounds. The air reeked of sulfur and burning meat. Black and sticky fluid from the creature's guts soaked him. He wiped his eyes and the blurry film obstructing his vision cleared. Shrapnel holes pitted the walls.

Strauss regained his senses and got back on his feet, thankful the creature's body had absorbed most of the explosive force. The detonation left the tables and the people on them unscathed. Strauss hobbled toward the central platform, frantic to escape before the planned artillery strike. He peered over his shoulder at Ivanova, still lying unconscious on the table.

I can't leave her to die here.

He staggered past Severinov's limp corpse and toward Ivanova.

"Wake up." Strauss tapped his hand on her face. No response. Strauss rifled through his pockets and found the four remaining tablets. He grabbed one and shoved it down her throat. As he did so, he spotted a gold Star of David necklace around her neck. Strauss just shook his head at the irony of it all, an SS soldier saving a Soviet Jew.

"Wake up!"

He waited for over a minute, his heart pumping as the seconds ticked away. *C'mon. Wake up!*

"Eh?" Ivanova mumbled as she regained consciousness.

"We've got to leave now!" Strauss looked at his watch. "We have three minutes before all hell breaks loose."

She groaned and nodded.

Cold and clammy hands throttled Strauss's neck. Strauss gasped for air. In all the confusion, Severinov must've approached Strauss from behind.

Ivanova yelled in Russian at Severinov, pleading with him.

Strauss dropped his last grenade in an effort to tear Severinov's hands away from his throat.

It was no use.

Desperate, Strauss rolled forward, taking Severinov with him. Severinov's body hit the next table with a loud thud. The impact broke Severinov's death grip.

"Ivanova, get the grenade!"

She surged to her feet and ripped the last grenade off Severinov's bandolier, narrowly escaping his thrashing arms. She sprinted to a table opposite hers, pushed it in front of her, and pulled the pin.

"Strauss! Behind the table! Now!"

He hopped past Severinov's reanimated corpse, snatched the other grenade off the floor, and dived behind the table beside Ivanova. She threw her grenade at Severinov. Strauss covered Ivanova with his body. He pulled the table over them both at an angle. The grenade exploded. A concussive bubble blew the table backward, then slammed them against the wall. Smoky shrapnel sprayed the table. Yet the table held firm, protecting Strauss and Ivanova from the white-hot shards of burning metal. Chunks of human flesh splattered the chamber walls.

When the dust settled, Strauss checked his watch again. "One minute!"

Strauss led Ivanova to the platform. Before they reached it and he had a chance to tap the panel, the platform began to rise. Something on the outside was trying to get in. Strauss pulled the pin on his last grenade and lobbed it onto the rising platform. They waited in silence.

After the explosion, Strauss reactivated the platform. Blood dripped from the stand as it descended from the ceiling. When the gore-spattered platform reached the floor, the pair stepped on it, Strauss activated the panel, and the two rose toward the ceiling.

The platform led to the surface of a black circular disk. The scattered remains of Soviet and German soldiers littered the ground. A score of separated body parts continued to writhe and crawl toward Strauss and

Ivanova. The dead men must have surrounded the disk the moment they'd sensed trouble.

Strauss looked at Ivanova. "We're out of time. We need to get the hell out of here."

Ivanova nodded.

After two minutes, they were climbing out of the crater. There were still no signs of artillery.

"Why didn't your people blow this place sky high?" Strauss said.

"I don't know. This makes no sense."

As they hiked down the knoll, hundreds of soldiers and dozens of T-34s had cordoned off the area.

"What the…?" Strauss said.

"*Hände hoch!*" A Soviet soldier pointed his rifle at Strauss.

Strauss raised his hands in the air. "What the hell is going on, Major?"

"I don't know. I'll get to the bottom of this. Don't worry. I will provide a full report of your bravery to STAVKA."

Her promise did little to comfort Strauss.

Ivanova faced the soldier and said something in Russian.

The soldier stared at her for several seconds. His eyes lit up. He then jabbered away excitedly.

"What's he saying?"

"He's praising me for my actions at the Red October Steel Works and telling me it's an honor to meet a Hero of the Soviet Union."

The mention of the Red October Steel Works brought back a torrent of horrific memories. Vivid images of Heinz's lifeless form. Blood on the streets. The desperate desire for oblivion's sweet release. Strauss fought against the crushing weight of his sorrow.

He inclined his head toward Ivanova as tears trickled down his cheeks. "I… I was also at the Red October Steel Works. So… so was my brother. They say a sniper killed him there. A female sniper."

Ivanova glanced away from Strauss, and then regarded him again with her deep blue eyes. "Please, call me Anna." For an instant, she avoided Strauss's gaze. "I was the only female sniper assigned there. I'm sorry. War makes us all do cruel things."

Strauss nodded as he wiped his cheeks with his hand.

The man ushered Strauss and Ivanova down the hill toward a command tent nestled near the old Tiger tank. As they ventured down the hill, they passed a number of high-ranking Soviet officers. Anna seemed troubled.

"What is it?" Strauss said.

"I've never seen so many senior officers in one place. Something's not right."

Anna asked their escort a question in Russian. She seemed disturbed by his answer. She turned to Strauss. "He's taking us to see Marshal Zhukov"

Even Strauss recognized the man's name. Zhukov had won the First Order of Suvorov for his actions in the defense of Stalingrad and had attained the rank of Marshal of the Soviet Union.

Why is he here and not focused on tasks more central to the Soviet war effort?

The three entered Zhukov's command tent. The Marshal sat alone behind a large field table covered with a map of the Kursk salient. Red acetate cards representing Soviet divisions with arrows pushing ahead of them conveyed a static snapshot of the fluidity of the front as the Soviets gave chase to retreating German divisions.

Both Anna and the Soviet soldier snapped to attention and saluted the marshal. Zhukov barked an order in Russian. The two relaxed their ramrod postures. He motioned to his escort, addressing him in Russian. The man saluted and grabbed Strauss by the shoulder. As the soldier ushered a limping Strauss out of the tent, Strauss heard the marshal interrogating Anna.

Chapter 4
Marseille

0130 Hours, 13 July 1943, Marseille, France

Captain Jimmy D'Alessio took a swig of Scotch. A Wurlitzer coin-operated phonograph played some jazzy Édith Piaf ditty in the dimly lit café. The only bit he could understand was "Jimmy, oh, oh, oh." *Thank God there aren't any fucking accordions in this song.*

Perched on his bar stool, D'Alessio casually surveyed the establishment. A group of locals a few tables over pointed and snickered at him. They chattered excitedly in French. Two of the men were five foot nothing, but more than made up for their Lilliputian statures by cranking up the volume of their voices. The other two were so tall they'd probably had to crouch to walk in the café. On the opposite end of the establishment, three disguised British Special Air Service operatives quietly imbibed their drinks, nervous as nuns in a brothel.

D'Alessio scowled at the boisterous Frenchmen. He'd studied German instead of French at Harvard. He couldn't understand one iota of what these frogs were saying, but he was damned sure it wasn't good. Annoyed, he raised two fingers and ordered another Scotch. As usual, the service was slow as hell. After about five minutes, the waiter sauntered over to D'Alessio's table and gave him another shot. The man's irritated expression sent D'Alessio a clear signal that serving him was a task beneath his exalted Gallic sensibilities.

Normally, D'Alessio just downed his Scotch like the uncouth, uncultured persona he'd worked so hard to cultivate. But today was different. He needed to keep his hands occupied while he stewed over what he imagined the frogs were saying about him.

For a part of France that the Germans had taken control of only seven months ago, the French seemed to be in unusually high spirits. D'Alessio was pretty damned sure he wouldn't have felt the same way if Hitler had handed America its ass not once, but twice.

The mood in France had now settled into a steady, complacent hum. The French had seemingly lowered their expectations for their country's destiny. It was as if the French had eschewed all vestiges of the national pride and glory that had harkened back to the Napoleonic era.

A scrawny Frenchman sitting at the table finished speaking and uproarious laughter boomed throughout the café. Whatever the Frenchman had said, his friends found it hilarious. From their glances and gestures, D'Alessio guessed that the joke was on him.

Normally, D'Alessio would have kept his mouth shut. After all, he didn't know French, was in an unfamiliar place, and was on the edge of drunk. But it also wasn't in D'Alessio's nature to take crap from anyone. Eating shit was an acquired taste for fancy people. And D'Alessio was the furthest thing from fancy.

D'Alessio knew speaking English here would risk blowing his cover, but he couldn't let someone insult him in another language. It just rubbed him the wrong way.

He downed his scotch, glared at the table and said, "Excuse me."

The waifish Frenchman looked back at D'Alessio. He stuttered in English. "Ah, yes?"

D'Alessio smiled. *Good. They understand me.*

"Why do the French plant trees on the side of the road?"

The Frenchman squinted at D'Alessio and shrugged. "I don't know."

"Germans like to march in the shade," D'Alessio said. His mouth widened into the biggest shit-eating grin this side of the Atlantic.

The Frenchman's expression contorted from confusion to a snarling rictus.

Good. My words had the intended effect.

The man huddled around his companions, speaking excitedly in French. From their expressions, the men hadn't taken too kindly to D'Alessio's observations on French horticulture.

Outnumbered four to one, D'Alessio waited, cracking his knuckles. With liquid courage from their cognac, and likely emboldened by the safety of their superior numbers, the Frenchmen rose from their table and strutted toward D'Alessio.

D'Alessio shook his head. Every briefing he'd had before coming here, his superiors had warned him not to venture far from the port of Marseille. He and his British comrades were supposed to observe and report. Nothing else.

But D'Alessio wanted a drink. And when D'Alessio wanted a drink, he got one.

The English-speaking Frenchman was a foot smaller than D'Alessio, but the man had the courage of a nine-foot tall Goliath. He got within inches of D'Alessio's chest, buoyed by the jeers of his companions. His curly moustache was waxed to perfection. His total baldness betrayed his middle age.

"So does the big tough American think he can come into my country all alone and insult it?" the man said.

D'Alessio smiled. "Which country? The one the Germans are occupying or the one my country is about to liberate from the Nazis?"

He swung at D'Alessio. D'Alessio dodged the blow and countered with a left hook. The man stumbled back. Someone sucker-punched D'Alessio in the back of the head.

The American staggered.

D'Alessio was unsteady on his feet. The bald man stepped forward. D'Alessio taunted him. "Four Frenchmen against one American? Doesn't seem like a fair fight to me. Looks like the odds are in my favor. Your head looks real nice and shiny Did you polish it this morning?."

The man made a quick jab at D'Alessio. D'Alessio tried to dodge it, but his face absorbed the blow. It stung. He shook it off. He thrust an uppercut to the man's stomach. The Frenchman crouched and groaned. D'Alessio followed up with a left hook then a right cross. The Frenchman stumbled off his feet.

A crowd was forming. D'Alessio turned to deal with the Frenchman who'd sucker punched him from behind. The red-haired man was also barely over five feet tall. True to his cheating form, he grabbed a chair and swung it at D'Alessio. D'Alessio sidestepped the blow. He shoved his shoulder into the man. The Frenchman crashed into a table. A slew of glass, wine, and food exploded everywhere.

D'Alessio liked to fight as much as the next man, but he began to worry things were spiraling out of control. Taking on four drunken men was manageable, but facing an outraged mob in a tiny space was suicide.

A few tables over, the Brits rose from their seats and joined the fight, adding an Anglo flavor to the night's festive atmosphere.

Bedlam!

A pencil-necked Brit with the face of a twelve-year old smashed a chair on a Frenchman's head. One of the two French giants took a swing at D'Alessio. The lone American pivoted away from the punch. He countered with a rapid succession of body blows to the giant's gut. The man folded like a lawn chair. The second French gargantuan approached, his face grimacing.

D'Alessio knew that if he didn't get the hell out of here soon, he'd never leave France alive.

He began to feel a bit tipsy as his last drink started to take hold. He'd had about five tonight. The crowd swayed unsteadily in his vision. He struggled to stay on his feet. D'Alessio whistled to his British comrades and pointed toward the front entrance. Dodging flying chairs, bottles, and forks, and an unruly French mob, D'Alessio fled.

Two burly Frenchman blocked his path. No matter how much D'Alessio thought he could break through, he knew he couldn't make it. So he sought another way out.

He raced back through the bar through a gauntlet of angry Frenchmen. He made his way toward the bathroom, harried by them.

He spotted a window at shoulder height at the far end of the loo. He ran to it. He tried to lift the window open. It wouldn't budge, so he kicked it in.

The bathroom doors burst open behind him. Angry voices followed. He crawled through glass shards, their sharp points lancing him with pain. He looked down on a dark alleyway about ten feet below.

He hesitated.

A man's hands clamped down on one of his ankles.

D'Alessio kicked back.

A man howled.

The American plunged headfirst toward the pavement. He crouched into a ball, an instant before impact. He hit the ground hard, rolling forward.

His breath whooshed out of him. Dizzy and disoriented, he stumbled to his feet. He glanced up and saw a man crawling through the window feet first.

Where are the others?

He hoped his British compatriots were all right. He wanted to go back into the café to rescue them, but the Harvard man inside him knew that would be foolish. The SAS boys could take care of themselves. For now, he needed to get out of Marseille before someone alerted the Germans.

He ran.

The world swayed around him. Drunk as a skunk, D'Alessio stumbled through the alley. He had no idea where he was. But his drunkenness hadn't completely clouded his judgment. He knew he'd have to make it to water to escape. So he navigated through the city guided by one rule: head downhill.

As he rounded the café entrance, a Frenchman yelled, *"Ne le laissez pas s'échapper!"*

A frenzy of movement.

A screaming mob surged toward him. D'Alessio sprinted downhill, around a corner and right into a German roadblock.

"Papiere!" a German soldier shouted from behind two coiled rolls of Dannert wire blocking the narrow street. Two other soldiers watched him from a motorcycle with a sidecar.

D'Alessio laughed. The Teutonic invaders had so little respect for the French that the Germans didn't even bother to learn the language.

"Ich bin Deutsch!" D'Alessio slurred. "That mob stole my papers and my uniform. They're going to lynch me for sleeping with a French woman," he said in Bavarian-accented German. He gestured at the approaching mob.

The German standing at the roadblock raised an eyebrow at D'Alessio. D'Alessio concentrated on his breathing. He tried to remain calm. If he showed any doubt, the gig would be up.

The crowd drew closer. The German stared at D'Alessio as if trying to make a decision. "What unit are you with?" the man asked.

D'Alessio looked over his shoulder at the approaching mob, and then turned his head back to the German. D'Alessio struggled to come up with a cover story. All the preparation he'd done prior to the mission escaped him. He couldn't remember which units the Germans had stationed in Marseille. D'Alessio spotted a Luger on the German's hip.

"I'm on leave. My cousin is French. She's to be married tomorrow and I drank a bit too much tonight," D'Alessio lied. "You know the French. They'll take advantage of you when you're at your weakest."

The two men on the motorcycle and sidecar nodded as if D'Alessio's blanket statement were as fundamental as the second law of Thermodynamics. The sentry didn't seem convinced.

In another minute, the mob would close the gap.

"C'mon, let him through," the soldier on the motorcycle said. "Do you really want to be responsible for failing to prevent the murder of a German soldier?"

D'Alessio nodded. "Your friend's right. If that crowd gets a hold of me, you know they'll kill me. Do you want that on your conscience?"

The man hesitated, and then nodded. "So be it."

He pulled two coiled strands of the Dannert wire aside and waved D'Alessio through.

"What are you doing?" a man yelled from the crowd in German. "He's an American!"

The German dropped the wire. He reached for his Luger. D'Alessio lunged at him, knocking the man to the pavement. The American reached for the Luger. Shots fired. Blood splattered D'Alessio's face. The German went limp.

The mob screamed. Panicked men and women scrambled in all directions. D'Alessio shielded himself with the soldier's body. A second shot ricocheted off the asphalt. He grabbed the Luger, and then played dead.

Two German-speaking voices whispered in the darkness. They got closer. D'Alessio waited. His heart pounded. Sweat dripped into his eyes. It stung.

When the two soldiers rolled the dead body off him, D'Alessio took two aimed shots of their chests. One soldier went down without a fight. The other popped off a round. An intense pain lanced through D'Alessio's upper left arm. D'Alessio fired back, hitting the last soldier between the eyes.

D'Alessio's arm burned. He smelled scorching meat. Smoke rose from his wound, punctuating a faint sizzle. He vomited.

D'Alessio rose to his feet. He bent down and grabbed two eight-round clips from the dead German. The crowd was gone, having fled the scene during the melee. An eerie silence enveloped slick streets.

A wireless set on the motorcycle crackled to life. "Panther Three, this is Panther Six, radio check, over," a voice said in German. D'Alessio swallowed hard. Soon the city would be swarming with Germans and dogs.

D'Alessio bolted toward the waterfront.

છ

0900 Hours, 14 July 1943, Tunis, Tunisia

Not one of the Nigerian soldiers was below six feet tall. Disheveled, drenched, dehydrated, and reeking of seawater, D'Alessio fell into a neatly and well-disciplined two queues of Nigerian soldiers. Stowing away on a Tunisian freighter hadn't been the most pleasant of experiences, but it was much better than the alternative.

The soldiers queued in front of a warehouse near the docks. A surly mustachioed British officer sat at a table about a hundred feet ahead. He said, "Achebe!"

A Nigerian at the head of the line saluted smartly and said, "Private Achebe, reporting for duty, Sir!"

About twenty Nigerians were between D'Alessio and the officer. When D'Alessio reached the head of the line, the British officer's eyes widened. "Who the bloody hell are you?"

"Captain James D'Alessio reporting for duty," he said in a parched voice. "I'm trying to find my ship. Its destination is Plymouth, England. Its name is SS Jeremiah O'Brien.

The British officer looked at D'Alessio with a mixture of confusion and awe. "You look a wreck old chap. What the bloody hell happened to you?"

"I spent some time in Marseille the night after last. Thought I'd have a drink."

"Are you bloody nuts, man? Do you know what happens to soldiers and sailors who venture too far from that port? There've been kidnappings and muggings out here. Not to mention it's been occupied by Jerry."

D'Alessio shrugged. "Can you help me find my ship?"

"Oh, bloody hell." The officer pointed. "It's about two kilometers in that direction."

"Thank you much," D'Alessio said, smiling.

&

0830 Hours, 16 July 1943, Secret Intelligence Branch, Office of Strategic Services, London, England

D'Alessio stood at attention before William Casey, the Director of Special Intelligence/OSS London. Casey sat back with his loafers propped up on his desk. His perfectly pressed pinstriped suit, slicked-back non-regulation hair, and bifocals pegged him as a professional bureaucrat. But D'Alessio didn't take appearances at face value. He knew that Casey was a hard, analytical man. His calm demeanor and disarming smile were likely nothing more than cultivated affectations.

"Captain D'Alessio, do you want to tell me why in God's green earth you started a goddamned fight in occupied France while you were supposed to be on a covert mission? Please give me something, anything, so I don't have to court martial you."

"Well, Sir, they insulted me."

"How the hell do you know that?"

"I could tell."

"D'Alessio, your file here says you speak German and Italian. It doesn't say you speak French."

"So?"

"Well, how the hell did you know what they were saying if you don't speak fucking French?"

"That's a fair point, Sir," D'Alessio said, smirking. "You know, Sir, that when someone's pointing at your table and snickering at you, you might not know exactly what they're saying, but you know it ain't good. And I'm American goddammit. I don't have to put up with that garbage."

D'Alessio knew he was playing Russian roulette with his career. It also unsettled him that Casey just might decide to send him back to the States in dishonor. But D'Alessio banked on the fact that Americans who spoke both fluent German and Italian were rare. And Americans who spoke both languages and had military training were rarer still.

Casey shook his head. "Captain D'Alessio, this is completely unacceptable. If we were back in the United States, I'd put you up for court martial, I'd forfeit your pay for thirty days, and I'd confine you to your barracks. But fortunately for you, we're in a goddamned war. While our forces are making progress in Operation Husky, we're still sustaining an alarming number of casualties in Sicily. Now, we need men more than ever.

I can't afford to send you back to the States in disgrace. So, here's what we're going to do. It says here you went to Harvard?"

"Yes, Sir."

The general looked up and scratched his head. "You've gotta be fucking kidding me."

"No, sir, I'm not fucking kidding you."

"Don't curse around me, goddammit."

"All right, Sir, I won't fucking curse around you."

Casey shook his head. "D'Alessio, you're an irresponsible drunkard, and because of that, I'm going to put you on the most dangerous possible mission. One where you're more than likely to be dead within a year."

"Well, Sir, I hope you don't plan to put me on something where my life will just be thrown away. I hope you'll send me somewhere where I have a fighting chance and can really make a difference."

"Oh you'll definitely have a fighting chance. It'll just be a slim one."

"Well, sir, is it the most dangerous mission out there?"

"Yes. But it won't just be one mission. It'll be a series of them."

"Outstanding. Tell me all about them."

"Fine. These missions are classified as codename TOOL. We got some Free Germans we're gonna parachute deep behind Nazi lines. These guys are gonna spy on their own people and feed us the information. They need someone who can shepherd them into place and manage them from our end.

"It says here that your German's pretty damn good. Hell, it says you've even got a Bavarian accent. So we're gonna give you the training you need, and within a year we're gonna drop your ass out of a perfectly good airplane deep into enemy territory with a bunch of angry Germans who probably won't like you."

"Got it?"

"Yes, Sir."

"You survive that, I'll make the trouble you caused here go away. Sound good?"

"Yes, Sir!"

Chapter 5
Bargaining

0200 Hours, 13 July 1943, Outside Prokhorovka, Russia

The alien toxin that had rendered Anna unconscious lingered in her system, mixing a noxious stew in her gut. The Pervitin jumpstart only made her feel worse. Her fuzzy mental state was the last thing she'd needed while debriefing Marshal Zhukov. She supposed it could've been worse. At least he wasn't Stalin.

Marshal Georgy Konstantinovich Zhukov had a brutish way about him, consistent with his poverty-stricken upbringing. She knew the man would have no patience for anything other than a straightforward and full accounting of her actions at the crater. "Why did my soldiers find you collaborating with a fascist invader?" he asked in a blunt and accusatory manner.

Despite her knowledge of the man, the question's brusqueness caught her off guard, and she hesitated. "Comrade Marshal, my men had responded to a distress call. When we'd arrived on scene, we captured Georg Strauss. He told us an outlandish tale about the dead rising from the crater. As a rational Soviet, I discounted the story until I saw signs that Strauss had massacred his own men. This made me curious, so I sent a squad to the crater to investigate. When my men failed to return, I took the rest of my unit to see what was delaying them. Along the way, we discovered one of my men lying unconscious on the ground. Before I could examine him, we were attacked."

Anna paused to give Zhukov a chance to comment, but his expression was impassive, so she continued her report, telling him of Strauss's actions, the automatons, and the strange oil-black viscera left behind from something Strauss insisted wasn't human.

After she had finished relaying her account, Zhukov stared at her as he twirled his fingers. Then he spoke. "Major Ivanova, you've put me into a bit of a pickle."

Her face flushed red. She felt confused. She'd expected Zhukov to question her story and to call her crazy. She'd been certain he would court martial her for aiding the enemy. Instead, he seemed to be blaming her for something else.

Zhukov's eyes bored into hers as he crossed his arms and said, "Major, I'm still not sure what I am to do with you. On the one hand, you are a famous war hero who is very useful in helping motivate and inspire our young heroes during this Great Patriotic War. On the other hand, no one can know what you've seen or experienced."

Anna's mouth dropped open. "Sir?"

"You've disrupted our nation's carefully laid plans, plans that Stalin has painstakingly constructed. In just one night, you've undone fifteen years of delicate diplomacy."

Blindsided, she had no idea what to say. What the hell was Zhukov talking about? What plans could have possibly involved mutilating the dead? "Sir, with all due respect, I don't understand. What have I done wrong?"

Zhukov pounded his fist on a field table. "You attacked our allies, you fool!"

Dumbfounded, Anna didn't know what to say. Zhukov continued. "Nearly fifteen years ago, our government instituted a classified program to develop technologies essential for manned space exploration. It had several early successes, most notably the launch of a liquid-fueled rocket.

"It wasn't long before traitors infested the program, so all concerned had to be eliminated. This set the program back several years. While our efforts had stalled in this field, recent Nazi advancements in rocketry have alarmed us. We suspect German scientists are working on a wonder weapon – a pilotless flying bomb. So we decided to accelerate our collaboration with the species you encountered at Kursk."

"The species at Kursk?"

"They're extraterrestrials from beyond our solar system. They've been observing us for decades. We have a long-standing agreement with them: in exchange for their technology, we allow them to experiment on the war dead from both sides. They also have our blessing to dissect any Nazi prisoners or other political undesirables we deliver to them. However, I am not here to speak about that. You have put me in a very delicate position, Major Ivanova. As such, you are no longer permitted to fraternize with other Red Army soldiers. The risk, no matter how small, of you leaking this state secret is far too high. Therefore, I'm reassigning you to Moscow."

For the briefest glimmer in time, Anna had hope. She was going to survive this encounter. Then she thought about what Zhukov had said about handing over prisoners to the extraterrestrials, and changed her mind. When the two men wearing overcoats and fedoras entered the Marshal's command tent, she became certain that her future was bleak.

"Ah, Mr. Genkin and Mr. Azarov, how punctual of you," Zhukov said. He then glanced at Anna. "Major Ivanova, these men will be escorting you to Moscow."

A dark memory resurfaced. She shuddered at the thought. The last time she'd seen men like this, she never saw her father again. The men's dull eyes, plastic smiles, and cheap suits marked the men as NKVD.

And they were going to shoot her.

Maybe not here, not now. But at some point, they'd put a bullet in her brain. Anna struggled to retain her composure. The only thing she could manage was to ask a question. "What of Strauss?"

Anna regretted her words as soon as they'd left her mouth. She couldn't fathom why she'd chosen to ask about Strauss or more alarmingly why she had decided to refer to him by name, humanizing him. Her life was on the line and all she could think about was a fascist. Yet the man had saved her life. The least she could do was save his.

Zhukov raised an eyebrow. "What of the fascist? What's he to you?"

She decided to play it straight. "Sir, I consider myself a woman of honor. My loyalty to the Motherland has never wavered. Georg Strauss had no obligation to save my life. In fact, he had more reason than most to kill me. But he didn't. He stuck his neck out for me. As a warrior, I'm sure you can understand why I feel duty bound to return the favor; why I must vouch for this man, who only yesterday was my enemy. Surely, as a man of honor, you can appreciate why I owe this man my life."

The hint of a smile cracked the stoic edifice of Marshal Zhukov's face. "You are indeed a true Hero of the Soviet Union, Major Ivanova. I do understand this solemn obligation, and I will, therefore, grant the man a reprieve. Genkin and Azarov will take you to the POW camp where we are holding Strauss. From there, he can accompany you to Moscow. I will allow him to serve you there in an intelligence capacity."

Major Ivanova blushed. "Thank you, Marshal Zhukov. It was an honor to meet you." Anna was about to salute the Marshal until she realized that the details surrounding her next assignment seemed a bit too hazy for her liking. "If I may ask one last question, sir?"

"Go ahead," Zhukov said.

"What exactly will I be doing in Moscow?"

"That's classified. You'll find out when you get there." He paused for moment as if in thought, and added, "These men will be taking your rifle for safekeeping. Because of your bravery at Stalingrad, I have decided that it should be displayed as a battlefield artifact in the Central Museum of the Red Army in Moscow as a testament to your heroism. And you will no longer have need of it in your next role. Dismissed."

Before Anna could stifle the ominous feeling that had swept over her at Zhukov's final words, Genkin confiscated her weapon while Anna clumsily rendered Zhukov a salute. After he returned it, she spun on her heels and left the command tent.

Once Anna learned of Strauss's location, she had to find a way to ditch Genkin and Azarov before they murdered her.

⁊〇

0230 Hours, 13 July 1943, Outside Prokhorovka, Russia

Anna huddled in the back of the American-imported Willys Jeep. She was surprised the agents weren't using a GAZ-67, a Soviet knock off of the iconic American vehicle. She expected the NKVD to show more loyalty to the Soviet regime. From time to time, her eyes drifted toward the jeep's cargo well where Genkin had stowed her Mosin-Nagant.

Genkin drove the jeep, while Azarov sat silently in the front passenger seat. The two were so plain as to be virtually indistinguishable from each other.

The jeep's headlights cast long cones of light into the darkness. The vehicle passed through several military checkpoints on its way to the POW camp. Closer to the front, such a brazen use of headlights at night would risk a court martial. Such a blatant lack of operational discipline would cost lives. But this far in the rear, it hardly mattered. And no one dared cross the NKVD.

The two men were quiet, almost too quiet for Anna's comfort. As the jeep trundled through the dark Russian countryside, Anna worried about her uncertain fate. She needed to do something, anything. Dying like a sheep was not an option for a wolf.

Anna broke the silence. "Did Marshal Zhukov tell you what my mission will be once I reach Moscow?"

Neither man bothered to answer her question, so Anna tried again. Only this time she yelled at the top of her lungs.

"The jeep jerked a bit to the right, as the startled driver reacted to Anna's sudden outburst. Now, neither man could ignore her anymore, but they still evaded her queries. Azarov turned and replied in monosyllables, "*Nyet.*"

Now that Anna had opened up a dialogue with these empty suits, she pushed her luck. "Which department are you with?"

"Logistics," Azarov replied.

"I see," Anna said, "Which unit?"

"That's not important," Azarov said as he waved his hand.

Anna was convinced she wasn't going to get any information from these two playing this game, so she'd have to take a different tack. But before doing so, she asked them one last question. "Where is Strauss being held?"

Surprisingly, Azarov answered, "There's a temporary POW camp about ten more kilometers down this road. We should be there in thirty minutes or so."

Anna nodded. "I see. That's too long for me to wait. I really need to urinate now."

Azarov chortled. "My, you're rather direct aren't you?"

"I am. Can we stop here so I can relieve myself?"

Azarov tapped Genkin on the shoulder, pointed, and said, "Pull over." He turned his head, glaring at Anna. "Make it quick."

She nodded. Genkin steered the jeep toward the shoulder of the rugged country road. As Anna emerged from the vehicle and headed toward a thicket, Azarov trailed her. Anna worried he might attempt to execute her as she ventured out into the brush. She made sure to watch Azarov out of the corner of her eye.

As she traveled deeper into the woods, she listened carefully for even the hint of a metallic click. Then again, Anna didn't care much for being on the defensive, so she decided to take a more aggressive approach.

"Excuse me," she said to the NKVD agent looming in the shadows, "I'd really prefer some privacy."

"I'm sorry, Major," Azarov said as he drew closer, "We have our orders. I'm not going to let you out of my sight."

"I see," Anna said. "Exactly where in Moscow are you taking me?"

Azarov shook his head and gave her the party line. "I'm sorry, Major, that's classified."

Once they got deeper into the thicket and could no longer see Genkin or the jeep, Anna turned and grabbed Azarov's testicles. Azarov squealed. Then Anna said, "Tell me where you're taking me or I'll rip your balls off and tell Genkin you tried to rape me."

The man whimpered, then lowered his head and said, "The Kremlin."

Anna knew the man was lying, but released him anyway. She then dropped her trousers in front of him, squatted, and did her business. It would've been suicide to turn her back on him after having pulled her little stunt. Once she finished, she followed Azarov back to the jeep. Before

Azarov could say anything, she said, "Genkin, your comrade here told me you were taking us to Lubyanka. Why?"

Genkin's face turned beet red. Anna had her answer. In the confusion, she grabbed his sidearm and shot him in the head. Azarov fumbled for his pistol. She put a bullet through his skull before he could react.

The horrors of Lubyanka prison were not an option for Anna. She would've preferred death to the suffering she would have endured there. Now, she was a fugitive. She needed to get to Strauss and fast. Together they'd have to find a way out of Russia. Her Ukrainian cousin could help smuggle her out of the Soviet Union, but she'd need Strauss's help to pass through German lines. Ultimately, she'd need to find a way to the Brits or the Americans. Someone on the outside needed to know what her nation was up to.

Anna grabbed her cherished rifle from the cargo well, hopped in the jeep, and drove toward the camp, racing against time. If someone discovered the two bodies before she reached Strauss, she'd never see him again.

Chapter 6
Escape

Zhukov's henchman loaded Strauss onto a truck and drove him to a ramshackle internment camp bristling with razor-sharp concertina wire and populated with gaunt and desperate men.

The camp reeked of stale sweat, urine, feces, gangrene, and trench rot. Roiling waves of vermin scurried about the camp like a living carpet. The flies swarmed so thick they became a second skin for many prisoners. Most detainees had white flakes infesting their body hair since the Soviets probably had never bothered to delouse them. The camp was a breeding ground for typhus.

For several long hours, Strauss traded stories with the German POWs. Most hadn't eaten since their capture. The Soviets had denied them medical treatment, starved them, and rationed water, presumably to reduce their numbers. Few men survived longer than a week and the NKVD machine-gunned anyone attempting escape.

"Strauss!" a surly male voice shouted from the camp perimeter.

Strauss shuffled forward, uncertain. His shin throbbed with pain.

"Strauss?" A massive ursine guard glared at him.

Strauss nodded. The man peeled back a strand of wire so Strauss could exit the enclosure. With regret, Strauss took one last look back at his countrymen. He wished he could help them, but for all he knew, the Soviets were going to put a bullet in his brain. Those he left behind watched him, their expressions a mixture of pity and longing.

But Strauss refused to let his circumstances sour his mood. He was optimistic until the guard led him into a ditch overflowing with corpses. Sensing the end, Strauss pulled out his locket to gaze at Inge one last time, kissed it, and said goodbye.

A hand tapped Strauss's shoulder from behind. Then a familiar voice spoke. "Strauss, I'm glad they didn't shoot you yet."

Strauss turned and trembled with the relief of a man who was only a moment earlier certain of death. "Anna, it's good to see you again."

Anna's face was impassive. Her gaze flickered from left to right, betraying a need for secrecy. She spoke to the guard in Russian.

The man saluted and left.

"Come." Anna pointed to an empty, American-supplied Jeep.

Strauss entered the vehicle. Anna cranked the engine. The engine puttered, but failed to start.

She looked over at Strauss. "If you try anything, I will shoot you," she said.

Strauss laughed.

Anna smirked as she turned the ignition again. "They want us both alive until we reach Moscow."

"Why wouldn't they want *you* alive? Why aren't they going to shoot *me*?"

"I'll explain everything once we get some distance between us and this camp. C'mon, c'mon," Anna muttered as she continued to fiddle with the ignition.

Out of the corner of his eye, Strauss noticed the guard hadn't left his post. He was responding to a radio transmission on a heavy wireless set near the camp's perimeter. The man looked up at Strauss and Anna. His eyes widened. He pulled out a pistol and marched toward Anna's jeep. He put his hand on the windshield and said something authoritatively in Russian. Anna and the guard argued back and forth. She pointed at the rank on her collar.

The man scrambled for his sidearm. Anna shot him in the face. She turned the ignition again. Finally, the engine roared to life. She turned toward Strauss and said, "Hold on," slamming her foot on the pedal and careening out of the camp.

The country was so dark Strauss couldn't see his hands even when he put them in front of his face. The jeep's headlights washed out everything else. Ahead, a Soviet soldier stepped into the middle of the dirt road, a rifle slung over his shoulder. He signaled for the jeep to halt. Anna stomped on the gas pedal. The man dove toward a ditch on the roadside.

"What the hell's going on?" Strauss shouted.

"We need to get to a farm on the outskirts of Kharkov. My cousin lives there. He'll help get us out of the Soviet Union."

Strauss held on to the jeep's door for dear life as Anna sped through the Russian countryside. Strauss was sweating. His heart raced. He craved more Pervitin. Even worse, his shoulder still burned and his shin throbbed. A bullet was still lodged in it. "But I thought you were a Hero of the Soviet Union," he yelled over the sound of the grinding engine.

"I was. I mean, I am. Because of that, Zhukov cannot openly kill me. He needs to send me back to Moscow first."

"I don't understand."

"It doesn't matter. All you need to know is that after what I've done tonight, Zhukov no longer needs to send me to Moscow. He no longer needs to make me disappear. He can now shoot me in broad daylight. And he will shoot you too if he finds you. You and I need each other. You need me to get you to German lines. I need you to get me through them."

Strauss found the whole situation ironic. After Anna had taken his brother's life, Strauss had saved hers. Now she was returning the favor. Strauss had never been good at processing his feelings, but he was a master of survival. His instincts told him to embrace this temporary alliance.

"Fine. Where are we heading now?"

"North," Anna declared.

"North? Kharkov's west."

"The NKVD expects me to go west. So we have to travel north instead, and then wend our way back to Kharkov."

"And what if your cousin gets us back to German lines? Then what? You're a Soviet Jew. I can't imagine your prospects are any better with my people than they are with yours. And why would you ever consider defecting to Germany?"

"I'm not going to defect. I'm going to do something else entirely," Anna said.

Strauss ignored her evasion. There'd be plenty of time for planning the escape. But the mysteries of the strange black disk, the power cube, the automatons, and the black cephalopod nagged at him.

"Did you warn your people?" Strauss asked.

Anna shook her head. "STAVKA knew what was at Kursk Crater. By killing that grotesque thing, you disrupted a long-standing arrangement that could have ended the war sooner. My status as a Hero of the Soviet Union and your use as a bargaining chip were the only things that kept us alive. Zhukov worried my execution would harm morale. I suspect he also wanted you alive so he could deliver you to those things to make amends for the incident. Otherwise, Zhukov would've had us shot immediately."

"Wait, what long-standing agreement? Did Stalin make a pact with these creatures?" Strauss's eyes shone wide with disbelief.

"In a way. In exchange for their technology, my leaders allow them to experiment on our dead, and in limited cases, on our living. My compatriots also encouraged the extraterrestrials to do the same to any fascists found within our borders."

"What are these things?"

"They're interstellar beings. Aside from that, Marshal Zhukov revealed nothing more."

Two weeks ago, Strauss would have considered Anna's tale the ravings of a lunatic. Not anymore. "So, where are we ultimately going?" he said.

"The United States. Rumor has it the Americans are also interested in space travel."

Strauss smiled. He had never been happier to be wrong about someone in his life.

&

2330 Hours, 17 July 1943, Northeast of Bryansk, Russia

Strauss swallowed his last Pervitin tablet. According to Anna, it was the fifth day of Operation Kutuzov. The last four days had been long and hard, and the Pervitin wasn't as potent as it used to be. He was constantly perspiring and in need of a fix. Four days ago, Anna had removed the bullet from Strauss's shin, but his lower leg still ached from the wound, especially after Anna had abandoned their jeep.

Anna's jeep had had mechanical problems, so they'd had to ditch it two kilometers behind them. Anna's insistence that they only travel at night only made the journey more arduous. For now, Strauss posed as Anna's prisoner to avoid detection.

As the two lumbered along yet another unfinished Soviet road, they rounded a corner and stumbled into a checkpoint. Piles of half-filled sandbags formed a temporary command post on the road's right shoulder. Two shovels lay idle on the ground in front of the sandbags. The position had a loaded *Dushka* twelve-point-seven-millimeter heavy machine gun mounted on a tripod. Two bored-looking soldiers glared at Strauss while Anna pretended to lead him toward the checkpoint. One soldier sported the weathered features of an experienced combat veteran, while the other had a chubby baby face.

The more grizzled soldier said something in Russian as he swung the *Dushka* toward Anna.

Anna's face collapsed into a snarl. She wagged her index finger at the man, lecturing him in Russian.

After glancing at Anna's rank, the man lowered his weapon and muttered what seemed to be a half-hearted apology.

Anna then chided them some more in Russian. She grabbed Strauss by the collar and attempted to lead him through the checkpoint.

Then, the older soldier seemed to have changed his mind, stepping back out into the road with his hand outstretched. He then said something in a more authoritative tone.

Strauss cast a sidelong glance at Anna and whispered, "What's he saying?"

Anna replied, "He says he's under strict orders not to let anyone pass, even field grade officers." Anna then looked back at the soldier and asked him another question in Russian. After he replied, Anna inclined her head toward Strauss and translated the exchange, "He says the NKVD brought in some special exploitation unit in covered Studebaker deuce-and-a-half trucks. He also claims he's been given the authority to shoot anyone who attempts to pass through this checkpoint without authorization, even general officers. Apparently, this operation is highly classified."

"So how do we get through this checkpoint?" Strauss asked.

Anna smiled, put her hand in her trouser pocket and pulled out a handful of rubles. She walked over to the soldiers and stuffed some rubles in each of their upper chest pockets on their *gymnasterka* tunics.

The elder soldier just shook his head. "*Nyet.*"

Anna nodded in response, turned around, and started to walk a few meters away from the checkpoint. Then, she turned abruptly, picked up a shovel and swung it toward the corporal's face, knocking him unconscious. When his comrade made for the heavy machine gun, Anna pointed her Mosin-Nagant rifle at him and barked an order. He raised his hands. Anna disarmed him and then patted him down. She then slung her rifle back over her shoulder, picked up the shovel again, and swung it at the second soldier, smashing him in the face. Unfortunately, for Anna, the man didn't pass out, but screamed, his broken nose bleeding profusely.

Anna watched the wounded man for a moment and then swung again, beating him in the head until he stopped moving. Her work complete, she shot a glance at Strauss who was completely at a loss for words at Anna's callousness. She then said, "Well, what are you waiting for? Remove your clothing."

Strauss blushed and felt slightly aroused.

Anna just laughed. "What, did you think I was going to jump you in an active war zone?"

"Ah, well, ah, I didn't…" Strauss said, embarrassed and uncertain how to react to Anna's blunt manner.

"You'll have plenty of time to relieve your urges once we make it to safety. Until then, you need a Soviet uniform to pass through our lines undetected." She pointed to the two unconscious soldiers. "You have your choice of uniforms, but be quick about it."

Strauss quickly removed the uniform from one of the men, and then took off his own uniform, replacing it with the Russian's. Anna watched, impassively.

Once Strauss was set, the pair continued their trek down the dark road. Strauss then faced Anna and said, "What do you think's going on up there?"

Anna paused for a moment as she considered Strauss's question. "Eleventh Guards Army reconnaissance is probably probing for weaknesses in the German lines. The last thing the Eleventh wants is to draw attention to its operations. That unit has this area locked down. No one goes in or out. My guess is that the Eleventh is conducting a delicate exploitation operation and is concealing its intentions at any cost. If the Germans catch one whiff of what the Eleventh is trying to do, it would destroy any chance the Red Army has of creating a breakthrough in this sector."

It made sense, but there was one flaw in Anna's logic. The Soviets had already been attacking the Germans for several days along this very axis of advance. They were likely already alert and fully engaged.

After some consideration, Strauss said, "I agree that the Eleventh Guards Army has some sort of secret to keep, but I don't think it has anything to do with some deep reconnaissance mission. It has to be something else entirely."

"Like what? Do you think this has something to do with the aliens?"

"I don't know. But I do know that it's something big, something your side really thinks is worth this much secrecy."

The patter of heavy automatic weapons fire erupted in the distance with the practiced cadence of well-trained soldiers. Muzzle flashes peppered the dark horizon. Periodically, the Germans launched parachute flares to illuminate the skyline. In stark contrast, the Soviets oddly did none of these things, nor had they initiated this ostensible offensive with any sort of artillery bombardment. For Strauss, this was a first for the Soviets. In every single Soviet offensive he'd ever encountered, the Red Army had always softened their objectives with artillery before moving their armor and infantry forward.

No. Strauss was certain something else was going on.

Anna and Strauss continued their march toward the front lines, using the sound of sporadic small arms fire to guide them. Strauss wondered why he'd always found himself following death, always moving in its direction, its dark embrace beckoning him toward its black web of oblivion.

Voices.

Anna raised her right hand, signaling Strauss to freeze in place. Then she waved her arm toward the ground, her palm facing downward. Strauss followed her lead and lay flat on his belly. He slowed his breathing so he could better concentrate on sounds beyond those of the ambient background noise.

Tat-tat-tat. Tat-tat-tat. *"Raus! Schnell!"* a voice yelled from the darkness. Strauss estimated the German who'd uttered it was no more than a hundred meters distant.

Another burst of machine gun fire ensued. A stomach-twisting scream followed. Closer to his position, Strauss heard more small arms fire. Its pattern sounded unusual, but Strauss couldn't quite put his finger on what was different about it. It was just wrong. Then it hit him: the Russians weren't firing in three-round bursts; they were taking one shot at a time.

Anna lay on the ground next to Strauss. He turned to her and whispered, "Does the Red Army have an ammunition shortage?"

"No," Anna said, "but I've also noticed my side's only firing single shots. Unless the Eleventh Guards Army has deployed a battalion of snipers, which is extremely unlikely given how concentrated Soviet forces are in this sector, I see no reason why our soldiers would completely disregard their training."

"We need to get closer to the front so we can figure out what the hell's going on."

"Agreed."

The pair slow-crawled forward, careful to avoid detection. It was hard for Strauss to see much in the darkness. It was only when the Germans launched a parachute flare, that Strauss and Anna got a snapshot of the nocturnal battlefield.

As far as Strauss could see, hordes of men shambled toward the German lines. Their manner appeared certain and deliberate, but they did not maneuver. They walked into the withering German fire without any apparent fear. When Strauss looked closer at the soldiers' silhouettes, he saw a mix of German and Soviet helms.

No, Strauss thought. *No, it can't be.*

Strauss watched as the Germans poured every caliber weapon they had into the automatons. Chunks of human meat slapped on the ground after each bullet struck home, but still the man-things lumbered forward, firing single, precise rifle shots at their human prey. Despite their slow and unnaturally cadenced gait, the attackers inexorably gained ground, and were poised to punch a massive gap into Wehrmacht defenses.

Shrieks and screams punctuated the automatons' advance as the Germans discovered only too late that their small arms fire was nearly useless against their dead aggressors. Any Allied army would've folded in a pell-mell rout, but not the disciplined and experienced Germans. The infantry conducted an orderly withdrawal to their secondary positions, while their forward artillery observers began calling fire missions on the undead. The Doppler whines of incoming artillery forced Strauss to spring to his feet and find cover somewhere in the open plain. He grabbed Anna, and they ran blindly in the night, Strauss desperately hoping the Germans would launch another parachute flare to guide them.

Tufts of dirt burst all around them, as German Howitzers delivered their explosive ordnance on the advancing corpse-men. Strauss spotted an abandoned German strongpoint with trenches extending two meters into the ground and covered with sandbags. Anna darted toward it. Strauss chased after her and grabbed her arm, pulling her in the opposite direction. Strauss pushed Anna into a smoking crater. He dove on top of her and shielded her with his body. A high-pitched whistle presaged several tons of artillery that rained down on the strongpoint.

He whispered into her ear, "Germans usually pre-register their strongpoints for subsequent artillery strikes in case they must abandon their positions. I'm surprised you didn't know about this technique."

Anna slapped Strauss in the face.

"What was that for?" Strauss said, his face stinging from Anna's blow.

"Before you throw me in a hole, you need to tell me why," she said with the authority of a drill sergeant.

"Fair enough."

Strauss wrapped his arms around Anna, holding her tight in a vain effort to protect her from raining shrapnel. Her body was warm, and the smell of her sweat was strangely arousing. The intensity of the moment and the risk of imminent death made him feel somehow closer to this woman.

As exploding rounds thundered around them, uprooting trees and churning earth, Anna cleared her throat.

"What's wrong?" Strauss yelled over the ruckus and chaos.

"Is it me that excites you or is it all that heavy artillery," Anna quipped.

Embarrassed, Strauss quickly shifted his hips away from Anna's backside. "My apologies," Strauss stammered. "I lost control of myself. It… ah, won't happen again."

Between the explosions, Anna kept chuckling.

Anna's reaction reminded him of his responsibility to Inge. That he had let himself go like that shamed him and wounded him deeper than Anna could have possibly imagined. The wages of guilt hung over his minor betrayal hung over him like a Sword of Damocles ever ready to sunder his honor.

Soon, the artillery strikes abated, and the sector grew quiet. Another flare illuminated the horizon as its tiny parachute slowly swayed toward the surface like a descending pendulum. In the interim, Strauss peeked up from the crater, where he found far fewer automatons advancing forward, but the ground seemed to writhe. Upon closer examination, Strauss observed crawling and squirming human limbs, some of which continued to slither toward the Germans.

The squeaking chassis and rumbling of a Tiger tank broke the silence as the Germans deployed their armored reserves. The fight was still in the balance, but Strauss sensed the Germans would soon stem the breach.

"Now's our chance!" Strauss told Anna.

The two stumbled to their feet and sprinted toward German lines, trying to mask their movement by shadowing the contour of gullies and rivulets snaking through the battlefield.

Along the path, Anna abruptly stopped in her tracks and took a knee. Reluctantly, Strauss followed her lead, trying his best to keep a low profile to avoid being spotted and shot.

When Strauss took a closer look at where Anna had stopped, he saw a man's disembodied head, peeled open like a tin can. The inside of the man's skull teemed with the licelike organisms Strauss had encountered at the Kursk Crater.

Anna had opened her small knapsack, and removed a Mason jar. She unscrewed it and dipped the jar into the man's skull, filling the container with the alien organisms.

Fighting back the urge to vomit, Strauss said, "What on earth are you doing?"

"Leverage," Anna answered matter-of-factly.

"Huh?"

"If the Nazis capture me, I'll now have something to trade; a story to tell. Even better, if we make it to the Americans, we'll now have indelible proof these entities exist."

Anna's logic made sense to Strauss, but he wasn't so sure it would be easy to execute, especially if his side decided to torture the information out of her.

Several meters from the skull, Strauss found the man's torso, and felt a sudden rush of euphoria when he discovered it was clothed in a German uniform.

Pervitin.

Strauss dropped everything and sprinted to the man's writhing husk, stripping it for any Pervitin he could find. When he found three tablets, he swallowed them, shutting off the world and praying for his pain to end. As he rested next to the trembling torso, he embraced oblivion.

Anna's slap jolted him back to reality. She regarded him with what seemed like a deeply disturbed and concerned look. "I am worried about you, Georg."

Georg. She'd never called him that before. What changed?

Anna continued. "We need to wean you off that drug. It's making you sick."

Strauss nodded as fast as he could to change the subject. "We need to get out of here, now."

Anna stared at him for another few seconds, her eyes tinged with what Strauss sensed was sorrow. Then, she nodded and they continued their advance forward.

Soon, the eye of the storm had passed and the battle raged anew as the Germans leveraged their armored firepower to mop up the remaining reanimated corpses. Scores of tanks rumbled past Anna and Strauss's position, with hundreds of infantry marching in the steel Panzers' wake as the fluid wave of the battlefront rolled east. Now, the pair could hear German voices issuing commands and plotting future missions. Still wearing Soviet uniforms, Strauss and Anna were careful to avoid detection, crawling on their bellies toward a nearby tree line, and feigned death when the Germans got too close.

The chaos worked in Strauss's and Anna's favor. As the Germans surged forward, the two used the cover of darkness to wend their way to the tree line. Once there, they made their way to a German supply depot, where they found an unoccupied *Kübelwagen*, which looked like a four-wheeled washtub.

Anna drove the vehicle off road to avoid German checkpoints, turning south toward Kharkov until the vehicle ran out of fuel in the predawn morning glow.

Chapter 7
Withdrawal

1245 Hours, 11 August 1943, Near Kharkov, Ukraine

Anna carried Strauss on her shoulders. She staggered across a great wheatfield. Through Strauss's hazy vision, he saw a ramshackle and smoke-scarred bleached farmhouse in the distance. Utterly exhausted and nauseated, Strauss lacked the energy to move. Were it not for Anna, he would've blown his brains out weeks ago.

He'd suspected that the roots of his deep depression lay in his relentless Pervitin addiction. He'd run out of pills in mid-July when he and Anna had fled from Soviet authorities. A day later, he'd collapsed. If Anna hadn't cared for and protected him, the NKVD would've put a bullet through his brain long ago.

If the Germans discovered Strauss, they'd hang him for collaborating with a Soviet officer—a Jew no less. Anna's people would probably hang her too, if they only could reach her here, behind German lines. With the NKVD behind, the Gestapo ahead, and nearly three thousand kilometers separating them from their planned transit point in Calais, Georg Strauss wasn't optimistic. But then again, he'd never been an optimist, despite surviving both the Battles of Stalingrad and Kursk, and a desperate encounter with a Soviet-allied extraterrestrial near Prokhorovka.

Anna weighed thirty-two kilograms less than Strauss, but by Strauss's rough estimation she'd probably hauled him nearly two kilometers by now. She breathed heavily, drenched in salty sweat. The stifling heat of the Ukrainian summer boiled both blood and water.

"Stay with me, Strauss!" she groaned. "You're going to make it if it kills me."

Strauss felt trapped between shame and gratitude in an emotional state further addled and confused by his drug-starved fever. How could he let himself be so weak that this woman had to go to superhuman lengths to drag him across this searing field, exposing her life and limb to danger?

About fifty meters from the homestead, near the edge of the wheat field, she lowered Strauss to the ground. She then got on her belly and pointed her rifle toward the farmhouse. She placed one eye against her scope.

"Take a look at this," she said. Anna handed Strauss the rifle and motioned for him to look through the sight.

Strauss barely had enough strength to raise his head, but after everything Anna had done for him, by sheer force of will, he forced his eye to the scope. Two men dressed in traditional Ukrainian garb stood on the farmhouse's porch. Their body language and watchfulness seemed out of place for run-of-the-mill Ukrainian peasants. A bundle of clothing rested in front of the cottage's threshold. The men carefully scanned the area around the house, as if they were protecting something or someone inside.

Strauss found the men's behavior odd. A real farmer would have been in the fields working the land at this time of day, not standing attentively on a porch. No, Strauss suspected the two men were anything but farmers. "Neither of those men is your cousin. Am I right?"

Anna nodded. "Something isn't right." She grabbed the rifle from Strauss and prepared a makeshift sniper platform by cobbling together a small mound of dirt. She then handed a fist-sized stone to Strauss. "I know you're weak, but I need you to throw this at them," she said, aiming her rifle at the men.

Strauss hardly had the energy to do anything, let alone throw a stone, but he did his best, tossing the rock about twenty meters, before falling back down to his stomach.

The rock fell far short of its intended target, but it landed with a loud thud. In less than a second, the men dropped to their bellies and each secured a rifle from beneath the clothing bundle on the farmhouse's doormat. Strauss recognized the weapon's make and model, as he knew it intimately—the Karabiner 98 Kurz—a bolt-action rifle—standard issue for the Waffen-SS.

Strauss watched the men scan the horizon through their iron sights. The instant before one of the men swung his rifle toward Anna, she fired a shot, exploding the man's head open like a melon. The sudden sound startled Strauss. He hadn't expected Anna to act so preemptively.

The second soldier aimed his rifle at Anna, but before he could squeeze off a shot, he was already dead. Shocked, Strauss watched the back of the man's skull explode into a ruin of bone fragments, blood, and gray matter as the shot struck home.

Strauss was amazed by Anna's proficiency with her rifle. He'd never seen another human being so skilled in its application. After her two kills, Anna remained still, her right eye fixed on her scope. She lay in wait, watching the farmhouse. She was so still that Strauss could hear himself breathing.

The silence was maddening, but Strauss understood why Anna had to be patient. For all she knew, there were other German soldiers in the farmhouse who'd likely respond to the bedlam outside. Strauss counted the seconds, which seemed to stretch on for minutes, and then for nearly half an hour.

He was in awe of Anna's perfect discipline.

Seemingly satisfied the path was clear, Anna hoisted Strauss onto her shoulders and carried him the last fifty meters to the farmhouse.

Up close, the cottage was smaller than Strauss had estimated from a distance. Its pyramidal thatched roof barely exceeded a height of three meters. Anna laid Strauss on the soft clothing bundle before the farmhouse's door, and he collapsed against its smoke-stained walls. Strauss tried to get back on his feet, but his legs failed him, and he vomited instead.

Something rustled inside the house.

Anna jumped to her feet, hands on her rifle. She stalked toward the wooden door and lifted a crude latch. She kicked the door open and peered into the house through her rifle's scope.

A man screamed in Bavarian-accented German, "Please don't shoot! Please!"

Anna yelled, "Strauss! In here. Now!"

Strauss stumbled upward, vomited again, and fell. Determined not to be helpless, he attempted to crawl forward, and failed. But still he tried until Anna slowly backpedaled out of the household, never losing eye contact with the mysterious man inside, her rifle trained on him. When she reached Strauss, she grabbed his jacket with her left hand, and dragged him into the farmhouse.

Once inside the single room cottage, Strauss fumbled to his knees and was surprised to find a blonde gentleman wearing a checkerboard-pattern sweater vest over a white shirt and blue tie, and khaki-colored chinos. The man sat on a thatched chair next to a roughhewn pine table in the room's center. A simple wooden frame bed stretched along the farmhouse's dull green back wall. A threadbare indigo blanket covered the bed.

The German somehow seemed familiar to Strauss, but Strauss couldn't quite put his finger on why he recognized the stranger.

The man's piercing blue eyes regarded Strauss with a penetrating glare. "You're German," he said.

Without thinking, Strauss nodded.

The man loudly exhaled. "Thank God!" He gestured toward Anna. "I thought this woman was going to kill me."

"This woman still might," Anna interrupted in German.

Despite his continuing weakness, Strauss stumbled forward on his knees, inserting himself between Anna and the man, facing Anna. "Anna, please. Something's not right here. Why would a German civilian be out here all alone, protected only by a plainclothes covert military escort?"

Anna lowered her rifle. Strauss turned back toward the strange man. "Who are you, and why are you out here so close to the front?"

The man hesitated and then said, "What unit are you with?"

Strauss traded glances with Anna. Speaking with the man was frustrating, but Strauss decided to play along for now. Sharing a little information could potentially go a long way. "My name is Georg Strauss, and my companion is Anna Ilyinichna Ivanova. My unit was the Third SS Totenkopf Panzergrenadier Division, Ninth Company, Third SS Panzer Regiment. I got separated from it during the Battle of Kursk. Anna here is a Ukrainian separatist who's helped smuggle me through Soviet lines. Now, answer my question: who are you?"

The man folded his arms across his chest, inclined his head slightly to the right, and furrowed his brow. "If you're a German soldier, then why are you both wearing Soviet uniforms?"

Strauss responded with an inadvertent snort. "We very well couldn't pass through Soviet lines wearing German uniforms."

"But you're no longer behind Soviet lines," the man interrupted.

If this guy continued to ply them for information without sharing anything in return, Strauss feared Anna might end the discussion with a bullet in the German's skull. "We've told you who we are, but you haven't identified yourself, and my partner's patience is running thin. If you want me to answer any more of your questions, you need to tell me who you are," Strauss said.

The man just stared at Strauss, smirking.

Anna swung her rifle back up at the strange German. "Enough! You have three seconds to tell me who you are and why you're here or I will shoot you where you stand."

The man's eyes widened and he raised his hands toward the ceiling. "Please, there's no need for this."

"THREE!"

"Please. Lower your weapon. I'll be happy to cooperate."

"TWO!"

"All right! All right! I'm a representative from the Kaiser Wilhelm Institute for Physics."

"ONE!"

Anna aimed her rifle at the man and put her finger on the trigger.

"My name is Werner Kessler! I'm here to conduct an experiment."

Strauss slowly pressed Anna's rifle toward the floor. "Anna, please. The man told us his name. Give him a chance to tell us his story." Strauss left out the fact that the man had a Prussian surname, but a Bavarian accent. But he didn't want Anna to shoot Werner before they figured out why the man was here.

Strauss looked back at Werner. "Go on."

Werner nodded. "I am performing certain meteorological experiments in an effort to control precipitation in this region."

"I see," Strauss said. "Where's your equipment?"

Werner hesitated and said, "It's not here yet. I should be receiving it any day now."

"Why were you here with a plainclothes security detachment?"

"I'm sorry, Mr. Strauss, but…"

Strauss interrupted, "Call me *Rottenführer* Strauss. I work for a living."

"Indeed. *Rottenführer*, as a military man yourself, I'm sure I don't need to explain to you the concept of military secrecy. My experiment here is classified. I've already said too much."

Anna pushed Strauss toward Werner, and again trained her rifle at the man. "Where is Yuri Vynnychenko?" Anna yelled.

Strauss was so weak that Anna's aggressive movements nearly made him swoon. Kessler caught Strauss before he collapsed to the floor, and then held the back of his hand against Strauss's face. "You're sweating and your skin is cold and clammy," he said. "Have you been using Pervitin lately? You seem to be showing symptoms of withdrawal."

Strauss noticed that Werner's words appeared to have diffused Anna's tension. "How can you tell?" she asked in a hopeful sounding tone, lowering her rifle.

The man's eyes locked on Anna's. "I've seen many German soldiers experience withdrawal symptoms after they've spent any meaningful period on the Eastern Front. In regard to your other question, I'm sorry to say that I don't know anyone by the name, Yuri…what did you say his surname was?"

"Vynnychenko," Anna replied, with a tinge of what sounded like spite.

"Yes. I don't know the man. The two sentries you slaughtered were the only two men here when I arrived. Speaking of which, why did you kill my security detail?"

Anna again became visibly upset, leveling her rifle at Werner. "Give me one reason why I shouldn't kill you where you stand?"

Werner gestured toward Strauss. "I'm the only one in this room who can treat your friend's Pervitin withdrawal. If you allow me to leave afterward, I will help him relieve his symptoms."

Anna mulled over Werner's proposal and then said, "I agree to your terms, but no one leaves this farmhouse until dark, and I will search you to remove any weapons."

Werner nodded, and then Anna patted him down finding nothing more than a cigarette lighter.

When Anna placed the cigarette lighter in her cargo pocket, Werner said, "*Fräulein* Ivanova, if I may ask for one tiny indulgence. My wife gave me that cigarette lighter shortly after our wedding. It means a great deal to me, and I should like to keep it. May I have it back?"

Anna appeared to regard Werner with some level of suspicion. She glanced at Strauss as if she were looking for his opinion. "Give it to him," he said. "It's harmless."

Anna hesitated for a moment and then returned the cigarette lighter to Werner. She helped Strauss up onto the wooden bed. The trio waited in an uncomfortable silence for the sun to set. Werner's eyes kept flickering back and forth between him and Anna. He acted as if he were considering something.

After this bizarre behavior continued for several minutes, Anna lost her patience. "What's wrong with you?" she asked in her usual blunt manner. "Why aren't you helping Strauss?"

Then Strauss realized why the man had seemed so familiar and why he'd had a Bavarian accent. This man wasn't Werner Kessler. He was the Nobel Prize-winning physicist, Werner Heisenberg. Strauss's eyes lit up in recognition and he said, "Your name is not Werner Kessler. It's Werner Heisenberg."

Werner's face blanched, and then his eyes seemed to register a decision. He flicked open the lighter and pressed a button where there should have been a flame.

The room appeared to shift to a negative image of itself – what was dark became light, what was light turned dark. Time faded like receding sound from a Doppler shift. There was no time or gravity. When Anna made for Strauss, her now weightless body floated toward the ceiling. Strauss too began to rise. Then the effect collapsed into itself as gravity returned, pulling Anna to the floor with a dull thud, and rendering her unconscious. Strauss fell too, but not as far nor as hard.

Strauss was too dumbfounded and weak to react. Werner stared at Strauss, weighing, calculating. The man's face changed again as he shot one last glimpse at Strauss, turned, and left the building.

In his feverish and weakened state, Strauss could do nothing. He just lay there on the bed until he lost consciousness.

Chapter 8

Rift

0330 Hours, 12 August 1943, Northwest of Kharkov, Ukraine

Night had fallen by the time Strauss woke. His limbs ached, but his fever had broken. He groaned and shivered. His craving for Pervitin still held a tight grip on him. He desperately hoped Heisenberg hadn't fled for good. Strauss believed the man was his only hope for staving off Strauss's crippling addiction.

Dazed and bruised, Anna lay on the floor where Strauss had seen her fall. He stumbled tentatively to his feet, and shook Anna awake.

"Wah?" Anna murmured. "What happened? Where's Heisenberg?"

Strauss shrugged. "I don't know. He must've taken off."

Anna rolled her eyes. "I'm certain he's fled. Let me search outside, just to make sure."

After about five minutes, Anna returned having found no sign of the physicist.

"What do you want to do?" Strauss asked.

"We need to find him. I'm not going to let that bastard get away with what he did. And we also need to understand exactly what happened here."

"Maybe he'll come back," Strauss said. "He's a well-regarded Nobel Prize winner. Surely he has honor."

Anna chuckled. "You are such an optimist. You only see the good in everyone, don't you? But if you came from where I have, you'd know better. You can't trust anyone, especially someone who was connected to the same people Heisenberg was."

"What do you mean?"

"He was working with the Waffen-SS."

"I was Waffen-SS"

"But you're different."

"How?"

"You're just—different."

The two stared at each other for a fleeting moment as Strauss tried to decipher what she'd meant. Then she changed the subject.

"What time is it?" she asked.

"I don't know."

Anna scratched her head. "Let's leave the cottage and see if we can track him down. He couldn't have gotten that far on foot."

Strauss raised an eyebrow at Anna and said, "Why do we need to chase him?"

Anna regarded Strauss as a mother would an ignorant son. "If I have to choose between Pervitin and Heisenberg, I choose Heisenberg. He's the only one we know of who can fix your problem. And he owes me that. We also need him to explain what he did in the cottage. It could be as important as the information we carry about the Soviet pact with the extraterrestrials. We need to find him." Anna's determined tone then shifted to one of concern. "How are you feeling?"

Strauss cleared his throat and said, "Fine, I guess. I still feel sick, but I can manage."

"Are you sure?"

"Yeah."

The two left the farmhouse, stepping out into the darkness. Just over the horizon, a blue light pulsated. The wind swirled past Anna and Strauss as if the flashing light were sucking it in. Jagged webs of lightning rippled across the sky above the peculiar phenomenon.

"What on Earth is that?" Strauss asked.

"I don't know," Anna replied, "but we need to take a look."

The pair headed toward the strange spectacle as Strauss wondered if the event was somehow linked to Heisenberg.

Katyusha rockets exploded in the distance near the light source. Strauss worried that he and Anna were getting too close to the front lines, and he was convinced that yet another Soviet offensive was now underway.

The duo pressed on, though the moderate physical exertion was taking its toll on Strauss. As they drew closer, they saw a swirling vortex in the distance, oriented toward the East. As they made their way toward it, it abruptly winked out.

Then all hell broke loose as sporadic small arms fire and roiling explosions erupted at the front.

Chapter 9
Carnage

The rising sun exposed a charred and battered battlefield. Anna supported Strauss as the two investigated the scene where they'd spied the strange vortex the night prior. Strauss seemed the worse for wear, and his condition appeared to be deteriorating. He often muttered to himself and was constantly picking at his skin.

Anna was deeply worried about him. She felt obligated to help him make it through. It wasn't his fault that he'd served a murderous regime. He was a victim of circumstance.

Does the pawn consider itself a tool? Anna wondered. *No. It does its duty. With honor.*

Anna saw Strauss as a tragic figure that had always chosen honor and duty over his own needs. He'd subsumed himself to the state. And because of that, she believed he was truly a man worth saving.

About two kilometers from the vortex site, Anna and Strauss started finding German bodies. As they moved closer toward Soviet lines, the corpses thinned out. Then they began finding Soviet dead. The first Soviet bodies they'd encountered had suffered from conventional injuries ranging from gunshot to shrapnel wounds. However, as they drew closer to the location of last evening's odd phenomenon, they discovered something else entirely.

A ruin of men and machines marred the vortex site. Anna had never seen anything of its kind. Soviet soldiers had been twisted and fused together in contorted shapes, their eyes wide with terror. Flesh and skin had somehow been transmogrified into random patterns of quartz, marble, granite, and copper, as well as other unknown minerals and metals. Ash blackened the churned up earth, and the air was ripe with the smell of sulfur and human putrefaction.

Anna and Strauss found several soldiers folded from the inside out, their organs exposed in some kind of grotesque petrification. Multi-headed and limbed human hydras dotted the landscape, their faces rictuses of pain and suffering. One man's torso was fused to a T-34 chassis, akin to an armored centaur constructed from tempered steel. Other tanks were twisted inside out. Anna struggled to process the unnatural human and material wreckage confronting her. Yet, despite all this, Anna puzzled why she hadn't seen the contorted remains of a single German soldier on this part of the battlefield.

"Do you see what I see or am I going mad?" Anna asked Strauss.

Strauss sighed. "What you see is real. It looks like we Germans have our own secrets too. It's obvious from the destruction here that the Führer has his own ace up his sleeve. I can only shudder to imagine what it is."

Anna winced at Strauss's thought, and worried that both regimes seemed to be unleashing forces that neither would ultimately be able to contain or control.

A man screamed.

Anna lowered Strauss to the ground and up against a mangled tank. "Wait here. I'll check it out." Anna swung her rifle down from her shoulder and slowly turned a corner to investigate.

To her horror, she saw a man's face merged with the broadside of a T-34. The tank was composed of skin, bone, and sinew rather than steel. On closer inspection, Anna judged that he was actually more boy than man. The draft had probably plucked him out of some godforsaken village in Astrakhan only to die as a horrific mockery of man and machine made flesh. Anna retched.

The man spotted Anna and screamed in Russian, "Please, help me! Don't let me die here. Please."

Anna steeled herself before she approached the soldier. She had no idea what to say. After all, what does one say to a half human abomination?

"What happened here?" she asked.

The man's eyes widened as if he were confused. But, in a moment of remarkable lucidity, he said, "They came from the white void that sparkled from the dark abyss. Four of them, flowing like ghosts, weaved among the living, transforming and ruining everything in their path. Their faces were both human and inhuman. They had albino skin and their eyes were solid pale blue orbs, lacking any glimmer of white. And they showed no mercy."

"What were they?"

"Huh? Oh my God! Momma, save me! Momma!"

Anna couldn't stand to watch the boy suffer any longer. She aimed her rifle at his face and pulled the trigger.

When Anna returned to Strauss, she said nothing. She helped him back on his feet and said, "We need to leave, now."

Anna forced a disheveled and weary Strauss back in the direction of the farmhouse. She wanted to flee the scene as quickly as possible. Yet Strauss no longer seemed to possess the stamina to move any further. "C'mon, you can do it," Anna lied.

Strauss struggled to make his way forward, sweating profusely. Soon, he began wheezing. Yet Anna still soldiered on toward Kharkov, nearly carrying Strauss on her back. She made it about a kilometer before Strauss crumbled into unconsciousness.

"Wake up!" Anna slapped Strauss, but he seemed oblivious to her efforts to revive him. She placed her index and middle fingers onto Strauss's carotid artery, finding a shallow and weak pulse.

"No, you can't do this to me!" Anna said. "It's not fair. Not again. Not now."

Memories of her father flooded her mind. He used to sing to her while he bounced her up and down on his knee. She still remembered how he'd smell of pine after returning from chopping wood in preparation for a long winter – the winter the men came to take him away.

"No, not again," she said aloud. She set Strauss in a small gully to hide him until she returned. Then, she began rummaging through the putrid corpses of German soldiers, scrambling to find any Pervitin tablets she could. Rifling through cargo pocket after cargo pocket of dead Wehrmacht soldiers, she had no luck. She reasoned that soldiers this close to the front lines had likely burned up their Pervitin rations. So she ventured further back from the front lines, hoping to find soldiers who hadn't completely consumed their tablets. But every meter she moved farther west, she risked stumbling into a Wehrmacht unit. And this close to the front, most soldiers shot first and asked questions later.

As she continued foraging through the dead, she found it very peculiar that there weren't many Germans along her path. It was as if the German High Command had deliberately kept forces in this sector relatively sparse. If the German leadership was anything like the Soviet High Command, the absence of regular soldiers was a sure sign they wanted to keep their methods here a secret. Given the disturbing scene she and Strauss had stumbled upon, she could understand why.

A bit further from the front, Anna came upon a supply lorry with a red cross painted against a white background. Anna smiled. If Pervitin were to be found anywhere in this sector, it would be here. It took her about a minute to find shelves stocked with small glass bottles. Anna cleared entire shelves in her haste to find the compound, and after about five minutes of searching, she found four glass containers of Pervitin.

Anna raced back to Strauss, so she could give him one more dose, just to get him back on his feet. She hated feeding his addiction, but out here, away from modern medical facilities, she didn't have much of a choice.

Wending her way through various gullies and draws to avoid detection, she returned to Strauss only to find a man standing in front of him.

Heisenberg.

Heisenberg turned as she approached him. His mouth opened in an expression of surprise when he saw her.

Anna lowered her rifle and fired.

Chapter 10
Lubyanka Lies

1330 Hours, 12 August 1943, Northwest of Kharkov, Ukraine

Heisenberg lay unconscious, propped up against a mangled T-34. By the time he'd awoken, Anna had finished removing the round from his shoulder and was applying a bandage to the wound.

He cowered, raising his unhurt left arm, palm facing outward, at Anna. "Please, don't kill me. Please!" he whimpered.

She smiled, taking pleasure in Heisenberg's reaction. *Good*, she thought, *the bastard ought to be afraid.*

"Why were you out here all alone?" she demanded.

"That's… that's classified," he said, regaining some of his composure.

She slapped him. "I could shoot you right here, right now, and there's nothing you or anyone could do to stop me. Sure, Strauss might've come to your aid yesterday, but because you abandoned him, he's too weak to help you today. Now, I'm in control. Either talk or die."

Heisenberg glared at her, regarding her in his particular cold analytical manner, always calculating, considering his options, and then deciding on a particular course of action. "Go ahead and shoot me then."

Anna sighed. His response didn't surprise her. She'd expected him to call her bluff, which is why she'd carefully considered her next gambit. Pulling out the enigmatic cigarette lighter that she'd pulled out of Heisenberg's pocket while he was unconscious, she popped it open and placed her thumb on the button, threatening to press it. "What's this?" she said.

He smirked, seemingly unaffected by her ploy. "I'm sorry, Fräulein, that's also classified."

"Then I'm sure you don't mind if I press this button," Anna replied.

"Go ahead," Heisenberg said.

Now she decided to call Heisenberg's bluff. So she pressed the button, and nothing happened. "Why didn't it work?" she said.

"My dear Fräulein," he said, smiling, "that's also classified."

Anna fumed, unslung her rifle and poked the rifle's muzzle into his gunshot wound.

The physicist howled. She fought to retain her composure. Slapping the man was one thing, but torturing him like this didn't sit right with her. If she continued using such methods, she'd be no better than the NKVD or the Gestapo. Yet, her very life was at stake. Without Strauss's help, her chances of passing through Nazi-occupied Europe were slim. His survival was inextricably linked to her own. *Clean hands are dead hands*, she decided.

Twisting her rifle tip in his wound, she said, "Tell me why it doesn't work?"

"Please! Stop! Please!" he wailed.

"Answer me," she said, trying not to lose her nerve after inflicting so much pain on the man.

"Fine!" he said. "It doesn't work because it's not charged."

She pulled the tip of her rifle out of the wound. "How do we charge it, then?"

"We can't. Not here," he said, breathing hard.

She motioned to stick the rifle back into his shoulder.

He raised his left arm, warding off another attack. "Please! I swear!"

"Then where do we charge it?"

"Only four or five recharging stations exist, spread throughout Poland and Germany. I'm sorry. I can't say anything more than that. You can torture me all you want, but not even I have that information."

She didn't believe him, but she sensed that any further physical pain was unlikely to yield any more useful intelligence. So she decided to raise the stakes.

Anna opened a small knapsack and removed a Mason jar teeming with squirming licelike organisms. Heisenberg cringed, then curled into a ball.

Her mouth cracked into a satisfying smirk. "So you're aware of these creatures, aren't you?"

He nodded.

"Tell me what they are."

Heisenberg's reaction worried her. He'd refused to reveal anything until she inflicted an immense amount of pain on him, but after she'd revealed the licelike organisms, he cracked open like a peanut.

"The *Schwartzwald* entities," he said matter-of-factly as if their mere mention were self-evident.

"Explain," she said.

"You don't know?" he said in a surprised tone. "Your government's been working with them for years."

"What I know is of no concern to you," she hedged. "For all you know, I could be using this question to test whether you're deceiving me. And if you do lie to me, you do so at your own peril."

"Look," he pleaded, "I don't know all that much about that. But I'll tell you everything I know."

"Go on."

"*Abwehr*-controlled Soviet agents have been sending back reports since 1929 detailing alleged cooperation between the Soviets and extraterrestrial intelligences. My superiors didn't put much stock in the reports, because the accounts seemed so outlandish. In fact, my superiors had suspected the reports were part of a deliberate Soviet misinformation campaign to root out traitors in their midst. The theory gained a lot of credence at the time particularly in light of Stalin's great military purge. Consequently, my superiors ignored the reports.

"Then something extraordinary happened in 1936. No one above my pay grade will speak of it, but it was important enough that the *Abwehr* began diverting huge sections of its Technical Air Intelligence division to examine reports of unidentified flying objects over German air space."

"What exactly happened in 1936?" she said, interrupting the scientist.

He quivered and said, "Please. Don't hurt me. I swear I have no idea what happened. I only know how German intelligence responded."

Anna eyed Heisenberg for several seconds, hoping he'd say more to fill the silence. But he said nothing more. She asked her next question. "Why are you here?"

"After the Soviets unleashed parasite-infested corpses against Wehrmacht units in Operation Kutuzov, the *Oberkommando der Wehrmacht* sent me here to conduct some experiments."

"What sort of experiments?"

"I had been working on several quantum gravity experiments that the Wehrmacht thought could serve the war effort. The Nazi government provided me with the device currently in your hands and asked me to test and study it. They mentioned that the device's designers had leveraged the foundations of my early work in relativistic quantum field theory to develop the technology.

"During the course of my trials I quickly learned how to use the device to nullify gravity fields over limited distances. It's how I disabled you and Strauss in the farmhouse. More importantly, I discovered that Reich scientists and engineers couldn't have possibly constructed the device using current metallurgical principles, let alone forge it in any of Earth's modern foundries."

"Are you saying it was created by extraterrestrials?"

"No," he said. "I have no data to support or refute that hypothesis. For all I know, my government could have some advanced scientific facilities secreted away in Antarctica."

She considered his story. While the events she'd experienced over the last several weeks seemed unreal, Heisenberg's tale seemed even more fantastical. She reached a firm conclusion. "You're lying. Tell me who designed this or I'll ram these creatures up your nose."

Quaking, he coiled into a protective human spring, rippling with nervous energy. "Please! I assure you, I've told you everything I know. Please!"

"Then tell me why your leaders sent you here, now, right after the first time the Soviets deployed the walking dead in one of their offensives. Tell me, Doctor Heisenberg, what have you unleashed on my people? Have you even seen the horrors you've wrought here," Anna gestured at the wreckage surrounding them, "the Pandora's box you opened, unleashing untold horrors on my people?"

He rested his left arm at his side and glared at her. "*I* unleashed horrors on *your* people? Why don't you ask Stalin about opening Pandora's box? My government didn't send me here until the Soviet Union exposed humanity to an alien infestation that threatens the extinction of our entire species. My government only sent me here to conduct an anti-gravity experiment at some distance from the front. I used the device to open a gravity void about three kilometers from this spot, waited for thirty minutes for the device to collect data on the vortex, and then I ended my experiment. That's it."

"Why then, here? Why couldn't you conduct this experiment back home in a secure German laboratory?"

"Because we couldn't be sure of the fallout from our experiments. What better way to mitigate risk than to expose that risk to your enemies?"

Anna began to revisit her assumptions about this man. Perhaps he was telling the truth. "You really don't know what happened out there, do you?"

"What do you mean?" he said.

"Get up."

Heisenberg got on his feet.

"Go," she commanded, pointing toward the east.

He complied. She shadowed him, her rifle tracking his every movement.

"Strauss!" Anna called. "You can come out now."

Heisenberg spun his head toward her. "But, I thought he was sick."

"He is, but I managed to scrounge up some Pervitin to keep him going until we reach a proper hospital."

A beaming Strauss emerged from the other side of the T-34. "Doctor Heisenberg. It's a pleasure to see you again. As you can see, I'm feeling much better."

Heisenberg scowled at her. "You do realize that if he keeps taking those pills, he could go psychotic."

"I do," she said. "But I'd rather he be psychotic than dead." She prodded Heisenberg with the tip of her rifle. "Keep moving."

Strauss walked over to Heisenberg, extending his hand toward the physicist. "Doctor, I trusted your words, and you betrayed them. I thought you were a man of honor. I'd be happy to forget about your betrayal if you stand by your original promise."

Heisenberg seemed perturbed by Strauss's words. "How dare you impugn my honor! You coerced me to make that promise. Surely, you cannot expect a man to honor an agreement made under duress."

Strauss stood in silence, probably pondering over Heisenberg's logic. Anna cut Heisenberg off. "I could care less about your honor. As far as I'm concerned, you're a genocidal fascist. You will do as I say, when I say or I will shoot you. And unlike you, my actions are consistent with my words." She jabbed Heisenberg with her rifle. "Now walk."

Heisenberg followed Strauss to the vortex site. As the physicist passed the perverted and misshapen corpses, and mangled machinery, his defiant tone gave way to something softer, almost remorseful. *"Mein Gott,"* Heisenberg whispered. "What on Earth happened here? Did I unwittingly unleash some terror from the vortex?" Heisenberg lowered his head. "If my government did this, than it is no better than yours," Heisenberg said, glancing back at Anna.

Anna nodded and said, "Both sides are doing everything they can to destroy each other, and in the process have unleashed forces beyond their control. Yet both the Germans and the Soviets have ignored the bigger picture. By weakening each other, they are strengthening forces with the power to enslave or exterminate the human race."

Heisenberg turned and fell to his knees and pled with her. "Please, let me come with you. I will do whatever I can to help you put an end to all this. I swear I had no idea. I will fulfill my promise to help wean Strauss off his Pervitin addiction. Please, just tell me what you plan to do?"

Strauss's eyes locked with Anna's. She shook her head, but Strauss spoke anyway. "We intend to head for the United States. The Americans must be informed about what's happening here. If the rank-and-file Soviet officer corps is in the dark about the *Schwartzwald* entities, then Stalin's allies probably are as well."

"Thank you for trusting me, Georg. I promise I won't let you down again," Heisenberg said. The physicist then shifted his head toward her. "Please. Let me help. You can keep the device. Just let me help you put an end to this insanity. Please."

Anna glanced at Strauss. Strauss nodded. She looked down at Heisenberg and said, "Fine, but if I even suspect you're going to betray us, I will personally castrate you, shove your testicles in your mouth, and slit your throat. Am I clear?"

Heisenberg nodded, and the trio headed back west.

Chapter 11
Scorched Earth

1245 Hours, 23 August 1943, Kharkov City Limits, Ukraine

Outside, the world burned. Anna, Strauss, and Heisenberg huddled in a grimy culvert, where they lay in stagnant pools of water and filth reeking of urine and human feces. They choked on the smoke from thousands of brush fires consuming the Ukrainian countryside. Heisenberg seemed especially nervous that the constant ebb and flow over control of Kharkov had left the trio behind Soviet lines.

The ground quaked as Soviet armor rumbled over the road above the culvert in pursuit of retreating Wehrmacht units. Despite the squalid conditions and horrible discomfort, Anna fastidiously cleaned her bolt action Mosin-Nagant PE sniper rifle, working her ribbed rod-cleaning jag into the rifle's bore.

Over the past two weeks, Strauss had nearly exhausted his Pervitin supply. This morning, he'd emptied his last two tablets of Pervitin from a glass container, and left them in his cargo pocket for use later that day.

Whenever he went a day or more without Pervitin, his withdrawal symptoms returned. Dehydration, exhaustion, and depravation would overwhelm him, making him feel entombed in his own skin. Then, if he went more than two days without his pills, he'd hallucinate, sometimes clawing at imagined spiders on his skin. What's worse, he hated that Anna had seen him in such a wretched state. He shuddered to contemplate what she must think of his weakness, his inability to kick his addiction.

He felt slightly better now, just well enough to function. But more often than not, Anna would find him plundering German corpses for Pervitin tablets, a necessity of his existence that shamed him. Yet she'd stuck with him. Maybe she'd felt guilty about killing his brother at Stalingrad. Perhaps she'd thought she owed him for rescuing her from the *Schwartzwald* entity at Kursk.

In the end, it didn't matter. Strauss didn't deserve her, and she didn't deserve to suffer him. Strauss's loyalty to Inge further complicated his complex relationship with Anna. He felt duty-bound to stay true to Inge, even though he hadn't heard from her in over a year.

"The Red Army has captured Kharkov," Anna said. Her words came across as if they were self-evident, a statement of fact expressed without malice or joy.

Anna had changed a great deal during their time together. When Strauss first met her, she'd been an ardent patriot, willing to suffer for her Motherland through the siege of Stalingrad. Now, she seemed to have almost completely disassociated herself from the Soviet Union. It was almost as if she'd blamed Stalin for unleashing this scourge on humanity.

Cramped in close quarters and breathing rancid air, the crushing tension tested the trio's sanity. Every time a tank rumbled over the road above, the culvert shook, rattling everyone's nerves. Strauss had had plenty of time to develop his own coping strategies, and Anna likely had too. But both Anna and Strauss required silence to maintain their calm. However, war was a new experience for Heisenberg. And the physicist didn't seem to have a clue how to cope. So in times of crisis, Heisenberg chatted incessantly. No matter what they tried, Strauss and Anna couldn't shut him up.

"Strauss," Heisenberg said, his voice uncertain and cracking, "what's the first meal you plan to have when you get back to Germany and civilization?"

Heisenberg was always talking about food. Who could blame him? Few people realize the convenience of modern day comforts until they get to the field. A soft bed, a hot meal, a warm shower, and a modern toilet may have been commonplace in German society, but on the Eastern Front, they were unobtainable luxuries. The mere mention of a hot meal would make Strauss salivate, his mouth dripping in anticipation of well-cooked meat.

The last thing Strauss wanted to do was chat, but given Heisenberg's inexperience and almost certain terror of being nearly alone and behind enemy lines, Strauss indulged the physicist. "I suppose a large medium rare steak would do the trick. How about you, Anna?"

The former Soviet sniper rolled her eyes and said, "Human flesh, and I'd probably start with yours, Werner."

Heisenberg snickered nervously. Ever since Anna and Heisenberg had met, Anna excelled at getting under the man's skin. Strauss didn't like it, but he understood why Anna held such contempt for the man. Yet, despite Anna's reservations, Strauss was confident he and Anna needed Heisenberg if they ever hoped to reach America. The physicist would be a valuable bargaining chip to the Americans in a way that a Waffen-SS sergeant and a defecting Soviet major would not. So Strauss did his best to reassure Heisenberg during their journey.

"Don't mind her, Doctor Heisenberg. She's just messing with you. What's the first thing you plan to eat when you get home?" Strauss said.

Heisenberg smiled and said, "If you don't mind, I'd like to keep that thought to myself. If I tell you, I'm worried I'll jinx my chances of ever reaching home again."

Strauss nodded. "But Herr Heisenberg, I thought you were a physicist, a man of logic and ready."

Heisenberg chuckled. "Indeed. I guess I'm a bit like the wave-particle duality of light. As light is both a particle and a wave, I'm both logical and superstitious – yet another of life's great paradoxes."

"I'm not sure I follow, but if you won't tell me about your first meal, at least tell me who you'd share it with."

Heisenberg's eyes gleamed. "I would share it with my wife, Elisabeth." He looked down, and then up at Strauss. The physicist had the glint of a tear in his eye. "I miss her so much. Sometimes you never truly realize how much you cherish someone until they are far away in space and time."

Strauss couldn't help but agree with Heisenberg. The man's sentiment unearthed more memories of Inge. Yet Strauss couldn't bear to think of her here and now. So he tried to take his mind off her.

"How about you, Anna?" Strauss said. "Did you leave anyone special behind?"

Anna blushed. She hesitated as if unsure of what to say. "I had a few flings here and there, but no one I'd consider special. This war has made such arrangements impossible." Then Anna said something that caught Strauss completely off guard. "Did you leave anyone behind?"

Now that Anna had turned the tables on Strauss, he no longer liked the question. He also wasn't even sure how to answer it. While it was true he was saving himself for Inge, something was incredibly alluring about Anna. She was decisive, bold, loyal, and intelligent, and he could imagine a future with her. But he also had a duty to Inge. He owed her his loyalty, and he owed Anna the truth.

Strauss took a deep breath. "I left behind a woman I care deeply about and to whom I made a promise—a promise to remain true to her until I return from the war."

The way Anna's eyelashes flickered ever so slightly betrayed her stoic expression, and Strauss could sense she was upset.

"What's your lover's name?" Anna said. The way she'd phrased the question made Strauss feel as if she was trying to diminish Inge's significance.

"Inge."

Then Anna said something that devastated Strauss. "This Inge is a very fortunate woman."

Strauss just nodded, unsure what to say. Should he tell Anna that she could just have easily been the object of his affection; that Anna had more in common with him than Inge ever did? War made a mess of everything, but it also created possibilities. Was Strauss making the right choice? Was Inge the right woman for him?

"Do you intend to marry this Inge?" Anna said, unwittingly shoving a dagger deeper into Strauss's heart.

Strauss hesitated, and then whispered, "I do."

Anna laughed. "You do realize that capitalism has destroyed the traditional familial unit. Good luck trying to raise a family when both husband and wife are forced to eke out a living without the help of a benevolent state. Only communism has adequate solutions to help workers properly raise a family."

"Say what you will, Anna, but I'll always be a man of tradition, and I will never be a communist," Strauss said.

"Have it your way," Anna said, "But don't say I didn't warn you."

Another T-34 rumbled over the culvert and stopped. Boots landed on the pavement.

Anna prepared her rifle, while Strauss loaded a Luger he'd appropriated from a German officer's corpse.

The soldiers above bantered in Russian. Their voices were getting closer.

Strauss cocked his Luger.

Three soldiers dropped down from the road, converging on the culvert, their rifles pointing at the trio. Their leader yelled some indecipherable order in Russian.

Anna looked at Strauss and whispered. "They're demanding we surrender our weapons and identify ourselves. They want to know why two soldiers from the Eleventh Guards Army are nowhere near the Eleventh Guards. They probably think we're deserters."

"What should we do?" Strauss whispered, hoping the soldiers didn't hear him speaking in German.

"Let me see if I can talk my way out of this," Anna said. She answered the men in Russian. As she did so, one soldier's eyes widened when he saw Heisenberg. He then pawed frantically at his military tunic's upper left cargo pocket. He extracted a leaflet, pointing excitedly at it while showing it to his leader. The excited soldier then pointed at Heisenberg.

Anna's placed her right cheek on her rifle, her eye staring down the length of the weapon through her scope. "They know who he is," Anna said.

"Who, Heisenberg?" Strauss asked.

"Yes."

One soldier pointed his weapon into the culvert and nattered excitedly. Anna pulled back the bolt on her rifle, chambering a round, and then shot the man in the chest, but not before he could fire off a round into the culvert.

Heisenberg screamed.

The other two soldiers bolted away from the culvert's entrance and out of Anna's field of fire.

A pool of blood slowly congealed under Heisenberg. Strauss cocked his Luger and pulled out his empty bottle of Pervitin. He waited, his heart pounding. If the soldiers were smart, they'd roll a grenade into the culvert and be done with it. So, Strauss needed to act fast or they'd all die in a fetid culvert covered in shit.

Strauss raised the bottle over his head and glanced at Anna. She crawled up to Strauss so they lay side by side. Strauss tossed the bottle out of the culvert. Two bullets followed: one from his left traveling on a downward angle, and the other one moving straight down from the road above.

Strauss nodded to Anna. "Now!"

Strauss pointed his Luger to his left and up, along the same trajectory as the first bullet. Anna stuck her rifle out of the culvert, pointing it up and backwards, firing it.

Two screams.

Strauss rolled out of the hole and turned only to find one man straddling the culvert with his hands on his groin, blood flowing down the blackened concrete. The other man, now on Strauss's right lay on the embankment, his left hand on his bloody left leg, but his right hand rested on the trigger of a rifle. With one arm, the man lowered his rifle and squeezed off a shot, narrowly missing Strauss's head by a quarter of a meter. Strauss aimed his Luger and fired, hitting the man in the chest.

The other man was fumbling for his weapon when Anna calmly slit his throat with her combat knife.

"We've got to hide these soldiers and get out of here," Anna said. "Our gunshots will attract attention, even in an environment as noisy as this."

Heisenberg screamed.

"What about him?" Strauss said.

"Leave him here. He'll be nothing but a liability, and we still don't know if we can trust him," Anna replied.

Strauss considered her point and then made his decision. "I can't do that. I'll carry him like you carried me."

"It's your funeral," Anna said. "Are you sure you can do without Pervitin?"

"I'll be all right for now. Plus, Heisenberg's the only one who will be able to make me better, right?"

Anna shrugged her shoulders. "Fine. Hurry up then."

Strauss crawled back into the filthy culvert and carefully pulled out Heisenberg, and then lowered the physicist to the ground. Because Heisenberg was caked in filth, Strauss couldn't quickly determine where the physicist had been shot.

Anna and Strauss stacked the three bodies in the hole before triaging Heisenberg.

Strauss knelt beside the wounded physicist. "Where are you hit?"

Heisenberg groaned, pointing to his abdomen.

"Water," Strauss said.

Anna tossed Strauss a canteen. He took out his knife and cut open Heisenberg's sweater and collared shirt. He then poured water on the wound to clean it as best he could. The smell of Heisenberg's intestinal viscera was overwhelming. From one look, Strauss knew Heisenberg was going to die, a slow and painful death. The wound, coupled with the certainty of sepsis, would kill him in less than a day.

Strauss had lived through so many of these moments; moments when he watched life leave a friend's eyes. And no matter how many times he'd watched a good man die, it never got any easier.

As Heinz had lain dying, Strauss's final words to his brother had been lies. Strauss had cradled his broken brother in his arms, watching over him in despair. Nearly a quarter of his brother's skull had been missing, and Heinz had been nearly catatonic. Strauss remembered the gut-wrenching hopelessness of it all in that forlorn tomb called Stalingrad. "You're gonna be all right," he'd lied to his brother as Heinz's eyes had rolled back into his head and his mouth had frothed in a seizure.

No. Heisenberg deserved to hear the truth. Strauss grabbed Heisenberg's head and fixed the physicist's eyes on Strauss's. "I'm sorry, friend, but you don't have much time left. Is there anything I can do to ease your passing?"

Heisenberg sat dumbfounded seemingly pondering Strauss's blunt admission. Strauss could see the man, who, even in death, appeared to be calculating, rationalizing, considering. Then, Heisenberg's eyes widened in what seemed like some deluded flash of brilliance. The physicist glanced toward Anna and said, "The organisms, do you still have them?"

Strauss instantly grasped the implications of Heisenberg's query. "No, it would only make things worse. You should die in dignity, not in horror."

"How many organisms did the automatons have in their skulls?" Heisenberg asked.

Strauss scratched his head, "I don't know, a handful?" Strauss looked toward Anna for confirmation, and she nodded.

"What if I were to let one infest my mind? Surely any chance at life would be better than none at all, no?" Heisenberg reasoned.

Strauss again looked to Anna for a decision and she said, "No, I'd rather not unleash any more of these things into the world."

"Please, it can enter my nasal cavity. Maybe my will can triumph over the parasite's."

"Anna, just let him do it. It's his decision, not ours," Strauss pleaded.

"But if the parasite takes over, he'll try to kill us. Is it really worth the risk?" Anna said.

"What if it were me? Would you let me die here or would you roll the dice?" Strauss asked.

Anna brooded. Strauss could tell she wasn't happy he framed the decision that way. Then she said, "Do it then. But I swear that if Heisenberg even walks funny after we do this, I will shoot his body into shreds. Remember: clean hands are dead hands."

Strauss nodded and turned toward Heisenberg. "You sure about this, Doctor?"

Heisenberg groaned and then said, "Yes. The pain is too much. If I don't do this, I'll die soon."

"Fine then. Anna, hand me the Mason jar," Strauss said.

Anna pulled out the jar. Inside, the licelike organisms writhed in black ooze. She opened the lid, placed the jar on the ground, and then scooped out a parasite with her knife. Strauss then closed the jar.

Strauss removed a tablet from his pocket and handed it to Heisenberg. "Take this if you feel yourself losing control to the parasite. Perhaps the Pervitin can keep you focused."

"Thank you, Strauss," Heisenberg said as he placed the tablet in the pocket of his chinos. "You're a true friend." Heisenberg then glanced toward Anna. "Do it."

Anna brought her knife tip to Heisenberg's nostril, and as if by instinct, the parasite forced itself into Heisenberg's nose. Heisenberg screamed, then convulsed until he passed out.

Both Anna and Strauss watched Heisenberg. Uncertain what to expect next, worry consumed Strauss and he was already beginning to regret his decision.

"Just to be safe, we should bind his hands and feet," Strauss said. Anna agreed, and the pair tied Heisenberg's hands and his feet together, and then dragged him several hundred meters down the embankment to a better hiding place. Anna and Strauss observed Heisenberg until the sun set, and then tried to get some sleep before another busy morning.

∞

Strauss woke to find Anna in a fury.

"Heisenberg's gone," she said in a tone dripping with contempt. "This time, he's on his own, and that's if he's even still alive."

Anna was in such a state, that Strauss knew better than to push his luck. There were only two conclusions Strauss could draw from the experience: either the parasite had taken over Heisenberg's body, in which case Anna and Strauss could do nothing to save the physicist; or Heisenberg had abandoned him and Anna for the second time, in which case, Heisenberg didn't deserve their help.

Either way, Heisenberg was now a lost cause, so the two resumed their journey west toward redemption.

Chapter 12
Triumph of the Will

0545 Hours, 24 August 1943, Kharkov, Ukraine

Heisenberg sailed through the dark void between galaxies. The memories of a thousand thousand generations washed over him. His myriad siblings writhed and pressed against him for warmth in space's cold vacuum. Two overriding directives dominated his thoughts—propagate and consume. Render all sentient life into our image.

The hives passed a bright golden sun and then drifted toward its habitable zone, where a lush, azure world teeming with life awaited them. When the queens learned that a sentient species occupied this planet, they organized their hives for synergistic hybridization.

The hives' hibernation pods burrowed into the regolith on the hidden far side of that world's one and only moon. There, they laid in wait until they learned more about the creatures they would soon metamorphose into a superior, more adaptable species.

Heisenberg woke from his vivid dream—a dream more like a stream of memories from a distant past. Despite having been asleep, he awoke midstride, marching toward the rising sun. A small cadre of men dressed in cheap suits and carrying submachine guns escorted him somewhere east.

He had no idea who these men were or where they were taking him, so he just decided to play along. When the men started speaking to one another in Russian, Heisenberg had a pretty good idea of where he was headed.

No, it can't be, he thought. *How the hell did I get here? Why was I sleepwalking among Russian-speaking operatives? Am I still in the Ukraine or have I crossed over into Soviet Russia?*

Then Heisenberg recalled his wound and the parasite inside him. He placed his hand on his belly. It had swollen into an infested black boil. Without the parasite, Heisenberg was certain he'd be dead by now.

He felt something reaching from the dark recesses of his mind, attempting to reassert control. The desire to fade away was almost uncontrollable. Heisenberg wanted nothing more than to sleep. But his rational mind struggled for dominance over his reptilian brain and the other consciousness, lurking inside his dark dreams.

Then Heisenberg remembered he had Pervitin. As he fought to remain conscious, he rifled through his pockets to find Strauss's parting gift. He placed the tablet in his mouth and prayed for clarity and focus.

Heisenberg waited for the boost of energy he needed to maintain control, but the soporific powers of the beast inside him were too strong to resist. Just as the dizziness and blackness nearly overcame him, a jolt of energy rushed through Heisenberg's limbs, coursing through his veins, and providing his brain the added boost it needed to silence the interloper in his mind.

The operatives marched along an unpaved road bisecting a dense wheatfield. The wheatfield was one of many in a patchwork of undulating golden waves stretching across an infinite horizon.

The men traveled for what seemed like several kilometers through an unchanging landscape. For all Heisenberg knew, they'd march forever until they dropped dead from exhaustion.

By the time the sun hovered in the midday sky, Heisenberg's escorts were drenched in sweat, and their pace had slackened. Yet Strauss felt neither pain nor exhaustion. His feet weren't sore, and he didn't perspire. Heisenberg suspected the parasite was responsible for his newly manifested superhuman endurance.

The group ascended a hill with a long, slow grade. After another hour, Heisenberg reached the summit. The hill dominated an auburn valley below, where a large bivouac site overflowing with field tents and covered with grassland camouflage rested.

The men halted for several minutes. Most pulled out their canteens and drank, before striking out for the laager site below.

Within the hour, Heisenberg's captors brought him to a field tent in the center of the encampment. Two burly men pushed him forward into the canvas enclosure.

Unfiltered pipe smoke wafted in Heisenberg's face when he entered the tent. The inside of the structure was high enough for a man to stand, but not wide enough to comfortably stretch one's arms. A makeshift wooden field table dominated the center of the tent. A thuggish man with black hair, a broad forehead, and widow's peak sat alone at the table, smoking a pipe while he reviewed various coffee-stained documents. Behind him stood three easels supporting several regional and tactical maps.

When Heisenberg entered, the man raised his bushy black eyebrows. He smiled and started speaking to Heisenberg in Russian. The man's tone seemed warm and friendly as if he were somehow familiar with Heisenberg, though Heisenberg had no recollection of meeting the man. When

Heisenberg failed to reply, the man stared at the physicist as if seeking some sort of answer or solving a complicated riddle.

Then the man's tone changed markedly from jovial to angry. He shouted questions at Heisenberg in rapid fire Russian. After about three minutes of railing, the man sat back and started laughing.

"Of course!" he said in heavily accented German. "If the human inside you temporarily regained control, you likely wouldn't understand Russian. Welcome to my temporary headquarters in the Ukraine, Doctor Heisenberg," the man said, rising from his table and extending his hand toward Heisenberg. "Allow me to introduce myself. My name is General Valentin Kravchenko, Head of the Special Technical Bureau at the NKVD USSR. I apologize for my manners. I was expecting someone else."

Heisenberg timidly shook Kravchenko's hand. The befuddled physicist could only conclude one thing: the Soviets knew what was inside him. Even worse, the Soviets appeared to have had a long-standing relationship with it. How was that possible?

"At this point, you're probably wondering why I seemed to be acting so familiar around you when you and I have never met, aren't you?"

Heisenberg had no idea where this was going, but he decided to humor Kravchenko. "Indeed. If you would be kind enough to explain, I'd greatly appreciate it."

"Ah, you Germans. Always so polite and efficient, except when you force yourselves upon people you consider subhuman. Then you act like a bunch of rabid jackals," Kravchenko said. "But I digress. The reason I know the parasite inside you so well is that the *Keldrahdi*, or what you Nazis call *Schwartzwald* entities, have a hive mind and possess genetic memories. Based on our observations, they transfer their memories telepathically across short distances. Therefore, the *Keldrahdi* entities inside you are very likely up to date on the most recent developments. A very handy adaptation if I may say so myself."

Heisenberg was at a loss for words. The fact that this Soviet official had so carelessly leaked what were almost certainly highly classified state secrets worried Heisenberg. The physicist suspected the man planned to shoot him once the interrogation ended.

Kravchenko continued. "What intrigues me, however, is how you were able to re-exert control over the parasitic entities inside you, or is it only one entity? Maybe that's it. How many of them are inside your mind, Doctor Heisenberg?"

Heisenberg considered avoiding the question so he could use the information as leverage to keep himself alive. Yet, somehow Kravchenko had already seemed to anticipate that. "If you think your keeping silent will stop me from extracting the information I require, you don't know me very well. I'm an artiste of the modern era. I paint in blood and enemies of the state are my canvass. I'll simply crack open your skull with a pair of pliers and dig it out myself."

"One," Heisenberg answered, deciding resistance was pointless.

"Very interesting," Kravchenko said, clasping his hands. Kravchenko then asked one of Heisenberg's escorts a question in Russian. The escort responded, *"Da."*

Kravchenko returned his attention to Heisenberg. "It seems the entity had been controlling you for some time, but you woke up. We've never seen that happen before. What's more interesting is that you've managed to retain control for some period of time. What's your secret?"

"My secret?" Heisenberg said.

"Yes, what mental techniques are you using to maintain control. After all, the longer the entity is inside you, the more it expands and the firmer its tendrils take root in your internal organs. Soon, it will be impossible for you to resist, and the *Keldrahdi* inside you will ultimately overpower your psyche."

"How… how could you possibly know that?" Heisenberg shuddered.

"How do you know that gravity exists?"

"Henry Cavendish's experiment and Newton's apple."

"Exactly. We know these things from careful and painstaking empirical studies."

"You… you put these parasites into living humans."

"Well, of course," Kravchenko said. "How else could we discover how quickly the entities take control of their hosts? The most talented artists don't become famous by avoiding risk. True art is a process that requires alternating cycles of creation and destruction, death and rebirth."

"How much time do I have?" Heisenberg said, tentatively.

"Well, the good news is that you've already survived longer than any other human being we've tested. The bad news is… well… you know. Which is why I find you so intriguing, Doctor Heisenberg. There's something about you that is an outlier, aside from your being a Nobel Laureate, of course. And I must know what it is. But we can save that discussion for another time. There's the matter of the vortex and the ghost men that wiped out an entire Motorized Rifle Regiment in less than three hours. Even the *Keldrahdi* couldn't explain what happened there. Perhaps you can enlighten me, Doctor Heisenberg?"

"I'm sorry. I can't help you with that," Heisenberg lied.

"Do not attempt to deceive me, Doctor. For some time, the *Keldrahdi* parasite inside you could access some of your latent memories. According to radio communications I've exchanged with my operatives, soldiers in the area spotted you operating a strange device within several kilometers of ground zero. Where is that device and who or what attacked my comrades?"

Heisenberg shrugged. He thought about denying the device's existence, but that would only delay the inevitable. He needed to end this discussion as soon as possible so he could focus on his escape. After all, the *Keldrahdi* inside him would almost certainly assume control once the effects of the Pervitin faded.

"I'm sorry, general. I can't help you. The last time I saw the device was shortly before the parasite infected me. Then I blacked out and ended up here. In regards to what happened to that Motorized Rifle Regiment, I'm sorry. I can't help you. I only triggered the device. I had no idea what it had unleashed. But I did witness its aftermath, and it was horrifying."

Kravchenko smiled. "Normally, Doctor Heisenberg, I wouldn't believe anything you said, but I know better. So far your testimony has been consistent with what the entity inside you had reported to my agents. One last thing: where are your two companions heading?"

Heisenberg clammed up. Strauss's quick thinking with the Pervitin, and Anna's foresight in gathering the parasites had saved Heisenberg's life. He owed it to both of them to keep their plans quiet. "I'm sorry, general, I'm unaware of their plans."

Kravchenko stared at Heisenberg for several seconds in complete silence and then said, "Are you certain, Doctor Heisenberg? Because if you're lying to me, my hospitality might turn into hostility."

"I'm certain," Heisenberg bluffed.

"A pity. I quite enjoyed our unencumbered free flow of information here," Kravchenko said. He directed his eyes toward one of Heisenberg's escorts and said something in Russian. Both men saluted, grabbed Heisenberg, and led him outside the tent. They transported him to a smaller tent, motioning him to go inside. Heisenberg found a small canvas cot waiting for him there.

Heisenberg peeked outside the tent to get a sense of his surroundings, but found the two men guarding the exit. The physicist was desperate to find a way out of the encampment before the parasite permanently exerted control over his body. So Heisenberg bided his time until darkness fell, when he planned to attempt an escape.

&

2250 Hours, 24 August 1943, Kharkov, Ukraine

Well after nightfall, Heisenberg stuck his head outside the flaps of his tent and discovered his guards had left. He found this development somewhat strange, but decided to capitalize on this sudden stroke of luck. As he slinked through the encampment, the relative lack of security astonished him. But at this point, it didn't matter. He needed to find some Pervitin to ensure he'd make it back to Germany in time for doctors to discover a method to surgically remove the parasite.

&

Colonel Nimerov marched into General Kravchenko's tent, clicked his heels together, and rendered a crisp salute. Kravchenko returned the salute and said, "I trust our friend is now on the move?"

The Colonel nodded. "Yes, Sir. Doctor Heisenberg is heading west as we suspected. We've sent several NKVD surveillance details to track him."

"Excellent. The operation appears to be going according to plan. Before long, we'll have the device, Major Ivanova, and Strauss. Then Comrade Stalin will stop breathing down our backs. See to it that the operation succeeds quickly."

Nimerov understood Kravchenko's subtext. They both knew that if they failed, the best they could hope for was a one-way ticket to Siberia's gulag archipelago.

Chapter 13
Reckoning

1830 Hours, 25 August 1943, Krasnograd, Ukraine

The three German soldiers manning the sandbag checkpoint wore torn and frayed uniforms. Two coils of razor-sharp Dannert wire blocked the dirt road. One rail thin German chain-smoked a cigarette as if each shot of nicotine might be his last. Another had a bloody bandage covering his left eye. And every man had his finger on his rifle's trigger.

Heisenberg approached the men cautiously, his hands held high. He'd traveled all night through Soviet-controlled territory disguised as a Ukrainian peasant.

The one-eyed man advanced toward Heisenberg. The German seemed more boy than man, and more bone than sinew. Based on the men's sickly condition, Heisenberg guessed they hadn't eaten or slept in several days. The thought that they'd used Pervitin to accomplish this feat secretly excited Heisenberg. In fact, he counted on it.

The man stopped about ten meters from Heisenberg, pointing his rifle at the physicist. "Stop there or I'll shoot."

Heisenberg complied.

The German pressed forward again, his rifle cradled in his right arm, while his left arm reached for Heisenberg's clothing. "Hans!" the man called. "Cover me while I search this peasant."

The chain-smoker's cigarette dangled lazily from his mouth, as he lifted his rifle, aimed it at Heisenberg, and then advanced steadily toward him.

The one-eyed soldier motioned for Heisenberg to lie face down on the dirt road, but his eyes widened when he saw Heisenberg's belly. "Whoa! Look at that gut! This guy looks pregnant."

Heisenberg ignored the insult and obeyed the soldier's instructions without complaint.

The soldier patted down Heisenberg, searching for weapons and other contraband. His task complete, the German said, "Identify yourself?"

"My name is Doctor Werner Heisenberg."

The three soldiers laughed in unison, until the man nearest Heisenberg abruptly ceased giggling. An expression of recognition registered on his face. The man's smile expanded into a wide gape. "Holy shit! This guy is a dead ringer for Werner Heisenberg. Check it out Hans!"

The soldier training his rifle on Heisenberg lowered it and strolled over to the physicist. His face expressed similar surprise. "You're right. This guy looks like the real ticket."

Heisenberg was getting impatient. Judging that the danger had passed, he decided to try his luck at giving orders for a change. "I'm so happy to have amused you. Now that I have your undivided attention, I need any supplies of Pervitin you have on hand. I also require access to a wireless set."

The men chortled, and then the third man, who remained protected behind the sandbags yelled, "What the hell is going on over there?"

The man then left his command post, and walked over to his men. "What the hell's going on here?" he repeated.

The smoker took a drag on his cigarette, and said, "Oh, this nutcase thinks he's Werner Heisenberg."

The man, who seemed a bit older than his two comrades, inclined his head toward Heisenberg and said, "Is that so?"

"It is. Now, I would appreciate it if you would provide me with the two items I requested."

"Do you take me for a fool?" the squad leader said. "I'm not going to give you something just because you say you're somebody. I'm gonna need some proof."

Heisenberg considered the man's request, thinking of ways to convince the men of his veracity. "I'll tell you what. If you give me a pencil and some paper, I'll provide you with a radio frequency. If you call that frequency and identify yourself as Quantum Knight Proxy, they will confirm I am who I say I am."

The squad leader squinted his eyes as if attempting to root out some imagined deception perpetrated by Heisenberg. The man then said, "And what happens if I don't do that?"

"What's your name?" Heisenberg asked.

"*Feldwebel* Müller."

"Well, if you don't at least attempt to confirm my identity, *SS-Obergruppenführer* Heydrich will almost certainly learn that *Feldwebel* Müller refused to help Doctor Werner Heisenberg, the German Nobel Laureate, complete a mission that was instrumental to the Fatherland's war effort. If you're comfortable with that risk, then don't help me."

The man barely hesitated before handing Heisenberg a dirty slip of paper and a graphite pencil. Heisenberg scribbled the frequency on the slip. The soldier grabbed the piece of paper and returned to his position behind the sandbags. He accessed his wireless set, switched to the specified frequency, and radioed for confirmation. "Any station, any station, this is Quantum Knight Proxy. Radio check, over."

Within seconds a voice answered, "Quantum Knight Proxy, this is Albatross One. Confirm Quantum Knight Actual is co-located, over."

"Albatross One, Quantum Knight Proxy. Negative. Contact claims to be Quantum Knight Actual. I require confirmation, over."

"Negative, Quantum Knight Proxy. Confirmation requires transmitter to know the proper frequency and code name. Quantum Knight Actual is the only operative with that combination. Break. If Quantum Knight Actual is co-located, put him on the net, over."

The soldier glanced at Heisenberg and waved for the physicist to come forward. As Heisenberg walked over to the sandbags, he said, "Can you supply me with the Pervitin I asked for?"

Müller nodded and motioned for the chain-smoker to do as Heisenberg requested. The soldier tossed Heisenberg a half full bottle of the drug. Heisenberg opened the bottle, removed two Pervitin tablets, and swallowed them. Heisenberg then grabbed the wireless speaker and said, "Albatross One, this is Quantum Knight Actual. SITREP follows."

"Quantum Knight, Albatross One. Send it."

"Quantum gravity test successful. Break. Positive contact with *Schwartzwald* entities. I've been infected. Request immediate medical assistance, over."

"Quantum Knight, Albatross One. Standby, over."

Heisenberg waited for several minutes.

"Quantum Knight, this is codename Heydrich. Do you have anything else to report?"

SS-Obergruppenführer Heydrich was actually on the communications net. Not good. Not good at all. If the *Obergruppenführer* asked about the device and Heisenberg reported it lost, it could mean Heisenberg's imprisonment or something far worse.

Heisenberg hesitated and then said, "Negative, over."

"Quantum Knight, Heydrich. We will transport you and the *Schwerkraft* Device to a medical facility run by the SS Technical Division. Break. What's your current location, over?"

Heisenberg panicked. There was no way he could avoid telling Heydrich the truth without making matters worse, so he decided to come clean sooner rather than later. "Codename Heydrich, Quantum Knight. *Schwerkraft* Device is lost. I say again: *Schwerkraft* Device is lost, over."

Heisenberg's heart pounded as he waited for Heydrich's response. "Quantum Knight, this is Codename Heydrich. Where did you lose the device, over?"

The physicist told Heydrich about Heisenberg's near death experience and the unconsciousness that followed after he merged with the parasite. He also related how Strauss and Anna had helped him survive. However, Heisenberg was loyal enough to his friends that he omitted any mention of their location or ultimate destination.

"Where did you last see them, over?"

Heisenberg again wavered. If he gave Heydrich their location, he'd send SS units to pursue, apprehend, and potentially kill them. He decided to provide Heydrich with perfect accuracy but limited precision. "Codename Heydrich, Quantum Knight. Last location was on a road outside Kharkov city limits heading west, over."

"Send grid, over."

"Negative knowledge, over."

"Roger. Sending SS units to intercept personnel around thirty-kilometer radius of Kharkov. Break. Send your grid coordinates for further instructions, over."

Heisenberg turned to Müller and said, "What are our grid coordinates?"

The soldier provided Heisenberg with their location, and Heisenberg transmitted the coordinates to Heydrich. Heydrich repeated the coordinates to ensure they were correct and Heisenberg confirmed them. "Standby," Heydrich transmitted.

Heisenberg waited for several minutes before receiving another transmission. "Quantum Knight. Proceed to the airfield at Checkpoint Zulu Six Alpha. The soldiers with you now are familiar with it and will escort you there."

"Roger," Heisenberg said.

"Heydrich out," the *Obergruppenführer* said, ending the transmission.

Heisenberg took a deep breath and followed the soldiers to Checkpoint Zulu Six Alpha.

Chapter 14
River Crossing

Anna watched the two-tiered, three-arch railway bridge through her binos. The bridge stretched across the New Dnieper stream of the Dnieper River towards Khortytsi Island. On the upper tier, a locomotive pulling cars teeming with German tanks and artillery pieces confirmed the rumors that the Germans had finally repaired the bridge.

On the lower tier, a long-gray stream of German troops marched steadily across the span. The swarming Soviet divisions on the Dnieper's eastern bank convinced Anna the bridge wouldn't be operational for much longer. Dark gray clouds hovered in the sky threatening to disgorge their cold ordnance. The wind carried the scent of an oncoming rainstorm.

Anna sought out a secluded ditch. Using her black entrenching spade, she dug a small hole where she would bury her waste. Several hundred meters beyond that ditch across a field, Strauss rested against the burned out hulk of a T-34. As Anna removed her grimy trousers, she watched Strauss from the corner of her eye like a protective mother wolf.

It had been a precarious few months for Anna. NKVD units had been hot on their trail. Anna had dyed her ginger hair blonde and had called in a favor from a fellow Ukrainian soldier to forge documents that would help her and Strauss secure passage through the multitude of Soviet divisions mobilizing outside of Wehrmacht-controlled Zaporizhia, one of the last German bridgeheads on the Dnieper's eastern bank.

For Strauss, life had been much harder. He'd played the part of a mute Soviet conscript, an Estonian Baltic German who'd suffered a head injury at Kursk. Strauss even had a bandage wrapped around his head to prove it. Anna's heart had always seized whenever they'd run into a Soviet checkpoint, and there'd been plenty of them between here and Kursk. She'd frequently worried that someone might check under Strauss's bandage to expose the deception.

The rain began to fall in a light drizzle. A catcall from the opposite end of the ditch surprised Anna. Three Soviet soldiers approached her, all of them snickering in a manner that unsettled her.

More beast than man, one soldier stood nearly two meters tall. His dull blue eyes and bushy red beard gave Anna a sense of how a serf must have looked before Peter the Great had forced men to shave. As the brute lumbered toward her, she could smell his rank rural musk, a scent like stale sweat mixed with sulfur. He stalked toward her like a pack leader, his two wolves in tow. His eyes focused squarely on her exposed genitals.

The rain now fell with increasing intensity. Anna scrambled to lift her trousers. The men drew closer. Out of the corner of her eye, she saw another squad of soldiers approaching Strauss from across the field. When she returned her attention to her own predicament, the bear-man grabbed her arm with his greasy and calloused hands. He leered at her like a hungry jackal.

"Nice finding you here, my pretty little *devotchka*," the giant man growled. "Things could soon get ugly with the fascists, and me and my boys are tense and tired. Whaddya say you help us all relax?"

Anna pushed away the man's muscle-corded arm. "Get your hands off me," she said with the air of someone who had been accustomed to commanding men.

The pack leader's mouth opened in what seemed like surprise, as if he wasn't quite sure how to react. Then, his eyes widened and his open mouth slowly curled into a sneer. "Well, well, you filthy little *suka*," he growled. "I thought you looked familiar. You're that major the NKVD's been looking for. I suppose they wouldn't mind if me and my men had a go at you first before we turned you in."

Anna trembled and was on the verge of panic; but panic wouldn't do. She searched frantically for a weapon, anything she could use to fight. Her rifle was several meters away, but it wouldn't be of any use in close quarters. Her spade was within reach, but if she grabbed it now, the three men would overpower her and use it against her. Then she saw one of the burly man's henchmen pull out a captured SS ceremonial dagger. She had to think fast.

"Wait. There's no need to be rough, boys," she cooed, "I'm a bit wanting myself. But I'd prefer a roll in the hay with the big boy first." She winked at the massive man to underscore her feigned interest.

The man puffed up his chest and smiled, exposing his rotten and crooked teeth. He started undoing the buttons on his trousers.

Anna waved her finger. "Now, now, this isn't any old romp in the hay. You're gonna be with a real lady. If you really wanna see what I've got, we're gonna need some privacy." she said, pointing toward a broken down jeep about two hundred meters from her current position. She grasped the brute's hand to lead him there.

"Bullshit. I'm not falling for your dirty tricks," the man said as he seized her. He forced her to the ground. Anna almost screamed, but she knew better than that. The last thing she wanted to do was draw more attention to herself. She'd been made, so there was only one thing left to do. She reached for his testicles, dug in her nails and twisted hard. The man squealed and rolled off her, collapsing into a fetal position.

She clutched a handful of mud and leapt to her feet. The man holding the dagger charged at her and lunged forward with the blade. She threw mud into his eyes and tried to dodge the knife. She felt a sharp pain as the soldier buried it into her left shoulder. She fell to the ground again, but used the momentum of her fall to spin away from her attacker. The soldier fell with her. In the melee, he lost his grip on the dagger.

In spite of her wound, Anna leaped to her feet. She ripped the dagger from her shoulder. An intense wave of pain rippled through her body. Both soldiers inched toward her, their eyes fixed on the bloody weapon.

Anna was in no shape to fight two male combatants head on. If they expected a knife fight, she'd have to surprise them with something else. So she hurled the dagger at one man's chest. The blade landed with a dull thud. When the other man saw his comrade collapse, his pace quickened, and his face twisted into a snarl.

She glanced to her right and saw her spade. The other man seemed to notice it too. Both Anna and her assailant scrambled toward it, but she narrowly reached it first.

As she bent to lift it from the mud, the man landed on top of her. He pounded her face with his fists. Absorbing the blows, Anna reached for the spade with her hand, stretching her arm as far as she could. Her fingers struggled to gain a grip on the shovel, the tip of her index finger glancing its handle.

The man continued to beat Anna. Her finger pressed the spade handle toward her. An instant later, she snatched it, and knocked the man unconscious with one savage blow.

She struggled to roll the unconscious man off her. The man's ringleader was back on his feet, limping toward Anna.

"I'm going to cut your tits off after I'm done with you, you filthy *suka!*" he grumbled.

Anna fought to wiggle out from under the man, but she estimated the pack leader would reach her before she could twist free. So, she hid the spade beneath her right arm.

To her surprise, the man did not rush headlong at her. Instead, he headed toward his dead comrade. He wrested the SS dagger from the man's chest and then grinned at Anna. "I'm gonna cut off your tits and lady parts with this," he said, brandishing the bloody dagger, "you dirty slut."

Anna pretended to struggle free as the man approached. He rolled his unconscious comrade off Anna to get at her. When he lunged at her, she slammed her spade into his left thigh, knocking him to the ground. She scrambled to her feet and ran toward her rifle. The brute limped after her. Anna reached her weapon first, aiming it at him and pulling the trigger. Anna's attacker fell, blood pooling in his chest.

She took three breaths before she realized her shot had triggered a flurry of activity beyond the ditch where she'd left Strauss. When she peeked across the field, she saw three soldiers rushing toward her position from the charred T-34 hulk. Five others continued to push and prod at Strauss, who'd likely refused to answer their questions.

Anna dropped to her knees and established a firing platform on the ragged lip of the ditch, and yelled in German, "Strauss, run!" Strauss elbowed a man in the face and then bolted toward Anna.

The major pulled back the handle of her rifle to unlock the bolt. A spent casing ejected from the breech, and the firing pin cocked. Anna locked the bolt back into place, aimed, and fired a round, knocking one advancing soldier off his feet.

Three rounds remained.

The other two attacking soldiers immediately dropped to their stomachs and established firing positions in the muddy no-man's land between them. The soldiers nearest Strauss sought cover behind the T-34 and then started firing their rifles. But Anna couldn't tell if they were aiming at her or Strauss.

The rain was now descending in torrents, and rivulets of water obscured the lens on Anna's scope. Anna pulled back the handle, ejecting the spent casing, and then jerked it forward again in one fluid motion honed from years of training. She picked up another stationary blob on her scope, wiped off the lens with a rag, and fired. A splash of blood like the juice from a smashed melon marked her third rifle kill.

Two rounds remained.

Strauss closed the distance fast, but not fast enough. Small tufts of smoke impacted the ground ahead, beside, and behind him. He appeared to be moving in slow motion. Then he fell. Anna's heart beat with increasing intensity. If she didn't act fast, they'd kill him. But shooting the soldiers behind the cover of a T-34 would take too long. Anna needed to do something radically different.

She rolled to her right to change position, while she simultaneously ejected another spent casing. A bullet whizzed by the left side of her head. She raised her rifle over the parapet, acquired the last survivor in no-man's land and fired. A man shrieked like a frenzied banshee. Anna peeked over the parapet and saw the man flailing his arms. She watched the soldiers behind the T-34 for a reaction. They'd stopped firing. Good. Anna ejected another spent casing and then waited.

One round remained.

Strauss had stumbled back to his feet half way across no-man's land. His movement stimulated wild bursts of small arms fire from behind the T-34.

Suppressive fire.

Anna's heart stopped. She'd screwed up. She'd intended the men to focus their efforts on rescuing the soldier in no-man's land, and hoped to use the distraction to save Strauss. But she hadn't counted on the fact that, in order to rescue their comrade, the Soviets would lay down suppressive fire. The purpose of this suppressive fire was to force her to keep her head down, so she couldn't shoot at the subunit of soldiers maneuvering forward to rescue their wounded comrade. Now Strauss was caught in the crossfire, and the bullets streaming across no-man's land just might kill the only other human being on earth Anna cared about.

Anna peered over the parapet again and, like clockwork, she saw a solitary soldier crawling toward the wounded man. They'd taken the bait. She just hadn't counted on the suppressive fire.

Stupid. Very stupid.

A wispy film of acrid smoke and haze malingered over no-man's land, burning Anna's eyes. She searched frantically for Strauss, chancing quick furtive glances amidst the withering rifle fire. Yet she could find no sign of him in the smoky chaos.

Anna waited several minutes for the soldier to reach his wounded comrade. Then she fired at the rescuer, killing him instantly. The wounded man howled even louder, obliging the others to commit yet another sacrificial lamb.

Having expended her last round, Anna crawled toward the dead men in her trench, plundering their still warm bodies for Mosin-Nagant clip strips. She reloaded her rifle with a five-round clip, and crawled back toward the parapet. She heard voices whispering nearby. Anna guessed they were no more than twenty meters in front of her.

When she glanced above the parapet, she saw four soldiers, one's rifle trained on her prior position, another hunkered down on his left scanning her section of the parapet, and two huddled together on her far left.

Where'd the fourth soldier come from? she thought. A second later, the answer became self-evident: Strauss.

Most sane soldiers who'd endured this much, and yet still remained hopelessly outnumbered, would surrender. The mental strain of such impossible odds was simply too much for most to endure. Not Anna. It was either her or them, and she had only one chance.

Anna slow-crawled to her right. Once she was in place, she picked up an old sardine can she found in the trench with her right hand. She wouldn't have time to sight her scope because the instant she exposed it, the men would make her location. Worse, she'd have to identify and kill Strauss's captor before he could execute Strauss. She needed a diversion.

Here goes nothing, Anna thought as she placed the barrel of her rifle toward the two men on the far left. Once she set her rifle, she lobbed the sardine can in the direction of the soldier farthest to her right. All three men fired at the can, while Anna lifted her rifle over the parapet, exposing her head and torso to her enemy, and fired a round at the man nearest Strauss. The man's head exploded on contact, spraying blood on her comrade.

Anna didn't even bother to take cover. Her training and experience taught her that her ruse was worth two kills. Anna shifted her rifle to her right, cocked back the bolt with the calm confidence of a professional sniper, aimed and fired, killing the second soldier. Anna ducked behind the parapet. A round nearly winged her right ear as the last soldier on her far right took his shot.

Anna rolled right, raised her rifle, identified her target, and fired, killing the man as he fumbled with his Mosin-Nagant.

Anna's heartbeat quickened. She carefully scanned no-man's land for any further signs of opposition. Finding nothing, she crawled toward Strauss.

The rain continued to pound no-man's land as Anna low-crawled through the silty muck toward two stationary human bodies.

Please don't be dead, she hoped. *Please.*

In minutes, she was within two meters of her destination. A puddle of blood, brains and gore decorated the two slumped figures. Anna girded herself for Strauss's death.

When she was within arm's length of the carcasses, she reached out and touched Strauss's corpse.

A head popped up and smiled. "Anna! I thought you'd never make it," Strauss whispered in German.

Anna didn't know whether to be relieved or angry. Like any proper Ukrainian woman she chose to express the latter emotion, and slapped Strauss. "Why the hell didn't you say anything? Why didn't you crawl toward me?"

Strauss shrugged his shoulders. "I wasn't sure it was you. Until I could be certain, I just played dead."

Anna couldn't decide whether to kiss him or slap him again, but the crescendo of voices in the distance prevented her from doing either. "C'mon," she said, "All that ruckus won't go unnoticed. This area will be crawling with Soviet soldiers in a few minutes."

Then Anna realized that her only option for survival was to head toward the city, behind German lines. Anna shivered at the thought. Would the Germans shoot her on sight or would they rape her first? She'd heard rumors about instances of both, but she didn't know how to separate truth from propaganda. Still, she was certain she didn't have a choice. Her life was in Strauss's hands now, and trusting him meant surrendering control, which was not something Anna did lightly.

Bullets started peppering the ground behind them in dull thumps, punctuating the pitter-patter of falling rain. The voices drew closer, but the soldiers approaching were still far enough away to be shrouded in a veil of smoke and rain.

Strauss and Anna sprinted blindly toward German lines. Then Anna hesitated. She never rushed headlong into anything. Snipers never did anything without forethought. Strauss seemed to operate by instinct.

Strauss turned back, his face in an apparent expression of confusion. "Anna, we need to go! Now!"

More bullets zinged by their heads, and Soviet soldiers emerged from the smoky mist. "Anna, now! I'll promise I'll protect you."

Half a dozen thoughts ran through Anna's mind. What about minefields? What if the German soldiers in this sector decided to shoot first and ask questions later? Too much uncertainty reigned, yet Strauss was blindly dragging them both into a maelstrom.

Strauss clutched Anna's arm and tried to pull her along, but Anna wouldn't budge. Strauss threw her over his shoulder and then darted toward her sworn enemies.

"No!" Anna screamed. "We can't rush headlong into German lines without a plan!"

"Have faith," Strauss said.

Soon, rounds from the German side whistled past the two fugitives. Strauss dropped to the ground, softening the impact of Anna's fall. He opened his military jacket and tore off a strip of his faded and grimy white shirt, tying it around the bayonet of his rifle like a flag. He lifted his rifle above his head and waved it toward the German lines. He yelled, "*Bitte nicht schießen!*"

The firing from the German lines ceased and a man shouted, "*Aufstehen! Hände hoch!*"

Strauss rose first, his hands held high. Anna hesitated, but Strauss motioned for her to follow his lead.

"*Vortreten! Schnell!*"

Strauss marched forward at a brisk pace, hands raised above his head. He nodded for Anna to do the same, so she followed his example, trembling in his wake.

The path toward the German lines was wrought with concrete debris and punctuated with coiled and razor-sharp Dannert wire concertina. Emaciated, wet, and filthy German men held vigil behind makeshift bunkers crafted from confiscated rail cars and automobiles.

While Anna feared what might happen next, she was relieved Strauss had safely guided them toward German lines without getting either of them shot.

Chapter 15
Debriefing

1930 Hours, 21 September 1943, Zaporizhia, Ukraine

Strauss sat rigidly on a roughhewn pine chair, uncertain of his fate. He tapped his foot against the chair while he scanned the abandoned Soviet primary school classroom. He was struck by how spartan it all was.

His skin felt cold and clammy. His head ached. His stomach throbbed with hunger. His lips were cracked and parched. His throat, dry. Thoughts of ending his own life brought him strange comfort.

Crisp Cyrillic characters worthy of imitation peppered the classroom's blackboard in precise geometric patterns. Three rows of six rectangular student desks were organized in columns of two. Each desk had four chairs. Strauss sat behind the middle front student desk. His stern interlocutor leaned on the dilapidated and wooden teacher's desk beneath the blackboard.

The intermittent whine of artillery was punctuated by violent explosions that rattled the school's mildewed walls. Somewhere beyond the confines of German-occupied Zaporizhia, the Red Army gathered, poised to capture one of the last remaining Wehrmacht outposts on the Dnieper

River's east bank. Sporadic gunfire underscored Strauss's dread of being inside a city under siege and unearthed tortured memories of Stalingrad.

At first, Strauss trusted that his country would reward him for his loyalty; that his fellow comrades-in-arms would understand the difficult choices he'd had to make. But the tall, lanky, and humorless Waffen-SS officer leaning on the teacher's desk made Strauss question whether his country would extend that same unwavering loyalty to him.

"Let's try again. Why did you abandon your unit?" the humorless officer said.

Exasperated, Strauss shrugged. "I told you my story. Either believe it or shoot me. At this point, I don't give a damn."

The man's facial muscles didn't budge. Strauss found it impossible to read him. The officer raised an eyebrow and said, "You do realize we're also interrogating your female companion?"

"So?"

"Well, if she fails to provide the same details you do, we'll expose your story for the farce it is, court martial you for desertion and treason, and then shoot you."

Strauss smiled. "Then I have nothing to worry about."

The officer's lips pursed. "You have everything to worry about, Georg. Your companion's story isn't consistent with yours."

Strauss was dumbfounded. Why on earth would Anna lie about any of this? Their story was so crazy, it'd be impossible for either of them to concoct every last detail on their own. What was her game? Why would she betray him with such callousness? Then Strauss realized what was really happening.

"You're lying," Strauss said. "You're making things up to get us to crack. You think one of us will tell you something more plausible, more believable. Something nice and tidy that you can pass on to your superiors.

I'm sorry to disappoint you, but I've been entirely truthful. I had also urged Anna to be forthright as well, because I had the absurd notion that my country might actually trust me."

The man scowled at Strauss, as if Strauss's last words had somehow besmirched the Reich's honor. Good. It deserved to have its reputation tarnished a bit. "A bit paranoid, aren't you," the man said in the tone of a doctor diagnosing a patient was some all-too-familiar malady.

"Where's Anna?" Strauss said.

The man's face returned to its mask of impassivity. Then he said, "She's being questioned."

"Is she safe?" Strauss said, his voice cracking and tinged with a hint of desperation.

"Your cooperation will go a long way in ensuring her safety."

"I've been cooperating. Please, there must be some way I can prove the events I've described are true. Just tell me what I need to do to convince you," Strauss pleaded. "We have proof. Surely, you've recovered the device?"

The man's eyes widened, "Device? What device?"

"You know. The cigarette lighter. Or at least it looks like a cigarette lighter."

The man still seemed confused. "Tell me more."

"Your men removed all my belongings when Anna and I surrendered. One of the items we carried was a cigarette lighter. But it's anything but. It's an antigravity device we acquired from Doctor Werner Heisenberg."

"Schmidt!" the officer yelled. A rat-like German enlisted man scurried into the room and saluted the officer. The officer returned the salute and said, "Bring me the bag of items we recovered from our two… err… guests."

Schmidt spun on his heels, left the room, and returned about two minutes later with a tattered burlap bag. The officer dumped the contents on the table. Strauss's eyes locked on to his almost empty bottle of Pervitin. He began to perspire at the sight.

The officer cracked a smile. "Ah, we heard you had a thing for *Panzerschokolade*," the officer said, snapping Strauss out of his addict's trance. *Panzerschokolade* or "tank chocolate" was a euphemism soldiers used for Pervitin. "Perhaps your experiences are the product of Pervitin-induced hallucinations?"

Strauss turned his head away in shame. He hesitated for a moment and then said, "Your point is a fair one, but what of Anna? She's no Pervitin addict, yet she's seen the same horrors I have. How do you explain that?"

"A fair point," the officer said. Then he held up the cigarette lighter. "Is this the so-called antigravity device?"

"It is."

The officer flipped open the lighter and seemed surprised to find a button instead of an igniter. "What happens if I push this?" the officer asked.

"Nothing," Strauss said, "it's uncharged."

"Forgive me if I don't take your word for it." The officer pressed the button. Nothing happened. He looked at Strauss and said, "And you acquired this from Doctor Werner Heisenberg?"

"I did," Strauss said with confidence.

"Well, then, wait here until I have an opportunity to corroborate your story. If what you say is true about this device, I will notify the *Obergruppenführer*. He's been looking for you and your companion for some time."

"*Obergruppenführer* who?"

"I'm sorry but that's classified. Wait here. Is there anything you'd like while you wait? Coffee? Tea? Field rations?"

Strauss's heartbeat quickened. "Pervitin."

&

1730 Hours, 22 September 1943, Zaporizhia, Ukraine

Strauss's story was so crazy, yet so accurate, that the Reich sent a dead man to speak with him. Standing well over two meters tall, *SS-Obergruppenführer* Reinhard Heydrich strode into the room. Strauss heart stopped. He was looking at a ghost.

"I, I thought you died last year," Strauss muttered, worried that he was hallucinating. Yet after taking the Pervitin, he doubted it. He was feeling much better. Euphoric, in fact. More alert. More alive. More in control.

"I nearly did," Heydrich said. "But I had a little help from my friends. The story is quite interesting actually, and since we have time, I think I'll tell you about it.

"According to *Abwehr* intelligence, the British Special Operations Executive launched a mission to assassinate me in Prague in May 1942. As is typical of the British, they didn't bother to carry out the operation themselves. They let their Czech and Slovak proxies do all their dirty work. The operation's codename was Anthropoid.

"They ambushed me at an intersection in a Prague suburb. One of the cowards took a pot shot at me in my open-top Mercedes, using a Sten submachine gun. As is typical of most British machinery, it jammed. I suppose I could've avoided the whole mess entirely, but I'm better than that. I am an Aryan warrior and do not submit to cowards, so I ordered my driver to stop the Mercedes. I left the vehicle and counterattacked. However, even Aryan supermen make mistakes. Mine almost proved fatal. The second assassin threw a converted anti-tank mine at the Mercedes, critically injuring me.

"But I didn't give up. I emerged from the smoke and wreckage, spurred by my fury. I chased my assassins several blocks before severe blood loss prevented me from venturing any further. To this day, I regret ending my pursuit because those sniveling cravens escaped my personal justice. I am even more outraged that even when the SS cornered the bastards in an Orthodox Cathedral, the assassins took their own lives. It was only after the Führer rounded up ten thousand Czechs and executed them to avenge me that I felt any sense of vindication."

The blood drained from Strauss's face. He had been certain that Heydrich had died. "But, but I read about your funeral ceremonies in both Prague and Berlin. How is it possible you survived?" Strauss said.

"Well, it's true that German doctors pronounced my death in early June of 1942. The official report says that I died from my wounds, and I nearly would have, if not for our descendants."

Now Strauss was confused. "What do you mean by descendants?"

Heydrich chuckled and said, "When Hitler spoke of a thousand-year Reich, it was a literal, not a figurative, concept. Without it, I wouldn't be alive today. And that's about all I can speak on the matter. I've already said too much."

Strauss desperately wanted to know more, but this was Reinhard Heydrich, the architect of the *Einsatzgruppen*, squads that traveled in the wake of the German occupation, executing Jews and other undesirables. He was the highest-ranking Nazi official Strauss had ever had the misfortune to meet, and the last thing Strauss wanted to do was give the man a reason to shoot him.

Heydrich picked up the cigarette lighter from the desk and playfully twirled it in his hands. "This," he said pointing to the device, "is the only reason I am here. This is why I believe your story. You have performed an invaluable service for the Fatherland. And you have other reasons to be proud of your family. They're doing wonderful things for our Führer.

unimaginable feats and wonders beyond description. I simply couldn't do justice in their telling."

"What have my parents done?" Strauss said, horrified of what they might have done to support Heydrich's twisted madness.

Heydrich snickered. "Oh, I'm not talking about your parents."

"Well, who else then? My brother perished at Stalingrad. I'm the only one left."

"Herr Strauss, your thinking is too linear. But I trust you will have an opportunity to meet these heroes in due course. Wait here and relax for a while. I will return later this evening with your next mission.

"By the way, given your newly minted relationship with Werner Heisenberg, I've been looking for you, your companion, and this device for some time. As a reward, I've taken the liberty to bring you these." Heydrich dropped a stack of faded letters on Strauss's desk. "I apologize it took so long for the Reich to deliver these, but we are fighting a war after all."

Inge.

A flood of emotions washed over Strauss. Remembrance and loss interspersed with longing and regret. Strauss yearned to read Inge's letters, but no matter how hard he tried, he couldn't get Anna out of his head.

Heydrich turned and started to leave the room, but Strauss couldn't hold it in any longer. "Sir," Strauss said. Heydrich stopped midstride.

"Go on," Heydrich said.

"How is my companion, Anna, doing?"

"There's no need to worry. The Reich won't hold your collaboration with a Jew against you. Anna's being sent on a train from Lvov to a large reeducation facility in Poland called Sobibór. She'll be fine. I'm sure you'll have a chance to see her again after the war. Worry not. We will take care of everything," Heydrich said before turning back and exiting the room.

Somehow Heydrich's promises didn't reassure Strauss.

Chapter 16
Progeny

Strauss had spent several gut-wrenching hours poring through Inge's letters. She'd written him at least once a week for the past two years. He read the letters in chronological order, because he feared if he'd read her latest correspondence, he'd have to wrest with the inevitable disappointment that she'd abandoned him.

Her early letters were filled with longing for his touch. She'd promised she would be a dutiful German woman and remain faithful to him while he defended the Reich. And she'd asserted she would serve her nation by rationing and keeping up his morale through her writing.

While her later letters despaired that she hadn't received any of his, she'd understood that the necessities of war made it difficult for the military to deliver his correspondence. Nonetheless, she'd vowed to continue writing him no matter what.

Strauss was in awe of this woman, dedicating her life to lessening the blow of war's cruelty on his psyche. And his admiration for Inge only made him feel guiltier for his association with Anna.

Then, one letter changed everything. Dated June twenty-third, nineteen forty-two, the letter said the following:

My Dearest Georg,

Yesterday, on the one-year anniversary of the Führer's great undertaking in the East, I gave birth to a son, Maximilian Heinz Strauss. I hope you will forgive me for presuming to adopt your surname, but since he is your son I felt it appropriate to provide him with your name lest others name him a bastard.

My family is very proud that we have the offspring of a bona fide member of the Waffen-SS in our household. Now, no one can ever doubt the racial purity of our son. Your elite status and our impeccable Nordic heritage even inspired Hans Reinhardt, the local Nazi official to visit the hospital to personally deliver Max's Greater Aryan certificate, for which I and your parents supplied all the necessary paperwork and documentation to complete. We were all very proud of little Max that day, and we hope that he walks in the footsteps of his brave father.

I hope to send you photos of Max and me as soon as they are developed. Be safe and continue to honor the Fatherland with you selfless sacrifice and honor. We will be anxiously awaiting and praying for your safe return.
Love,
Inge

Strauss wiped a tear from his eye. A son. He had a son—a son with a middle name that honored Strauss's brother. The Almighty seemed to have had a hand in everything, for Inge would have had no way of knowing that Heinz would die later in 1942. Maybe all Strauss had been through, all he'd survived, had a purpose. From now on, whatever happened, he had a reason to make it out of this war alive, and he would now do so at any cost.

Anxious to learn more about his now one-year old son, Strauss tore through the remaining letters until he got to one dated January 4, 1943:

My Dearest Georg,

It is with the utmost heartfelt sorrow that I learned of your brother's death whilst defending the Fatherland's honor at Stalingrad. I've prayed for you both on every night since you left Augsburg.

The newspapers are calling the fight for the city, the "War of the Rats." We hear rumors of cold, starvation, soldiers crawling and fighting in the sewers, and even tales of cannibalism. I pray that none of these stories are true, and hope you return home soon.

Love,

Inge

Inge's letter triggered a flood of horrific images. Strauss saw his brother's head spraying chunks of bone, brain, and blood into the snow.

Alone and in relative safety, Strauss had time to ruminate over Heinz's death. He also struggled with the revelation he had a son. Strauss worried that he'd never live to meet his boy. In essence, one death and one life conspired to create a burden that was too much for Strauss to bear. Isolated in the dark classroom, Strauss broke down, letting loose a torrent of tears.

Strauss cried for nearly an hour before realizing that Heydrich might return at any minute. If Strauss was to finish reading Inge's correspondence, he had to get a hold of himself. And so he read on. He learned his son's first word was "tank." Inge shared his son's many other firsts that mark the beautiful marvels of childhood and life. He stared at photos of his young lover and their son, basking in the myriad possibilities of a new life. Then he read a letter dated August 14, 1943:

My Dearest Georg,

I wish I could tell you this news in person, but the war and the great distances involved make that impossible. The conflict has been extremely hard on my family and yours. Both are struggling to make ends meet in an era of extreme rationing and more frequent allied bombing campaigns. Your son was showing some signs of malnourishment, and I feared I lacked the resources to care adequately for him. However, Herr Reinhardt graciously informed me of a special service for young single mothers like me called the Lebensborn program. It encourages single women to offer their children for adoption, if their fathers are members of the SS.

I realize that this course of action may seem extreme. However, you'll be happy to know that the only families eligible to adopt our child will be racially pure and healthy SS families. I trust it will comfort you that our child will be raised by one of your own.

When you return home, I'll give you all the details. Please know, that I did not come to this decision lightly. As a mother, I did only what I believed would provide the best life for Max. I still miss you intensely, and yearn for your touch again in this life and in the next.

Love,

Inge

In the course of two hours, Strauss had learned he'd had a son and then that he'd lost one. The emotional ups and downs were excruciating, and Strauss's feelings for Inge had become even more complex. Should he love her even more for bearing him a son or should he despise her for selfishly abandoning him to strangers?

And then there was Anna…

As Strauss tried to reconcile all of his conflicting emotions, he heard the click of boots approaching from outside his classroom. Seconds later, Heydrich returned.

"Have you had a chance to finish reading your correspondence?" Heydrich said in what sounded like half-hearted interest.

Strauss nodded.

Heydrich regarded Strauss's face with more interest, "What? Is something wrong? You seem… depressed."

"My son," Strauss struggled to find the right words, "has been adopted."

Heydrich blinked. "Indeed. I am quite aware of your son's status. You should be proud of him. He's brought your family and the Fatherland tremendous honor."

Strauss stared at Heydrich, incredulous. "He's one year old. What could he possibly have done that brought honor to the family?"

"I'll explain later," Heydrich said, "but I'm not here for that now. I'm here to brief you on an upcoming mission for tomorrow evening. The Fatherland needs you now more than ever. This mission is vitally important, and could go a long way to winning a strategic victory in Soviet Russia. But I must first ask one critical question: do you recall the grid coordinates for the disk you'd observed at Prokhorovka?"

"How could I forget?"

"Excellent. I want you to lead a small unit to the site of the Prokhorovka crater."

"But that's impossible," Strauss interrupted, "the Soviets now control that area."

Heydrich's impassive face twisted into a snarl. "Don't ever interrupt me again, Strauss."

The lack of an "or else" was enough to put Strauss back into his place. "My apologies, Sir."

Apparently satisfied with Strauss's remorse, Heydrich continued. "An aircraft will fly you over Soviet airspace, and your team with parachute into the sector. You will lead the team, which includes several demolition experts, to the site, where they will place explosives to destroy the structure.

"Pending a successful mission, a Nazi agent will rendezvous with you and your team, and lead you all back to Germany. If you complete your objectives, I'll grant you leave to see your lover, Inge, and I promise to also do my best to reunite you with your son."

"Thank you, sir. If you will indulge me, may I make one request?"

"Do you accept the mission?" Heydrich said.

"I do."

"Then make your request."

"If I successfully complete this mission, can you arrange for me to visit Anna?"

Heydrich glared at Strauss for several seconds and then said, "I'll see what I can do, but I can make no promises."

Strauss smiled and shook Heydrich's hand. "Then consider it done, Sir."

Strauss saluted Heydrich. Heydrich returned the salute and left the room. For the first time in a long while, Strauss was hopeful.

☙

2230 Hours, 23 September 1943, Outside Prokhorovka, Russia

Strauss huddled on the floor of a Ju-52 aircraft, his body tightly wound in a cramped parachute harness. Two shivering German engineers from the *Fallschirmjäger* airborne infantry accompanied him on this mad jaunt over Soviet Russia's hostile skies. How only three men outfitted with several kilograms of explosives could safely drop into Soviet territory at night and complete this mission seemed impossible to Strauss. But it was all that was standing between him seeing his son, Inge, and potentially Anna, so Strauss did what he had to, no matter how insane.

Unlike his two companions, Strauss had had no jump training aside from a ten-minute tutorial just before he'd boarded the aircraft. It was only beginning to dawn on him that on his maiden jump he would literally be leaping out of a moving aircraft and into a high volume of Soviet anti-aircraft artillery fire. Then, he'd have to expertly steer his parachute to the correct drop zone under the shroud of darkness. He would then have to find and then organize his team, and then navigate through enemy territory at night. All the while, thousands of Soviet soldiers would be hunting him and his men in a sector over which the Wehrmacht had no operational control and where Strauss didn't speak the local language. One of the engineers spoke a little Russian, but if that man landed in a tree during the drop, Strauss would be out of luck.

The only solace Strauss had was that all three soldiers carried the *Fallschirmjägergewehr* 42, one of Germany's most advanced automatic rifles. Bandoliers teeming with bullets crisscrossed their chests, providing them with enough firepower to hold back a company of determined Soviet soldiers.

Mere minutes after their pilot announced they'd crossed into Soviet airspace, the black sky lit up with Soviet anti-aircraft artillery fire. Each time a round exploded near the fuselage, the aircraft rocked. Yet, for some strange reason, despite the high volume of rounds peppering the sky, nothing came close to scathing the aircraft.

"Five minutes!" the pilot yelled. The men fumbled to their feet and checked their gear. Strauss moved to the front of the queue. Since he was leading this mission, he felt it was important that he should be the first man out of the aircraft.

"One minute!"

Strauss shifted to the aircraft's port side toward a door just aft of the Ju-52's wing. Strauss opened the door and prepared for the jump. Wind swirled into the cabin, making it difficult for Strauss to hear. *Feldwebel* Zimmerman, who was positioned behind Strauss, tapped Strauss on the shoulder and yelled, "Remember to keep your feet and knees together. The last thing you want is to break a leg on impact."

Strauss nodded, awaiting the signal to jump. "Go!" the pilot yelled, and before Strauss realized he was in free fall, he was already out the door, his ripcord tugging against his back. In moments, a furious free fall decelerated as his chute opened and he floated toward the surface.

The sky lit up with explosions as the Soviets continued to fire anti-aircraft artillery at the Ju-52. But for now, Strauss sensed that the initial danger seemed to have passed.

In seconds, the ground rose toward Strauss. He prepared to land, keeping his feet and knees together as he braced for impact.

Strauss hit the surface fast and at a slight angle. His feet slammed into the ground, and then he twisted to his side rolling into the momentum of his landing. He scrambled to his feet, cut the chute's risers, and then rolled up his chute. Collecting his chute was critical because if the Soviets found any sign of where Strauss's team had landed, they could more easily triangulate his team's position. Strauss heard the other two paratroopers land nearby.

Once he'd conducted a quick inventory of his equipment, Strauss pulled out his map along with a red-lens flashlight to determine his bearing. Strauss was encouraged by the fact that he could see the eerie green strobe light in the distance. They didn't land too far from their objective.

After gathering the other men, the trio crept forward toward a nearby ridge. When they arrived there, they crawled toward its lip to recon the next terrain feature. From his vantage point, Strauss could see thousands of Soviet soldiers and hundreds of tanks in the valley, cordoning off the crater. Using his binoculars, he scanned the area, confirming the black disk still occupied the crater's center.

Strauss pointed toward the structure and its emerald strobe light. "That, gentlemen, is our objective."

The men regarded Strauss as if he were insane, and Strauss almost agreed with their assessment. Getting through that much security to reach the crater seemed impossible.

Zimmerman spoke up first. "Strauss, do you have any idea how we're supposed to make it through all that security? This looks like a suicide mission to me."

"Yeah, they really shafted us on this one, but I think I have an idea. Hear me out," Strauss said.

Strauss laid out his plan. After he finished delivering his operations order, the men appeared calmer, and they headed in the direction of the crater, careful to avoid heavy concentrations of troops.

Strauss ordered the team members to remove their helmets, so the Soviets wouldn't identify them as German troops based on their silhouettes. They checked their weapons, and fixed bayonets before venturing out toward the outskirts of the enemy's security perimeter.

Strauss led the men away from the roads and through dense wheatfields, hoping the local civilians had cleared out most of the mines by now. Given the intensity of the war effort, Strauss worried that the Soviets would be more occupied with activity closer to the front rather than wasting their effort sanitizing old battlefields in rear areas like Kursk. Either way, Strauss didn't have much of a choice but to push forward.

Strauss led his team toward the low-lying grassland where he'd found the wrecked Tiger. Before leaving the wheatfield, Strauss crawled toward its edge. He surveyed the open area that led to a gently sloping knoll beyond which lay the crater.

The sector around the crater had a strong Soviet presence, though the Red Army didn't seem to have as much personnel there as it did on that fateful summer night when Strauss had first stumbled onto the *Schwartzwald* entity.

The two engineers laid prone to Strauss's right, awaiting his orders.

"What's next, chief?" Zimmerman said.

"Well, we won't be able to sneak in wearing this," Strauss whispered, gesturing toward his Wehrmacht uniform, "but if we steal some Soviet uniforms, we might have a chance."

Zimmerman looked at Strauss as if a horn were growing out of his forehead. "How the hell are we supposed to do that?"

"Patience, my friend," Strauss said. "We just wait for nature to call one of them. Then, we slit their throat. After all, everyone eats, bleeds, shits, and pisses. Easy as one-two-three."

"You're telling me that our mission requires three Soviet soldiers to take a piss near this wheatfield before dawn, and before we can finish our mission?"

"That's not what I'm saying. The first two fellows who take a piss will be very lucky men, because we won't kill them. They'll show us where all the other Soviets go to relieve themselves. Then, we'll set an ambush at that spot before the next two arrive, and so on."

"Why two?"

"Because, the Soviets, like us, operate in two-man buddy teams. If they don't practice the same level of discipline this far from the front, then we'll only have to wait for one of them to show us where their field expedient toilet is."

"Why are you leading this mission again?" Zimmerman asked Strauss.

"Because I survived Stalingrad and Kursk, and killed a *Schwartzwald* entity. Does my resume meet your standards?" Strauss said.

Zimmerman kept his mouth shut after that.

After about five minutes, a soldier approached the edge of the wheatfield about fifty meters to the left of Strauss's position. The man walked in unsteady movements, randomly meandering left and right, and nearly falling over during the process.

Strauss pointed at the soldier. "Change of plans. That one's drunk and very close to our position. He's mine."

Strauss rapidly low-crawled toward the drunken soldier before the Soviet reached the wheatfield's edge. Strauss waited until the man stumbled about a meter into the wheatfield and pulled down his trousers. Knife in hand, Strauss crawled behind the soldier. Then he slowly rose behind him. He seized the man's mouth and snapped it backward with his right hand, while slicing the man's neck with his left. Strauss fell backward to minimize the volume of blood that might spatter on the man's uniform.

In less than five minutes, Strauss had his very own Soviet uniform as well as the instant respect of two skeptical *Luftwaffe* engineers.

Strauss crawled back into position and motioned for Zimmerman to set up an ambush near the dead soldier. Just as the man began crawling into position, the world went topsy-turvy.

Rays of focused light streamed through the valley at human height. Each time Strauss observed a beam, its intensity was so great he could see the contours of the crater as if it were almost daylight.

The rays didn't seem random either – each one struck a target with precision. Strauss watched a beam as thick as his arm hit a T-34 tank. The ray's shimmering energy enveloped the tank's hull as if it were catching on fire. But somehow, it seemed more focused than that. It was as if someone were erasing the picture of a tank from a black-and-white drawing, blotting it out of existence. After the glimmering energy dissipated, the tank and its crew lay frozen in place. Both tank and crew had the same hue and texture of human flesh. It was as if the beam had somehow fused the tank's and soldiers' molecular structures.

Strauss watched in horror as the beams twisted men and tanks inside out. The rays morphed others into steel, marble, and any other number of random substances. Whatever was behind this attack, it created a mutilated grotesquery in its wake. The carnage forged a chaotic path all the way to the crater's precipice.

One man's bloody torso slid off a stricken T-34, his shrill squealing echoing through the valley like slaughtered swine. Men were firing their weapons randomly, sometimes at each other, as the nightmarish assault sowed discord and death among the Soviets.

Where some saw panic, Strauss saw opportunity. Strauss tapped Zimmerman on the shoulder and said, "Don't worry about the uniforms. On my count of three, sprint toward the crater. Pass it on."

Zimmerman looked at Strauss as if Strauss were a flying pig. The engineer then sullenly nodded, and passed along the orders to Kaufmann, the other engineer.

When it appeared that the mysterious attacker had eliminated most of the Soviet units between Strauss's team and their objective, and the rest of the Soviets had fled, Strauss gave the order, "One-Two-Three! Go!"

The men followed Strauss in a dead sprint up the knoll. The sounds of rifle and machine gun fire reverberated throughout the valley, but the smoke and chaos these weapons generated helped camouflage Strauss's advance.

By the time the team was half way up the hill, the crater erupted in a flash of light, briefly turning night into day before winking out.

In minutes, the team had crested the knoll. Three meters from the summit, Strauss signaled for his men to low-crawl the remaining distance to avoid drawing attention from anything lurking inside the crater.

Before Strauss glanced over the crater's lip, he waited for several minutes for his eyes to readjust to the darkness. When he eventually peered into the crater, a gust of arctic-chilled air blasted him in the face, forcing him to pull back. He girded himself for a second look, and when he glanced over the lip a second time, he was surprised to see a remarkable lack of activity. It was as if everything inside the crater were frozen in time.

As Strauss's vision sharpened, Strauss saw scores of ice-covered German and Soviet soldiers. He crawled back from the crater's edge and said, "It's pretty damn cold down there, but it seems clear. Just ignore the ice statues and head toward the black disk."

The men followed Strauss into the crater. Along the way, they passed frozen cadavers. Several of the automatons had fallen, apparently in midstride.

When Strauss went to examine one of the corpses, Zimmerman tried to pull Strauss's hand away. Strauss glanced back at Zimmerman, smiled, and said, "Don't worry. They don't bite… anymore."

The corpses were cold to the touch as if they'd been immersed in liquid nitrogen. Yet, they didn't have the telltale blue-white color associated with that compound. Aside from their rigid composition and cold touch, they looked exactly the same, as they would've before the strange beam struck the crater.

"What do you think is responsible for all this?" Zimmerman whispered.

"I don't know, but whatever it is, it's making our mission a hell of a lot easier. What's that saying? Oh, yeah, don't look a gift horse in the mouth," Strauss said.

The men behind Strauss were shivering, but Strauss couldn't tell if it was because of the crater's temperature or their fear. At this point, it didn't matter much; they'd nearly reached their objective. All the engineers had to do was climb into the disk, set up the explosives, and detonate them.

Strauss motioned for the two engineers to follow him onto the disk, where he led them to the large conical structure rising from its center. When they reached the structure, Strauss realized he had no idea how to gain access to the inside of the disk. Strauss patted his hand around the cone's outer surface seeking any impressions or extrusions that might trigger an opening. After rooting around for several seconds, he found a circular impression the size of a human hand and pressed it. A hitherto unseen door materialized and slid open. Beyond the door, Strauss saw the platform he'd ascended in his last encounter with the *Schwartzwald* entity. Wasting no time, Strauss entered the platform with the two engineers in tow. Triggered by their weight, the platform descended toward the craft's floor.

As the platform elevator descended, Strauss could hear tapping below. He pointed at his automatic rifle and then at the two engineers, to signal them to be ready for a firefight.

Strauss could see parts of the room at a steep angle. Honeycombs of human brains, floating in green fluid, still surrounded the room. Strauss heard more tapping. Then he saw a flash of luminous white skin.

The elevator grew closer to its destination, widening Strauss's vantage point. Four creatures had attached strange devices to several of the honeycombs. Panels of light floated in the air all around them. A pair of eyes fixed on Strauss. Zimmerman raised his rifle, but Strauss forced Zimmerman's arm down. The things below looked nothing like the *Schwartzwald* entity Strauss had faced here. Despite the creatures' apparent awareness that Strauss and his men were entering the chamber, they ignored Strauss's team.

When the platform reached the floor, Zimmerman and Kaufmann were shaking. Strauss led by example and calmly stepped off the platform, gesturing for the engineers to follow. The men tentatively obeyed Strauss's instructions.

Strauss did his best to make slow, non-threatening movements. Still, the man-things seemed to regard Strauss and his men as if they were nothing more than spiders: useful for killing bugs, but worth killing if they got too close.

The creatures' eyes had a human-like quality about them, yet they also exhibited an alien otherness. Their bulbous skulls appeared to be larger and much more angular than a human's. A thin, barely noticeable layer of white hair covered their heads like some sort of fuzz. Their irises were dull blue and covered the entirety of their eyes. The creatures' arms were corded with muscle and were as long as their legs. They also had an extra joint between their forearms and wrist. The creatures' similarly powerful legs had knees that appeared to face backwards. But upon closer inspection, their lower knees were more like ankles, similar to those of a dog or a cat. All four creatures wore simple gray coveralls.

Strauss pointed to the honeycombed wall behind him. "Start prepping your explosives. Don't make any sudden movement. I'll cover you if they try anything."

Zimmerman and his companion nodded, still shaking. They skulked toward the wall, removed their rucksacks, and started attaching explosives to the wall.

As Strauss observed the man-things, he observed that they seemed to move half a tick faster than modern soldiers. He also noticed that one had stopped its work and was staring at Strauss's engineers.

"Slowly boys," Strauss reminded the men, "we don't want to alarm these things with any sudden movement."

Strauss glanced behind him to see the men attaching detonation cord to their bombs, and then back at the man-things. The one observing the engineers started moving its mouth, but Strauss could not hear any sound.

Before Strauss could react, the creature raised its arm and fired two translucent beams at the two engineers in quick succession before calmly returning to its work.

Strauss slowly backed away from the creatures and toward his men. He crouched and checked each of their pulses. While their heart rates were low, their hearts were still beating. He checked their backs to see if they had any wounds, and they appeared to be unharmed.

Given the damage these creatures had wrought on the Soviets, Strauss judged that if they'd wanted him and his men dead, they'd have killed them. But they didn't. They only acted hostile when Strauss's men had threatened to destroy the craft.

Strauss decided to try a different tack. He put his back up against the wall and watched the strange beings work.

Sensing he was somewhat safe, provided he didn't interfere with the creatures' work, he tried speaking to them. "My name is Georg Strauss and I'm a member of the German military. Who are you and what is your mission?"

The man-things ignored him and continued about their work. Several minutes later, the platform ascended back toward the ceiling. One of the creatures approached the center of the chamber and pressed what appeared to be a pressure sensor on the floor. A light shined from the ceiling, creating a three-dimensional display made entirely of light and covered in strange runes. The creature in the chamber's center began pressing buttons made of nothing but air and light.

Suddenly, seating platforms rose from the floor, wherever a man or creature sat or stood. Then, metallic harnesses materialized around their bodies. The creature in the chamber's center pressed more buttons. Strauss closely watched the man-thing carefully, trying to recall as much information as he could about how to operate the craft.

The man-thing pressed a circular green button on the luminous console with a "T"-like rune. The disk began to hum and vibrate. It then pressed an "F"-like rune on a green background and the interior of the craft became perfectly translucent. As Strauss looked ahead, he could see the west-facing wall of the crater. Below, he could see dirt, and above, the stars.

Then, the creature pressed an "S"-like rune on a green background, hurtling the saucer upward. In an instant, Strauss could see lights in Istanbul, which stood in stark contrast to the rest of Europe, which was shrouded in darkness because of mandatory blackouts. With one final push of an ellipsoid-shaped blue button with a "U"-like rune, the craft accelerated forward toward a destination unknown.

Chapter 17
Sick Transit

1230 Hours, 22 September 1943, Between Lvov and Sobibór, Poland

Coughing and wheezing, the huddled masses of three generations of European Jewry sweltered in the claustrophobic confines of a ten-meter long and windowless freight wagon. The thick, humid air reeked of stale sweat, rot, and piss, stewing into a potent, nauseous miasma. Over a hundred sickly men, women and children stood barefoot in a space fit for half that sum.

The Germans had herded Anna and the other Jews onto about twenty rail cars at Lvov, but not before some enterprising SS enlisted man had confiscated Anna's socks and boots. Two hours after the Nazis had loaded the wagons' delicate human cargo, the locomotive whistled and the trains groaned forward. By that point, the bottom of Anna's exposed feet had been thoroughly scalded by the thick layer of quick lime used to sterilize the cattle car's floor.

Between the teeming throngs of humanity pressing against each other in the rail wagon and the stifling heat simmering inside the fetid furnace, Anna labored to breathe. Her shoulder still throbbed from the knife wound she'd suffered at Zaporizhia. But if Strauss hadn't demanded medical attention when they'd surrendered to the Wehrmacht, her wound would've had a festering infection by now. Yet, in these wretched conditions, she worried her stitches might come loose, exposing the wound to even more virulent germs.

The wagon's sole sanitary bucket brimmed with feces. The searing temperatures only exacerbated the putrid stench of human filth. Soon the heat and aroma became so overbearing in the cramped conditions that people vomited, usually emptying their stomachs on other passengers.

After several hours, people started passing out. Anna suspected some even died. She watched helplessly as a small boy, no older than five, struggled for air. His mother sobbed uncontrollably as she lay pinned against the wall on the opposite side of the car, unable to save her son as he collapsed in a lifeless heap.

A frail elderly woman slumped onto the floor shortly after the boy died, her struggle to compete for the freight car's limited oxygen supply ending in failure. Then an elderly man dropped. Each time, the other passengers left them where they lay. But once it was clear the fallen had perished, the survivors vied for the newly vacant real estate, stampeding over the corpses in a callous, but necessary, rite of survival.

But the suffering and inhumanity didn't end there. Many more expired along the journey. Despite the horrific deprivations Anna had hitherto endured in this Great Patriotic War, she couldn't help but contrast the atrocities she'd seen on the battlefield with the banal indifference tired, suffering, and starving civilians tolerated as they watched each other fade away.

At least there was honor in the hunt. The German wolf and the Russian bear were well matched. But here, Anna was trapped in an overstuffed chicken coop. When one chicken died, the survivors trampled over its carcass. In this wretched coffin, battlefield prowess or even luck held no sway over life or death; age, health, and a ruthless selfishness to survive mattered far more.

When Anna had to void her bowels, she just dropped her trousers and defecated in place. Countless humiliations like standing in her own feces, and the horror of her journey fueled Anna's hatred for the Germans. She also began to wonder if Strauss had abandoned her to this torturous fate.

No. Strauss couldn't possibly be aware of her situation. How could he be? He would never have allowed her to be herded into a freight wagon like some animal.

Anna was convinced now, more than ever, that her commissars had been right. The Nazi regime was the archetype of the ultimate fascist state—the consequence of capitalist self-interest in a political emergency—where the worker was a commodity to be bought, sold, traded, and slaughtered. The workers of the world had to unite against this bloodthirsty and genocidal juggernaut, lest the hoarders of wealth enslave them and their progeny for all time.

At that moment, Anna's hatred for the Germans consumed her. Her *raison d'être* was now killing Germans. Except for Strauss, all members of the so-called "master race" were fair game.

The train made frequent stops during the passage. During the first stopover, Anna had hoped the Germans would unload the dead and provide the passengers with a chance to clean out their filthy car. But the Germans did no such thing.

Another locomotive towing a host of freight cars thundered past the station. Anna guessed these trains carried vital military cargo to the Eastern Front, to which the Nazis assigned higher priority than the human beings suffering and dying in these rolling coffins.

Each minute a locomotive whined past, Anna let her fury and hatred simmer and grow. Every time the trains ground to a halt, she thought, *Keep feeding the meat grinder, you fascist bastards, for my people hunger for the flesh of your pathetic Aryan man-children.*

Day faded into night, and the trains trundled onward. Heat's oppressive wrath waned, while exhaustion's dark specter waxed. The pain from Anna's charred and blistered feet made it nearly impossible to stand. She fought to remain upright, because if she collapsed, the others would crush her.

At the far end of the car, diagonal from Anna's position, two men screamed at one another in a mishmash of two languages, one Russian, the other Polish. Then the Russian-speaking man shoved the other. The Pole reacted by punching the Russian in the mouth.

Pandemonium erupted.

A wave of violence lurched the car's inhabitants to and fro. The sick and elderly groaned. If someone didn't stop the chaos, more people would needlessly die.

The Red Army had taught its officer cadets that leaders abhor a vacuum. Anna instinctively reached for a rifle that wasn't there. Her heart pounded, and she began to hyperventilate as she grasped for a solution to the crisis.

"Stop!" she yelled, but her voice was too weak and parched from dehydration to reach anyone's ears.

Anna wrestled to press her way toward the car's opposite end, but the wall of flesh was impassable. With a life of its own, it pushed back, pinioning Anna in place.

She had never known such helplessness. Fighting against an overwhelming desire to settle for things as they were, she despaired that this is how things were meant to be. After all, not everyone deserves happiness.

Suppressing her anguish, the former Soviet officer grappled for a solution. The panic in the car spiraled to a fever pitch. The pushing and shoving had spread from one end of the wagon to the other like a plague.

Then, for the briefest instant in time, she saw the dead boy's face, inexplicably unmarred after dozens of passengers had trampled upon his dead body. In her mind's eye, Anna saw the child the same way Strauss must've seen his dying brother, Heinz after she'd blown off his head at Stalingrad. Innocence lost, but renewed again in the glow of death's cold embrace.

A tear rolled down her cheek as an avalanche of memories overpowered her. The images in her mind harkened back to a childhood of deprivation as a poor Jewish peasant in the Ukraine. Her Russian father, Ilya, had settled on a farm outside Donetsk after marrying Anna's Ukrainian mother. She shivered when she recalled the strange men cloaked in greatcoats and wearing fedoras who'd visited her tiny farmhouse so many years ago. Their forced smiles and unctuous manner alerted an eight-year old Anna that something had been amiss.

Before the men had arrived at her home, Anna's father had slaughtered all the family's livestock, and the household had eaten like kings for a week. At the time, Anna had found her father's behavior odd. But a famished child didn't ask questions when her father presented her with a feast.

But once these *Cheka* men had invaded her home, Anna had begun to have an inkling for why her father had destroyed his livestock. The men seemed very intent on understanding why, grilling him about whether his act was in retaliation against the Red Army for confiscating his grain stores the prior year. No matter how many ways they'd framed the question, Anna's father had responded with one stubborn word: food.

So the men took him away, and Anna never saw her father again. Ever since, she associated government agents with the smell and taste of swine. The SS men overseeing this horrific operation were no different.

As arguments in half a dozen tongues reached a fever pitch, and the passengers verged on ripping each other apart, Anna realized they all possessed a common bond. They were of one tribe, one people united by a history of persecution and hardship. Her father's exacting Hebrew lessons had had a purpose after all. With a deep heart and firm voice, Anna fought past her thirst and pain, and hummed the rhythm of the *Hatikvah*.

The men and women around her began to echo the melody, bolstering it with new voices. Then, an old woman barely clinging to life sang out the first verse in Hebrew:

"As long as deep in the heart."

An adolescent girl joined in:

"The soul of a Jew yearns,"

Men added their baritone voices to the chorus:

"And forward to the East"

And on they sung, until the freight car boomed with one unified voice of a people who would not be sublimated, defeated, or denied liberty:

"To Zion, an eye looks

Our hope will not be lost,

The hope of two thousand years,

To be a free nation in our land,

The land of Zion and Jerusalem."

And on and on it went, through the night and into the sunrise, the testimony of a proud people who had rediscovered their purpose and their will to overcome the worst of hardships.

A tear streamed down Anna's cheek. If she could not be near her family in these dark times, she would bring family to her, and with them, hope.

Chapter 18

Sobibór

Early the next morning, the trains squealed to a halt. The passengers pounded feverishly on the door, demanding release. The cargo doors screeched open. The rising sun nearly blinded Anna after she'd been cooped up for so long with so little light and ventilation.

As Anna's eyes adjusted to the brightness, a German officer commanded, *"Heraus! Schnell, schnell!"*

An orgy of frantic fumbling ensued as people who'd been standing stiffly for hours suddenly had to move forward, and quickly. Men and women wearing black and white striped uniforms began shouting in a Babel of languages as varied as German, Polish, Russian, and Ukrainian, as well as others Anna didn't recognize.

The Germans separated the men from the women and children. She also watched what appeared to be a secondary sorting process as the men and women in striped uniforms moved down the lines, removing the old and infirm. It was all so typically German—well organized and efficient. And it all happened so fast that Anna barely had any time to wonder where it was all leading.

Amidst all the herding of men, women, and children off the trains and onto a railway platform, a tall man with delicate features sat in a wooden folding chair. He wore a lily-white lab coat, posing as a doctor. But from the man's bearing, Anna knew that simply wasn't the case. He seemed more military than medicine man.

"*Guten morgen!*" the man addressed the harried passengers in a pleasant, soothing voice, "I'm *Oberscharführer* Hermann Michel." Michel then paused while his black-and-white striped confederates repeated his introduction in a barrage of various languages.

Then he continued. "Welcome to Sobibór. Sobibór is a transit camp for those fortunate enough to be resettled east. Here, you will all have the opportunity to work while you wait for the next resettlement trains to arrive. But before you can be assigned to your work details, we understand that you've all endured a very long and arduous trip. As such, we ask that you remove your precious belongings and give them to one of our trusted *Sonderkommandos* here," he said, pointing to several of the striped personnel. "They will ensure that your items are returned after you have an opportunity to take care of your personal hygiene and undergo a thorough medical exam. We wouldn't want any of you to get sick on the way to the Promised Land."

Michel smiled and then said, "And with that, my apologies in advance for the immodesty of my request, but I ask that you all remove your clothing now so that we can quickly get you cleaned up and provide you with work clothes."

A stocky German soldier rushed up to Michel, tapped him on the shoulder, whispered something into his ear, and then handed him a document. Michel nodded, stared at the slip of paper, and then again addressed the crowd. "Oh, I also forgot to mention that some of you will be joining a work detail immediately. If I call your name, keep your clothing on, and please form a line behind the platform immediately after you turn in your belongings."

He began reading names from the sheet. "Abramovich. Izrailov. Pechersky." And on and on. Anna soon recognized a pattern. All the names were Russian or Ukrainian surnames, and most of those stepping forward were healthy young men. Then Michel said, "Ivanova."

That's it, she thought, *the names are all Russian and Ukrainian because the Germans seem to be separating Soviet prisoners of war from the other Jews.*

Now Anna was truly worried. Were the Germans going to separate the soldiers and execute them? Should she try to hide among the others to survive? As she waited for the *Sonderkommandos* to collect her meager belongings, she struggled with the dilemma. The Germans had ignored the terms of the Geneva Convention before. But then again, so had the Soviets.

However, that had been at the front, where rigid compliance with the Convention regarding POWs sometimes threatened the survival of one's unit. Then again, what protections did civilians really have? The Geneva Convention probably protected her as a soldier far more than it did the civilians. So, she rolled the dice and stepped forward. Worst case, she'd self-selected into a population that had had military training. If the Germans intended to execute them, the POWs would have a better chance at fighting back.

Several meters away, Anna heard commotion in the crowd. An elderly man had slapped an SS officer. Anna grinned at the man's gumption. The SS officer stumbled backward, stunned. Out of the corner of her eye, Anna saw another SS officer march toward the scene of the transgression.

The man was impeccably dressed, his uniform creased and pressed, and he wore immaculately clean white gloves. The officer calmly grabbed the old man and pulled him to the front of the platform. The German removed a Luger from a holster on his belt, and shot the elder pointblank in the temple. A wave of screams swept over the crowd, followed by a deathly silence. His point made, the SS officer spun on his heels and calmly strolled away from the passengers. Two *Sonderkommandos* scurried in his wake, dragging the man's corpse out of sight.

Anna felt an overwhelming urge to do something. Anything. It was in her nature to act. She could no more detach that aspect from herself than she could separate her arm. But, she had also honed her survival instincts from engagement after engagement in a very long and unforgiving war. She knew from that experience that remaining inconspicuous in this place and at this particular time was the key to staying alive. So she bided her time by joining the formation of POWs, hoping for the best.

Separated from the other civilians, the Soviet POWs marched in a column of two toward the main entrance of the camp. As Anna took in her surroundings, the area was heavily wooded and swampy. But most importantly, it was isolated.

Metal fences, teeming with triple-strand concertina wire and punctuated by several watchtowers, surrounded the camp's perimeter. With the experienced eyes of a trained sniper, Anna noticed small tufts of dirt beyond the metal fencing: minefields. Toward the far eastern edge of the camp, Anna spotted what appeared to be a row of charcoal-black monoliths.

The rising sun had just crested the trees, and Anna covered her eyes to shield them from the piercing light. The POWs stood at various states of attention without anyone in particular ordering them to do so. Anna just chuckled.

Old habits died hard.

After the civilians had entered the camp and were well out of sight, Anna heard what sounded like some sort of engine buzzing in the distance. She saw faint wisps of smoke rising from the far eastern edge of the camp, the sun's rays refracting through the haze. Soon, a gray vapor crept through the camp as the engine continued to vibrate. The fog's scent of lead mixed with burning petrol reminded Anna of diesel fuel.

After about ten minutes, the black monoliths vibrated and shone a dull blue. Then the engine noise stopped, and their glow slowly faded.

A raging SS officer stormed in front of her formation immediately after the engine stopped, underscoring the significance of what had just occurred. Anna had no idea what it was, but it felt ominous. When she recognized the man as the white-gloved sociopath who'd killed the old man in cold blood, she was certain something was very wrong here.

"*Sonderkommandos!* Atten-Shun!" he yelled in German-accented Russian. Despite their wretched condition, the Russian and Ukrainian POWs snapped to attention, slaves to their military training. The man then addressed the group in German as one of the *Sonderkommandos* processing the POWs translated the officer's words to Russian.

"At ease," the man said. The POWs relaxed their ramrod postures. "Welcome to Sobibór. I'm SS *Hauptsturmführer* Franz Reichleitner, commandant of this camp. The good news is that you will live today, and for as long as you prove useful in helping us run this camp efficiently. It can be hard and frequently unpleasant work, but if you listen to the *Sonderkommandos* assigned to you, you'll be able to eke out a tolerable existence here in peace and away from the horrors and travails of war. While many of you may find your next few days gruesome, it won't be long before your work starts to take more of a routine veneer."

Anna wondered what could possibly be gruesome about removing and storing valuables for people. Perhaps the Germans had more modesty when it came to nakedness?

Reichleitner pointed toward the camp entrance. "We run a very precise operation here. In one to two hours, we unload a human cargo of twenty to forty rail wagons, remove their valuables, strip them, march them through the woods along the *Himmelsraße*, and process them efficiently. Your role will be to help process the human cargo at the front-end and back-end. Those of you assigned to reception, will remove our guests' belongings and help them queue in the appropriate lines: women, children, and the old and infirm on one side, and soldiers and healthy skilled men and women on the other."

Calm, efficient, and clinical, Reichleitner was the very model of the professional SS officer. He pointed toward the northwestern edge of the camp and said, "For those of you chosen for cleanup and sanitation duty in Lager III, the bookend to our operation here, you will be briefed about your roles after you enter that area and are issued your uniforms. That is all."

After Reichleitner left, a striped *Sonderkommando* marched toward the head of the formation and called the POWs to attention. He then marched the POWs into the camp, while various SS soldiers lurked on the periphery, conveying an implicit threat of violence if anyone attempted to deviate from the prescribed path.

As Anna made her way into the camp, she heard men snickering behind her. "I'm gonna fuck that one," a voice said in fluent German.

"No you're not. She's mine!" another said.

From the voices' proximity and the very limited number of women in the work detail, Anna had no doubt she was their target.

Once the POWs were within the camp's gates, the *Sonderkommando* ordered them to stop and remove their clothing. Several other *Sonderkommandos* hosed them down in rapid succession. Anna suffered the indignity as hundreds of men gawked at her naked body.

The POWs' *Sonderkommando* leader then ordered them to report to a barracks building where each of them received a black-and-white striped uniform. The *Sonderkommandos* then led them to their cramped living quarters, where they each had little more than one square meter for sleeping space.

Once clean and dressed, Anna and the other newly minted *Sonderkommandos* reported to yet another formation where they each received some water and a small chunk of stale bread. Anna devoured her portion in two bites, but her hunger was far from sated. Her feet still burned from the quick lime, and her shoulder wound ached, though she was glad to see that her stitches were still in place.

As Anna waited for the next set of instructions, a rail-thin *Sonderkommando* tapped her on the shoulder and pointed to two German soldiers skulking near the edge of the perimeter. "Those two have ordered you to report to them at once," the man said.

"Why?" she said.

The man's face turned red and his eyes widened. "It's not my place to ask. It's best you just do what they say, and at the double quick. Laggards don't live for very long around here."

"Fine," Anna said, so she made her way toward the two soldiers. As she drew closer, they both smirked and jeered at her. *"Sprechen Sie Deutsch?"* one asked.

"Ja, ich spreche fließend Deutsch."

"Ausgezeichnet!" the other exclaimed.

Anna knew what their game was, and frankly, she had been terrified from the onset that SS soldiers here might abuse female prisoners. But she heard them out, playing for time.

The first man continued in German. "Have you had a chance to see your quarters," he said, adding a derisive smirk to underscore his apparent sarcasm.

"I have," Anna said, using brevity as a passive form of resistance.

"And what do you think of it?"

"I am thankful I have a roof over my head and a place to sleep away from the front," Anna said, evasively.

The man's smirk vanished, shifting to a frown. "I see. Well, if you ever need a friend, just ask for old Fritz, all right?"

"I will," Anna said. "Is that all?"

From the scowl on Fritz's face, Anna knew she was pushing her luck. "Yeah, watch both your attitude and your back. The next time I call you, I won't give you a choice. Dismissed."

Anna turned and marched back to the common area. As she did so, she heard the men whispering to one another. Their murmuring grew more intense and animated until Fritz summoned her back. "I've changed my mind. If you don't get over here now, I'll shoot you."

She turned and calmly walked back over to the unsavory men, wracking her brain to find a way, any way, out.

∽

The two men led Anna into an administrative area of the camp where the Germans housed members of the Sobibór garrison. While organized with the efficiency of German military precision, the barracks building looked almost pleasant; a small touch of civilization in the midst of the isolated Polish hinterland. But Anna knew better than to let a thin veneer of comfort lull her into a false sense of security.

Anna passed a trio of German guards. One of them shouted to Fritz, "That one looks like a good one, but she smells like a bear. Surely, you're going to do more than just hose her off."

Fritz stopped the procession, turning to the man with a wide smile. "But of course, Adolf. I'm no barbarian." Then he grabbed Anna's arms and led her toward the wooden barracks building.

Along the way, Anna could not help but notice how both closed and isolated this remote German outpost was. With what she estimated were twenty to thirty proper SS guards and five to six times as many non-Jewish Ukrainian auxiliaries, it wouldn't be impossible to overcome the security if the inmates could arm themselves. Unfortunately, the Germans and Ukrainians possessed the only instruments of violence in the camp. Even if Anna seized a weapon from one of the guards, and if the others didn't kill her first, she'd die bleeding, ensnared by the twisted triple-strand concertina wire. And if she were fortunate enough to make it past those obstacles and the guards shooting at her from the watchtowers, she'd probably step on a mine on the camp's outskirts. And if, by a miracle, she managed to fight that far, the roving bands of soldiers and dogs the Germans would almost certainly send out to recover her would likely recapture her, sealing her fate.

No, acting alone here wouldn't work at all. She'd be dead in a fortnight. She needed to organize a team of conspirators: a collection of Soviet POWs and camp insiders who knew the compound inside and out. Until then, she had to do whatever was necessary to survive.

Entering the barracks, Fritz and his heavyset companion forced Anna up a simple wooden staircase, leading to a second-floor hallway. They led her down the narrow corridor, passing several doors along both walls spaced at regular intervals. Halfway down the hall, Fritz turned right, opened a door, and beckoned toward Anna.

When Anna entered the room, a naked and bruised brunette lay on one of the room's two beds. She stared at Anna for several seconds, seemingly in shock, and then screamed. The woman yelled something in Polish at Anna. A curse? No, it was too long to be a curse. Perhaps it was a warning.

The woman repeated her message over and over again. *Yes*, Anna judged. *It was most definitely a warning.*

Fritz's corpulent companion entered, and led the kicking and screaming woman out into the hall. Anna used the brief distraction to survey the room. The space was tight, as the Germans seemed to have designed it with an eye for efficiency, minimizing form and maximizing function. Yet, as most soldiers are wont to do in every army, Fritz and his companion did their best to bring their own comfort in this lice-infested camp.

Fritz handed Anna a clean white towel and escorted her out of the room, toward the end of the hall and into a latrine. Past a series of open troughs along each wall, an open shower stood at the far end of latrine, its showerheads spaced at regular intervals. "Strip and clean yourself," he said.

"Some privacy, please," Anna said, knowing full well how Fritz would respond.

"You are no longer entitled to privacy in this camp. Do as you are told and there will be no trouble," he said as his right hand brushed the handle of his sidearm holstered on his thigh.

Anna hesitated as a well of anger surged inside her. Who was this bastard telling her what to do? Did he expect her to blindly follow his commands?

Then the man rushed forward, drew his pistol and pointed at Anna's temple. "Remove your clothes, Jewess, or I'll blow out your brains and no one will ever know the difference. If you haven't figured it out by now, life's pretty cheap in this camp. Only the useful survive. And right now, I find you useful. Don't try to convince me otherwise. Now take off your clothes."

Anna fought to stifle her rage, channeling each boiling impulse to grab the man's weapon into unfastening another button on her uniform.

Once naked and stripped of her dignity, Anna glowered at Fritz, the anger seething through her eyes. She had nothing but contempt for this small man. She'd piled better men than Fritz like cordwood at Stalingrad, which made this humiliation even more difficult to swallow.

"That's a good girl," Fritz gloated, handing Anna a bar of soap, "Now turn on the water and wash yourself with this."

She reluctantly obeyed, convincing herself, albeit unsuccessfully, that at least he'd given her the opportunity to scrub the grime from her bruised and battered body.

After she'd lathered her body with soap and finally felt human again, Fritz laughed at her and said, "The best part about meeting a new Jewish whore is watching her reaction when I tell her that soap was manufactured here, using the fat from other dead Jewish whores."

Then he claimed her.

⁖

After Fritz finished, he'd returned her striped uniform and had two Ukrainians escort her back to the Jewish barracks.

For the first time in her life, Anna simultaneously felt shame, helplessness, and anger. She trudged with her head down, and she wanted to die. A woman used to having power over life and death, Anna was now a victim of power wielded by capricious masters. She felt as though she could no more influence her fate than humanity could stop a tornado.

Yet, when she passed Soviet POWs on her way to her quarters, she saw a wave of recognition wash across their faces. When she'd been covered in dirt and grime, no one had noticed her. Now, her presence inspired a certain and indescribable glow of hope among her countrymen. Soon, word spread among the *Sonderkommandos* that a bona fide Hero of the Soviet Union was in their midst, and it wasn't long before the camp resistance came calling.

Chapter 19
Fortress Antarctica

0530 Hours, 24 September 1943, Neuschwabenland, Antarctica

Strauss watched how the strange pilots handled the disk. By this point in the journey, Strauss was confident he could pilot the saucer on his own, albeit at a much slower velocity.

The disk had zipped around the curvature of the Earth, accelerating over the continent of Africa. At the current velocity, Strauss's mind could barely recognize the terrain below. It was nearly impossible for him to navigate. Then, just as suddenly as the craft had accelerated, it decelerated.

Through the translucent floor Strauss saw a white waste with no recognizable terrain features. Then the craft hovered in position and slowly descended toward the surface. To Strauss, it somehow felt as if the disk used its own gravity to bring objects to it, rather than the other way around.

Once the saucer was about fifty meters above the icy crags, it resumed its lateral movement, wending over desolate windswept wolds in hypervelocity nape-of-the earth flight.

The craft decelerated as a mountain resolved into view. As the disk drew closer, Strauss saw what appeared to be a hangar bay chiseled into the mountainside. In seconds, the vessel was inside the hangar and hovering above a dull gray metallic surface. When Strauss glanced through the craft's transparent floor, he saw a black sun emblazoned on a white circular background on the hangar deck.

Several black-garbed soldiers entered the hangar from somewhere inside the mountain. As they got closer, he immediately recognized the distinctive *Stahlhelm* worn by Wehrmacht troops.

By Strauss's count, about twelve soldiers had entered the hangar. They hustled to form a circle around the disk. Once they closed that protective circle, the craft hovered to the surface, landing effortlessly.

Trying not to draw too much attention to himself, Strauss surreptitiously checked his compass to get a bearing on his location. The instant he did so, the compass's needle started bending upwards, pointing to the sky.

Where on Earth could that happen? he wondered.

Once the craft was stationary, the strange creatures powered down the saucer. The translucent walls became opaque, and the restraints and chairs melded back into the floor and wall. The beings activated a hydraulic system, lowering the platform elevator. Once the platform reached the floor, the creatures climbed aboard and ascended toward the outer surface of the craft.

Strauss wanted to follow the strange entities out of the vessel, but he knew better than to take that risk. While the beings rose toward the ceiling, Strauss dragged the unconscious engineers toward the platform's edge.

Seconds after the platform reached the ceiling Strauss activated it again. Once it descended back to the floor, Strauss loaded his two stunned comrades onto the platform, joining them as it re-ascended.

When Strauss emerged from the craft's conical structure, he saw an entity hand an SS officer Heisenberg's antigravity device. The two saluted each other and then both exited the room, leaving Strauss and his men surrounded by eleven soldiers.

Were the Germans also collaborating with extraterrestrials? Strauss wondered.

He climbed off the craft, leaving the unconscious engineers lying on the disk's sleek surface. The soldiers watched Strauss's movements the same way a child might watch a moving car, with passing interest, but with no real alarm.

A pulsating blue light appeared in the chamber accompanied by a strong breeze and a sucking sound, reminding Strauss of the vortex he and Anna had observed outside Kharkov.

Anna.

Strauss wondered where she was now. He worried that his failure to destroy the disk would prevent him from ever seeing her again. But, he still had hope. He suspected that Heydrich hadn't been entirely forthright about Strauss's mission. The fact that Strauss now found himself in what appeared to be a remote SS base, gave him hope that his mission had been successful. After all, he was confident Heydrich would consider capturing the disk a better outcome than destroying it.

Before Strauss could formulate a plan of action, the pulsing light winked out and the strange sucking sound stopped. In less than a minute, the SS officer returned to the hangar.

The man's impassive face opened into a smile when he saw Strauss. The man, who had a muscular build and was well over two meters tall, approached Strauss. The officer's SS uniform was coal black and it bore a unit patch on the man's upper arms that Strauss didn't recognize—a black sun on a white circular background – the same emblem on the hangar floor.

The officer extended his right hand toward Strauss. "Congratulations, Herr Strauss. It's an absolute pleasure to make your acquaintance. My name is *SS-Standartenführer* Hans Hönig, and I am third in command of our facility here. With your help, our operatives have seized our very own *Schwartzwald* entity craft. Using it, we can begin to turn the tables on the Soviets. Then, when the Führer begins fielding new wonder weapons over the next several months, our victory over Communism will be complete."

The man's introduction raised so many questions for Strauss that he didn't know where to begin, so he just shook the man's hand. "Ah, Thank you," Strauss said.

"Excellent. Will you be staying long enough to dine with us?" Hönig said, seemingly oblivious to the fact that Strauss didn't know where he was much less what he'd be eating for dinner.

"Well, *Standartenführer*," Strauss said, "I'm really not sure. Actually, I have no idea where I am right now. Can you help me out a bit, please?"

Hönig's face registered shock. "Why, we're in *Neuschwabenland*. In Antarctica."

"We're in Antarctica?" Strauss said, dumbfounded.

"Heydrich didn't brief you?"

"Not exactly. My mission was to seek and destroy the craft, not capture it. Speaking of which, who were those alien operatives piloting the disk? Are we also working with extraterrestrials?"

The man's expression shifted from one of shock to one of suspicion. "I think I may already have said too much. If Heydrich didn't brief you on any of this, I'm sure he had his reasons."

"Fine," Strauss said in resignation. "Can you at least tell me when I can see Anna Ivanova? And Inge Prager?"

"Who?"

"What? Is that classified too?"

"Unlikely. I just have no idea who you're talking about."

"Would it be possible for me to speak to Heydrich?"

"Yes," Hönig said, "The next U-Boot should be docking here in about two months. You can hitch a ride home with the submariners then."

"But, but that's not possible. I need to get back to the Eastern Front as soon as possible. People's lives depend on me!" Strauss pleaded.

Hönig laughed. "Only a few hours removed from being behind Soviet lines and you already want to get back into the fight. Heydrich said you were one hell of a Teutonic warrior, but I had no idea. Take some time to rest and relax. You'll be returning to the front soon enough."

Hönig's words failed to reassure Strauss. "If I can't get out of here soon, do you have a radio I can use to contact Heydrich?"

Hönig nodded. "It's in the command center, and you're welcome to try, but you'll have to wait in line to use the Enigma machine. We're trying to save on transmission costs. Also, it'll take a few weeks for a low priority message to reach its destination. The message must be relayed from communication hubs in South America and then retransmitted to Germany. By the time it's encrypted, and then decrypted, the message could take several weeks to reach its intended recipient."

"But this isn't a low priority message. My friend's life is at stake," Strauss said.

He was now certain Heydrich hadn't been entirely straight with him. Strauss also entertained the notion that Heydrich had never expected Strauss to survive the demolition mission.

Hönig smiled. "Georg, when it involves a woman, every man's message is high priority."

Hönig's apparent attempt at levity failed to amuse Strauss. "Fine," Strauss said, "Where do I need to go to transmit the message, and when's the soonest I can do it?"

Hönig pointed beyond the hangar toward a man-made cavern bored into the mountainside. "Right this way," he said.

ℬ

0630 Hours, 30 September 1943, Bletchley Park, Milton Keynes, Buckinghamshire, England

The military section's Teletype Model 15 clacked into operation on the second floor of Bletchley Park's Victorian mansion. The machine's typebars pounded impressions on a plain white loose-leaf sheet. In twelve seconds, it printed a single line of text before executing a carriage return and beginning another line. The machine was no bigger than a small desk, but punched well above its weight in the information war.

The Hut Six folks had decoded the Enigma encrypted message from intercepted German transmissions. The men and women in Hut Three then translated the German into English and relayed the message here. More than half a dozen single-story wooden huts marred the natural beauty of the manor, their chimneys spewing smoke into the crisp country air.

Today, the Bletchley folks flagged another Enigma intercept for high priority analysis.

MESSAGE DECRYPT FOLLOWS:

TO: DIRECTOR REINHARD HEYDRICH, ORDER OF THE BLACK SUN
SUBJECT: SITUATION REPORT, OPERATION APOLLO
DATE: 24 SEPTEMBER 1943
MISSION COMPLETE. CHARIOT AND SCHWERKRAFT DEVICE SECURE. NO CASUALTIES. REQUEST FULL CLEARANCE FOR STRAUSS ON PROJECT POCKET. DESPITE LEADING KEY OPERATIONAL EFFORT, HE WAS UNAWARE OF BLACK SUN ORDER. STRAUSS COULD BE OUTSTANDING ASSET IF ALLOWED INTO FOLD. RECOMMEND STRAUSS FOR IRON CROSS, FIRST CLASS FOR ACTIONS IN KURSK. REQUEST INFORMATION ON ANNA IVANOVA AND INGE PRAGER TO PROVIDE COMFORT TO WAR HERO.

Captain D'Alessio swiped the sheet off the Teletype and read it. The British "leftenant" manning the communications station scowled at the brash American.

D'Alessio noticed, swaggered back toward the Brit, and said, "What? The Queen tell you I can't take a piece of paper? Well, fuck the Queen."

D'Alessio smiled inside when he said that. These Brits, with all their pomp and tradition, couldn't see their social structure for what it really was: a rigged caste system based on slavish devotion to an inbred monarchy. As far as D'Alessio was concerned, the monarchy could wipe his ass.

The "Leftenant" stood up, apparently itching for a confrontation with D'Alessio. *Today could turn out to be an interesting day after all*, D'Alessio thought. He'd always wanted to knock out a limey.

The Brit marched up to D'Alessio and said, "Apologize, you Yankee grease ball."

Oh, it was definitely gonna be an interesting day. "What did you call me?" D'Alessio said, invading the Brit's personal space.

"I called you a Yankee, Yank!"

"No, after that. Did you call me a fucking grease ball?"

The Brit puffed up his chest. "Yeah, mate, I bloody called you a grease ball, too."

"That ain't gonna be the only thing you 'bloody' do today," D'Alessio said before he knocked the Brit out cold.

All activity in the communications center stopped. Everyone stared at D'Alessio. D'Alessio just shrugged. "Whatchya looking at?" he said at no one in particular, glowering.

Silence.

Satisfied with his little bit of fun for the day, D'Alessio read the contents on the Teletype sheet. "Holy shit!" D'Alessio exclaimed, "This transmission mentions the *Schwerkraft* Device!"

Everyone in the office glared at D'Alessio. Man, the Brits were one uptight people. "Sorry," D'Alessio said holding his beefy hands up in a sign of contrition. "From now on, I promise to be a good boy," he said, while making the sign of the cross like an altar boy.

More silence.

D'Alessio just couldn't help himself. "Who's in charge here?"

A heavy set, balding man wearing bifocals pointed down the hall, and said, "That would be Colonel Tiltman. His office is the last room in that direction."

D'Alessio grinned, shook the man's hand, and said, "Thank you, Sir. You are a gentlemen and a scholar."

The man harrumphed. D'Alessio made his way down the hallway until he reached the room. He rapped three times on its large oaken door.

"Enter!" Colonel Tiltman said.

D'Alessio opened the door, marched toward the colonel's desk, saluted and said, "Captain Jimmy D'Alessio, reporting for duty, Sir." As D'Alessio looked around the room, he was surprised to see Peter Rabbit wallpaper.

Colonel Tiltman glared at D'Alessio, while D'Alessio held his salute. After an uncomfortable silence, the colonel returned the salute and said, "What's your purpose here?"

"I'm the OSS liaison for the War Anomalies Response Team."

Tiltman raised an eyebrow. "WART?"

"Yeah, yeah, yeah. If I hear somebody say that cheesy shit again, I'll knock 'em out. Only this time, I'll hit 'em so hard it'll make it seem like I gave the other guy a nice massage." D'Alessio said.

Colonel Tiltman scowled. "So, you're the source of the recent commotion this morning, aren't you?"

D'Alessio raised his hands in surrender. "Guilty as charged, Sir."

"I'll have you know, Captain D'Alessio, that we are not cowboys here. I expect officers under this roof, be they British or American, to obey basic standards of decorum. You are not to assault anyone ever again while you're here. If you do, I'll beat the bloody hell out of you myself," Tiltman said, winking at D'Alessio.

"Fantastic, Sir. You and me are gonna get along swell," D'Alessio smiled and inclined his head toward the wallpaper, "Sir, if I may ask, what the fuck is that on the wall?"

Colonel Tiltman chortled. "You Americans certainly don't mince words. Before the military appropriated this mansion for our code-breaking operations, it used to be a child's room."

D'Alessio shook his head in faux disappointment. "And here I thought I finally found a man who shared my love for Peter Rabbit."

The colonel laughed again, and then said, "Now that all the awkward bits are out of the way, how may we be of service to you Yanks?"

"Sir, the reason I'm here is that I have authority from Churchill himself to assemble a team of your best cryptanalysts and interpreters to work on a classified project. Here's the paperwork." D'Alessio handed the colonel a stack of documents.

The Brit's affinity with D'Alessio didn't diminish his officiousness. The colonel took his time scrutinizing the document in a bureaucratic love affair that threatened to make D'Alessio's head explode.

After about ten minutes, the colonel appeared satisfied. He directed D'Alessio down the hall toward another room. The room was a giant safe protected by a steel door with a combination lock.

"I will assign two of my best cryptanalysts and two of my best German interpreters to you," Tiltman said. Then he handed D'Alessio a strip of paper with a set of numbers. "This is the room's combination. Our rules require that nothing leaves that room, no matter what. Do you understand?"

"Of course," D'Alessio said, smiling. "In the interim, I want you to monitor any traffic that contains any of the following names or references: The *Schwerkraft* Device, the Chariot, Operation Apollo, Heydrich, Strauss, Hans Hönig, Anna Ivanova, Inge Prager, the Order of the Black Sun, and Project Pocket. If you code-breakers hear anything, please have them alert me immediately any time of day or night. Here's my local number if I'm not in the office." D'Alessio handed Tiltman his number, saluted the colonel, and left the office glowing.

Today was going to be a good day.

Chapter 20
Pechersky's Promise

1600 Hours, 14 October 1943, Sobibór, Poland

"One of my men will place it by the door at sixteen hundred hours and not a minute sooner," Alexander Pechersky had warned her.

Anna had been waiting for this day since she'd arrived at Sobibór. Between the guards' capriciousness and Fritz's unwanted attention, the thought of what she would do to Fritz and his comrades today had sustained her for three horrific weeks.

Rumors that the Nazis were planning on shutting down the camp had reached the *Sonderkommandos* by midsummer. Many speculated that as part of the shutdown, the Germans were going to exterminate the camp workers to cover their tracks. Spurred by these rumors, a small group of *Sonderkommandos* had begun planning an uprising in earnest. But it wasn't until the Soviet POWs had arrived in the camp along with Alexander Pechersky, that Leon Feldhendler, a Polish Jew, had the muscle he needed to pull off an escape.

Anna had her doubts about the plan, which required the conspirators to surreptitiously kill as many SS personnel and Ukrainian camp guards as possible. That way, the conspirators could waltz out the front gate, altogether bypassing the concertina wire, watchtowers, and minefields. Anna believed the plan was ambitious and unrealistic, but she preferred to die fighting for her freedom to being slaughtered like a slave.

Fritz forced himself on her that afternoon—a daily indignity that hardened Anna's hatred for the Germans. She kept telling herself her suffering was essential for her survival; that it was temporary. But deep down, she knew the scars from this experience would never fade and the anger would never die. All she could do was channel the hatred; store it up for one final violent eruption.

At sixteen hundred hours precisely, Anna heard a rap at Fritz's door. She lay on his bunk, his limp arms wrapped around her naked and bruised body. He snored, then stirred at the sound of the knock. Moments later, he fell back to sleep. Anna attempted to wiggle gently out of his slumbering embrace, praying she didn't disturb him. She shifted her weight away from him, and he stirred again.

Anna shuddered. If she moved too fast, she'd wake Fritz up. Too slow, and someone would discover what waited for her in the hallway.

She paused, waiting for Fritz to settle. Then, she employed a sequence of careful movements, balancing and counterbalancing, to wrest free from his embrace without waking him.

Free, Anna tiptoed toward the door, and carefully turned the knob. The door creaked as she pushed it open. Anna heard rustling behind her. She spun her head over her shoulder. Fritz grabbed her close-cropped hair, and slammed her head into the door.

A flash of light, then her head rang like a bell. She stumbled backward, her head throbbing.

Fritz slammed her to the floor.

"You filthy, sneaky Jew whore!" he yelled as he kneed her repeatedly in the face.

A sharp pain rippled from her nose to the rest of her face like a rock impacting a stagnant pond. Hot blood streamed from her nose, over her upper lip, and into her mouth, its salty tang lingering on her tongue. She wondered if her nose was broken, like her. Her eyes watered. Maybe she was meant to die here, alone, and in the wilderness. Perhaps it was her destiny. After all, not everyone deserved a good life.

Fritz nearly pummeled her into unconsciousness. Just before she was about to pass out, he began taunting her. "You know why you'll never escape? Because you are a filthy verminous Jew, unworthy of survival."

Then he grinned.

His self-righteous contempt worked like gasoline, fueling her fury. Fuming with anger, she couldn't take it anymore. How could she ever let this coward of a man kill her? This pathetic excuse for a warrior who would go as far as murdering helpless woman and children to avoid the front.

Anna slammed the heel of her open palm into Fritz's face, breaking his nose and unleashing a torrent of blood. Fritz reeled back, howling. She gripped and twisted his testicles. His howl crescendoed into an ear-splitting squeal.

She scrambled back on her feet and surged toward the door. She opened it. Leaning against the wall, Pechersky's promise waited, enticing her to unleash the hidden potential of its violence.

Seizing the hatchet that the prisoners had made secretly in their workshops, she stormed toward Fritz. He covered his wreck of a nose with one hand, while the other cupped the ruin Anna had made of his genitals. "No! Please, don't," he murmured.

She struggled for words, fumbling for a way to express the shame he'd made her endure. The despair and the depth of her depression and sorrow screamed for release.

But Anna had no words. The hatchet would speak for her. So she buried it in his head, over and over again until his skull was a mash of blood, meat, and bone.

She ripped the key Fritz kept around his neck to open his barracks room safe. She removed his Luger. Anna dressed in his uniform, loaded the pistol and stuffed the spare bullets in her pockets. Then she grabbed the hatchet and fled.

Her heart quickened, propelled by a mix of equal parts fear and exhilaration. Her face throbbed, but the adrenaline pumping through her veins helped dull the pain.

In the hallway, she stumbled into a German soldier rushing toward Fritz's room. The man had probably been racing to investigate the source of the disturbance. When his eyes locked with Anna's, he hesitated, likely confused by finding her dressed in an oversized German uniform. Anna buried her hatchet in his head, using that brief delay to her advantage.

She would've preferred the pistol, but Pechersky had been unequivocally clear: no one was to use firearms unless absolutely necessary. The more Germans they killed covertly, the more likely the mission would succeed.

The man's limp body slumped to the ground as Anna labored to dislodge the hatchet from his skull. Anna yanked the weapon, finally freeing it, but overcompensated and hit the wall behind her. She heard rustling in the barracks rooms, so she sprinted toward the stairs.

Before Anna reached the stairwell, two Germans emerged from rooms at the far end of the hall and blocked her path.

In such close quarters fighting, Anna knew that both men would ultimately overcome her using their weight advantage. So Anna pulled out the Luger without breaking her stride and squeezed off two shots, each bullet hitting center of mass.

The shots rang out louder than she'd expected, as the sounds reverberated off the barracks walls. Now the world presented sound with a muffled hum. The after echo of the gunshots resonated in her eardrums with a ghostly whine.

She burst out of the barracks building to find German soldiers and their Ukrainian lapdogs mustering outside. She popped off two more shots as she stumbled into two surprised and dazed Ukrainians on her way out of the barracks building.

Outside, the Germans scrambled to organize. The several hundred prisoners in the yard had only begun pressing forward toward the front gate.

Now that Anna had fired her Luger, she had to take more drastic action for the plan to succeed, so she sprinted toward the nearest watchtower.

The guard on the ground watching the tower's ladder spotted her and trained his rifle on her. Anna put a bullet in his chest before he had a chance to pull the trigger.

She shoved her Luger in her trouser cargo pocket and seized the man's rifle. Bullets zipped toward her from above, ricocheting off the ground. Anna took cover under the one of the crossbeams at the base of the tower, crouching to make her body as small a target as possible.

In between the soldier's three-round bursts, Anna exposed herself long enough to pop off a shot. The man slumped over and tumbled from the tower, hitting the ground with a loud thud. Having silenced the one watchtower gunman, Anna slung the rifle over her back and climbed a ladder until she reached the structure's upper platform. There, she established a firing platform.

Pandemonium reigned below. A German guard blew a whistle in a futile attempt to force the crowd back into line. Anna heard him shout, "Hey you motherfuckers, didn't you hear my goddamn whistle? Get in squads of three. Stop acting like cattle!"

An ax took him from behind.

Guards on Sobibór's other watchtowers fired at Anna. She kept her head down and took cover, trying to catch glimpses of them. She cocked the bolt back on her rifle, took aim and fired, dropping another guard.

The Germans and Ukrainians below started firing indiscriminately into the crowd. Men and women screamed. A widespread panic threatened to devolve into a stampede.

Then, Anna heard Pechersky's commanding voice, "Forward! For the Motherland, forward!"

A core of Russian POW's surged against the guards, massacring them with hatchets, axes, truncheons, and any other crude tools the POWs managed to cobble together and use as weapons. The other prisoners scurried in random directions. Some fainted, after weeks or months of ceaseless work and malnutrition had robbed them of the energy, but not the will, necessary to fight.

Soon, scores of prisoners were dropping like cockroaches. The German response was becoming more organized. Anna continued to duel with the guards on the other watchtowers. They were now concentrating their fire on her. Pinned down, she struggled to acquire new targets. But each time she raised her head to get a glimpse of the enemy, bullets zipped all around her.

A machine gun emplacement at one tower raked hers with withering fire. She kept her head down and prayed they left her for dead. At least the men occupying the watchtowers were wasting their efforts on her instead of shooting at the prisoners below.

The great mass of humanity was now gathering near the fences. Several Soviet POWs pulled out stolen bolt cutters and feverishly cut a hole through one of the fences. The crowd pressing them from behind surged through the opening, widening it. The crowd's combined weight forced entire sections of fencing to buckle and fall.

With horror, Anna watched as the great throng of humanity began to cross the hidden minefields at the camp's edge.

This couldn't be happening. Pechersky had planned for this contingency. The Soviet POWs were supposed to throw stones at the mines to diffuse them, and lay down wooden planks to clear a path through them. But in the panic to flee from the shooting, no one had bothered.

Anna watched helplessly as the prisoners rushed to their deaths, body parts catapulting through the air in a macabre fireworks display.

The men on the watchtower had since given up on Anna and were now fully engaged in a firefight on the ground with several prisoners armed with stolen automatic weapons. She used her tactical pause to identify the location of the watchtower machine gunner. She took aim at the man. She squeezed the trigger and watched his body go limp and then tumble end over end onto the cold ground. The scene of the man plummeting to his death mesmerized Anna, both real and surreal.

A bullet zipped over her head, yanking her back into reality. The last watchtower guard. She took cover behind one of tower's crossbeams. She mounted her rifle, aimed, and put a bullet through the man's forehead.

Out of rifle ammunition, Anna scrambled down the watchtower ladder. Once she reached the surface, she bolted toward the breach in the fence. Sporadic small arms fire whizzed past her as she raced toward the breach. Sprinting through the gap, she was careful to follow the path the dead had cleared for her with their warm corpses. She passed scores of severed heads and limbs. Blood was everywhere.

Hundreds of surviving prisoners neared the tree line beyond the camp's edge. Bullets zipped and popped all around her. She ran for her life.

She ran for home. And she ran for Strauss. She couldn't stop. She was exhausted and weak, but the forest was her salvation.

If only she could make it.

Seconds later, she disappeared into the protective embrace of a dense old growth oak and birch forest along with the other haggard and terrified survivors. A man ahead of her wheezed loudly. A woman crouched on Anna's left sobbed uncontrollably. But most continued their desperate flight into the woods. Anna was no different.

As she trampled through the forest, she smiled. It was the first time she had known peace in months. While she still had a long way to go to get to freedom, the horrors she'd endured at Sobibór were behind her. And now, for the moment, she was in the company of her people making her way back home.

Chapter 21
Foo Fighters

Anna was dead.

After weeks of waiting, Strauss had finally received Heydrich's clinical response. Now Strauss wanted to kill the man.

Heydrich's curt and perfunctory note had informed Strauss that several weeks ago Heydrich had sent Anna to a resettlement camp called Sobibór. In the interim, the prisoners there had launched a rebellion, which the SS put down. Now the SS was razing the camp.

Heydrich offered no apology, no condolences, and no expression of grief, just a clinical report of Anna's demise.

Then Heydrich had the gall to order Strauss to remain in place and await further instructions for his next mission. Heydrich's ham-fisted message motivated Strauss to ignore the order.

But Strauss decided to take his insubordination to a whole new level. Within an hour of receiving Heydrich's callous dispatch, Strauss raided the base's pharmacy for enough Pervitin to last him several weeks. He approached Hönig in the base's command center and said, "Sir, I just received classified orders from Heydrich. I will need immediate access to the craft. Heydrich needs me to complete a high priority mission, and he expects a report within the next several hours – once I'm operating over European airspace."

Hönig eyed Strauss suspiciously. "Let me get this straight. You're asking me to grant you access to a device that was seized in the single most important intelligence coup in human history. Let me see your orders."

Strauss shook his head. "I'm sorry, sir. They're for my eyes only. If you don't believe me, you can always send a message to Heydrich."

"But with retransmission and decryption time, it could take weeks," Hönig said.

Strauss was counting on it. "Alternatively, you could deny me permission to carry out my orders. In which case you'd have to answer to Heydrich."

Hönig still seemed skeptical. His hand moved toward the Luger holstered on his hip.

Strauss stared directly into Hönig's eyes and told him the truth, "While I can't tell you the mission, I can tell you that lives depend on it. I hope you'll trust me, because I've never let the Reich down."

Hönig nodded. He relaxed the grip on his pistol. "Indeed. No one can doubt your honor and skill as a true German soldier. I'll grant you access, but be quick about it."

Strauss turned to head toward the craft, but stopped midstride and decided to try his luck. "Oh, one more thing," Strauss said, "I'm going to need the antigravity device while I'm inside the craft."

"Well, I don't know about that," Hönig hedged.

"Heydrich will be disappointed, Sir."

Hönig vacillated and then said, "Fine. Wait here. I'll bring it to you."

"Excellent. Thank you, sir. I'll be sure to mention your name to Heydrich and how instrumental you've been in helping me complete my mission."

Hönig beamed. "Why, there's no need to do that. It's my honor to serve." Hönig left the room. He returned several minutes later with the device and handed it to Strauss.

"Thank you," Strauss said. He then walked calmly toward the hangar bay, doing his best to avoid triggering any suspicion. He wiped off a bead of sweat that dotted his brow.

"Wait," Hönig said, "I'm sure Heydrich won't mind if I accompany you inside the craft. While your orders may be classified, my orders are to keep that disk secure. If your orders from Heydrich had conflicted with mine, I'm sure he would have amended my orders. So, in the absence of such an amendment, I'm duty bound to follow my standing orders."

"Really, Sir, it's not necessary."

Hönig gripped Strauss's shoulder. "No, I insist."

Strauss worried that Hönig suspected something was awry. And Hönig was right. So Strauss had to modify his plan. It wouldn't be the first time, and it certainly wouldn't be the last.

Hönig shadowed Strauss into the craft, watching Strauss like a hawk. Once both men stepped off the platform, Strauss realized that no matter what happened, Hönig would now be joining him for the trip, dead or alive.

So be it.

Strauss walked toward the center of the disk and said, "You might want to put your back against the wall."

"Excuse me?" Hönig said approaching Strauss. "I will do no such…"

Strauss activated the pressure sensor with his boot. The craft came to life as a pilot's chair rose from the floor, and its harness wrapped itself around Strauss. Circular panels of light appeared, hovering in the air. Strauss pressed a circular green button with the "T"-like rune, powering up the vessel. The disk shook in response.

At first, Hönig seemed disoriented and confused. Then, appearing to regain his bearing, he resumed his advance toward Strauss.

Strauss had activated the disk's optics, making the walls translucent. Hönig grabbed Strauss's shoulder a split second before Strauss pressed the "S" rune, forcing the craft upward and slamming Hönig to the floor. Strauss glanced over at Hönig, who lay sprawled against a wall, and the man appeared to be unconscious.

Strauss reactivated the seat and harness system, tying Hönig down, so intense gravitational forces wouldn't crush him during the flight. Strauss had no desire to harm Hönig. The man had only ever been kind to Strauss. Once Hönig was secured, Strauss pressed the "U" rune to accelerate forward toward his ultimate destination: the United States.

As Strauss passed over the Southern Atlantic Ocean and then over Argentina, he couldn't help but think about Anna. If she were in his place, would she just accept someone's word that he were dead, especially someone as manipulative and unreliable as Heydrich? While Strauss doubted Anna's survival, his gut said otherwise. And he owed her a debt for helping him reach safety and deal with his addiction. Even if the chance she'd survived was less than one percent, Strauss still thought it was a risk worth taking.

Strauss chose loyalty over duty and honor. And though he was unwilling to admit it, he chose love. He changed course and spiraled toward Poland.

&

2100 Hours, 15 October 1943, Outside Sobibór, Poland

Strauss slowed the craft as he got closer to Europe. He surveyed the surface below. He'd just crossed over the Mediterranean Sea and was about to pass over Sicily when his disk experienced some turbulence.

The craft spasmed again. Strauss glanced behind him and through the translucent walls. Two disks pursued his saucer from above. The instant

Strauss detected their presence, one craft fired a bright green energy pulse, rattling Strauss's disk on impact.

Unsure what to do, Strauss operated on pure instinct, pulling the craft into a steep dive. The ground raced up to meet him.

Undaunted, the hunters traced Strauss's trajectory, diving with Strauss's craft and shadowing his every move. Strauss's disk bobbed and weaved through valleys, gullies, and ravines. But no matter what Strauss did, he couldn't shake his pursuers.

Unable to lose the hunters, Strauss focused squarely on reaching Poland. He increased his altitude, accelerating upward. He needed to reach a height where he could more easily navigate. On his way up, the disk's hull sparked, followed by a wisp of smoke.

What the heck was that? Strauss thought.

Seconds later, two American aircraft buzzed beneath Strauss's craft, banking in opposite directions, probably for a second pass. Though at Strauss's current rate of ascent, he'd be long gone before they'd have a chance to set up another strafing run. But the Americans weren't Strauss's biggest problem; his other pursuers worried him far more.

The enemy disks continued firing their energy beams. After each successive strike, Strauss's disk became less responsive and increasingly difficult to handle. He figured it could take two or three hits at most, before he'd lose control and crash. So once he was at a sufficient altitude for navigation, Strauss flew hard and fast toward Lublin in Eastern Poland, reaching the city in minutes.

His pursuers increased their rate of fire, as Strauss descended toward the surface. He wished he'd seen the man-things operate the craft's weapons during his trip to Antarctica. Alas, he had no such luck, and his ignorance of those systems would now be his undoing.

One strike, and the craft wobbled. A second strike and it shook. But after the third strike, the disk began to rapidly lose altitude, hurtling toward the surface.

It had all happened so fast. Strauss was convinced he was going to die. Nothing built by man could survive a crash at these extreme velocities.

A massive fireball enveloped the disk. The friction from the Earth's atmosphere and the craft's high velocity made it impossible for Strauss to control his landing. So he closed his eyes and braced for death.

A massive flash of light heralded the disk's impact, followed by a cloud of smoke and debris. When the dust settled, the outside of the craft was shrouded in darkness. By the light of the console systems, Strauss glanced over at Hönig, and the man still seemed to be unconscious, but breathing.

Good.

Strauss felt bad about what he'd done to the man. Hönig had done nothing wrong, only his duty, something Strauss had shirked by coming to Poland instead of the United States. And now, Strauss was starting to regret his decision. After all, he'd prioritized the life of one woman over the lives of every human on Earth.

And only then did Strauss realize he'd survived what would have been a devastating crash for anything constructed with modern human technology.

After catching his breath, Strauss worried his pursuers were still out there, waiting to recover the craft, and potentially, the antigravity device. So, Strauss disabled the craft's systems, lowered the platform, placed Hönig on it, and rose to the surface.

The air outside was thick with smog and heavy particulates, making it difficult for Strauss to breathe without coughing up brown phlegm. While dark, the smog appeared to glow, illuminated by several points of light beyond.

As the fallout settled on the ground, Strauss found himself inside a massive crater. The smoldering brush fires raging inside the depression and on the surface above were hot coals in the darkness.

Two luminous emerald spotlights shined on the crater from above. When Strauss glanced up, he saw two disks converging and descending on his position.

Not good. Not good at all, Strauss thought.

He wondered why they hadn't killed him by now. Then, placing his hand in his pocket and gripping the antigravity device, he had a pretty good idea why.

Strauss climbed off the disk and into the crater, searching for a way out. He traveled toward the crater's edge, but the nearly four-meter walls were too steep.

Desperate, Strauss searched for objects he could use to climb out of the hole. Meanwhile, the descending craft had passed out of his line of sight, which was blocked by the crater's walls.

Without a visual on the enemy disk, Strauss's imagination went to work, conjuring up images of *Schwartzwald* entities tearing him apart. He had to think fast. Strauss spotted some head-sized stones strewn all about the crater. He gathered them near the crater's edge, stacking them into a crude series of steps leading out of the crater.

After he finished stacking two stone platforms, he heard the eerie call of what sounded like a bird, reminiscent of an American whippoorwill, just beyond the crater's edge.

Strauss felt uneasy. He was worried that whatever was stalking him from the darkness beyond was getting closer. So he redoubled his efforts.

Just beyond the crater's edge, a tendril unfurled, grasping from the blackness.

Strauss was out of time.

Two writhing *Schwartzwald* entities dropped into the crater. Their vertical maws whistled like whippoorwills. They lumbered toward Strauss. He stood helpless, cornered like a rat.

Strauss had survived so many brushes with death his luck had probably run its course. For the briefest of moments, he made peace with death.

Then he remembered what these creatures did to the dead, infesting them with their parasites, and using them to propagate their foul race. *No,* Strauss vowed, *I won't be a meat puppet.*

Strauss opened the cigarette lighter, aimed it at his attackers, and pressed the red button.

Chapter 22

Intercept

Military operations in Italy had the cryptanalyst teams monitoring German Army and Luftwaffe communications working overtime in Hut Six. Even D'Alessio's small team was working feverishly to decrypt German radio communications intercepted from Italy. Bletchley Park's victory here could make the difference between success and failure for the United States Fifth Army. Detailed information about enemy positions along the Volturno line could help the Americans achieve a decisive penetration of German defenses.

"Sir, we intercepted another message from Heydrich to this Strauss figure," an orderly said, handing D'Alessio a Teletype printout.

D'Alessio scanned the message, confused. "The Germans are razing Sobibór? Anna is likely dead? What the hell is all this about? And now Heydrich wants this Strauss to take on a new mission? What the fuck? I need answers here, not more riddles!"

The orderly blinked. D'Alessio clasped his chin with his hand, deep in thought. He was also trying to rein in his temper. If he kept flying off the handle like that, his men would start holding things back from him if they weren't already.

"Okay," D'Alessio said, "Can someone find Sobibór on a map and tell me where it is?"

"Sounds Polish," Lucy Knox, one of D'Alessio's British interpreters said as she clutched a map of Poland and spread it on the table in D'Alessio's office.

"Yes, here it is," Lucy said, pointing at the map. "It looks like it's a small village on the outskirts of Lublin."

D'Alessio scratched his head. "Well, that's random."

"Lucy, what do you make of all this?" D'Alessio said.

"Well, Sir, there's only one of two conclusions I can make. One: it's a reference to the actual physical location and two: it's a code for something else."

"Suppose it's code," D'Alessio said, "What could the Nazis be referencing when they use the codename, Sobibór?"

"Sir, without any more transmissions or context, I simply don't have enough information to draw any conclusions."

"I see," D'Alessio pounded his fist on the table to release his simmering anger. Again, he struggled to hold back his temper. "Thank you, Lucy. Continue to monitor the net and let me know if you hear anything new."

"Yes, Sir," Lucy saluted and left the room.

D'Alessio mulled over the code hypothesis for a few more seconds and then called Lucy back into the room. "Hey, Lucy, ever hear of Ockham's Razor?"

Lucy returned to the room. "Whose razor?"

"Ockham's Razor. It's an idea attributed to the medieval philosopher, William of Ockham. It essentially says that between two competing hypotheses, the one with the fewest assumptions or simplest explanation is likely to be the correct one. Applying the logic of Ockham's Razor to this scenario would suggest that Heydrich references Sobibór because he's actually referring to the physical location."

"I see, Sir. What are your orders?"

"Continue to monitor the net for references to Sobibór, as well as all the other tags we've been monitoring."

"Yes, sir," Lucy said, before leaving the room.

D'Alessio decided to follow Lucy, and passed several monitoring stations where translators worked feverishly to translate decoded radio traffic from the ongoing battle in Italy.

Five minutes later, Lucy rushed up to D'Alessio. "Sir, an intelligence officer attached to the U.S. Fifth Army just called and instructed you to monitor a very specific U.S. military frequency. He says it's your 'very special sort of weird.'"

D'Alessio's eyes lit up in excitement, and kissed Lucy on the forehead. "You may have just made my night, Lucy!"

Lucy grimaced, and said in her usual sardonic tone, "I live to serve, Sir."

D'Alessio and Lucy returned to D'Alessio's office and huddled over a wireless set.

"Three contacts identified over Italian airspace. Break. Estimate that bogeys traveled at well over of one thousand miles per hour. Over," an American pilot transmitted.

"Blackhawk One, this is Blackhawk Six. Describe contact. Over," a second American radioed.

"Three jet black disks, traveling in a triangular formation in excess of over one thousand miles an hour. Break. Two of the disks fired green rays at the third. Break. When the first craft entered our airspace, we engaged with Papa Five One Mustangs with no effect. Over."

"Blackhawk One. Blackhawk Six. Could you determine if there was a unit designation on the craft or anything that might identify nation of origin? Over."

"Blackhawk Six. Negative. Over."

"Blackhawk One, this is Six. Would you classify contact as foo fighter over?"

"Affirmative. Over."

"Blackhawk One, continue to follow and report. Do not break contact. I say again, do not break contact. Over."

"Negative, Blackhawk Six. Bogeys accelerated northeast at a high rate of speed and out of our designated airspace. Over."

"Roger, Blackhawk One. Continue prior mission hunting Jerry. Happy hunting. Blackhawk Six. Out."

D'Alessio switched off the radio, turned toward Lucy, smiled, and said, "I have a hunch where those craft are heading. I have some operatives on the ground in Poland. I'll give you their frequencies and call signs. Reach out to them and ask them to monitor air traffic over Eastern Poland. If you hear anything, radio the air traffic control center in Watton, England and ask them to pass the information along to me when I arrive."

"Where are you going, sir?"

D'Alessio's eyes lit up and he grabbed his coat. "I finally have my mission, Lucy. Toodle-oo!"

&

2110 Hours, 15 October 1943, Outside Sobibór, Poland

After hiking all night through the forest with over fifty other survivors, Anna felt both exhausted and exhilarated. Just before sunrise, Pechersky had ordered the survivors to separate and spread out to avoid attracting German attention. Avoiding daylight, most of the fugitives huddled under the meager cover of bushes and trees, barely sleeping. By sunset, Anna couldn't believe the Germans hadn't discovered them while they'd slumbered.

Anna scurried through the forest in single file with ten others. Everyone moved much slower than they had the prior evening, likely exhausted from nearly two days of flight. Several meters ahead of them, the woods opened up into a small field that stretched for about a hundred meters and then ended at another tree line.

A light flashed over the horizon near the Polish-Ukrainian border. Anna quietly counted, "One one thousand, two one thousand, three one thous…"

A loud boom sounded and the ground quaked. Anna addressed her comrades. "Something just crash-landed. Judging from the time lapse between the flash and the boom, whatever fell from sky landed about a klick to the east. If we're lucky, it's a Soviet aircraft. If it is, and the pilot survived, he might have a radio we could use to contact the Red Army. Let's get to the crash site before the Germans do," Anna said as she headed toward the site, which was illuminated by dozens of brushfires.

Anna had no intention of radioing the Red Army her whereabouts, given her status as a Soviet fugitive. But she saw value in reporting the crash to the Soviets. At best, they might send aircraft or paratroopers to the site, distracting the Germans from pursuing the escapees.

"Wait," Shlomo said, "Shouldn't we be avoiding attention? The Germans will be swarming all over that wreck."

Shlomo had a good point, but Anna's gut told her that heading toward the explosion was her best bet. If the others chose not to follow, that was their prerogative.

"That's a fair point, Shlomo," Anna said, "The Germans will be converging on that site. However, it's also the last place they'd expect to find us. We're heading east anyway. Plus, if we find the pilot before the Germans do, we can radio the Soviets for help. And the closer we get to the frontlines, the easier it'll be for us to get lost in the confusion. The Soviets are a more pressing concern to the Germans than we are.

"If you'd rather wait and hide here, so be it. I'm heading toward the crash." Anna marched toward the smoldering fires on the horizon.

All ten men surprised Anna and followed her toward the site. As they drew closer to their destination, dogs barked in the distance. "German shepherds," Shlomo said.

"Shoot the dogs so the Germans can't track us as effectively."

The barking grew louder. Anna cocked her Luger.

A man in an SS uniform emerged from the darkness, toward the fugitives. He kept looking over his shoulder, as if he were running from something rather than toward them. Shlomo aimed his rifle at the man and fired, chipping the bark off a nearby pine tree, but missing his target.

Anna forced Shlomo's rifle down. Shlomo glowered at her. "Can't you see he's running from something?" Anna said.

"So? He's a Nazi, woman. What other excuse do I need?"

"He's more useful as a hostage, no?"

Shlomo rolled his eyes, hesitated, and then said, "Fine. What's your plan?"

"Let me try something first," Anna said before yelling, "Strauss! Is that you?"

The soldier stopped dead in his tracks. "Anna?"

Anna's eyes welled up with tears. She turned to Shlomo, "Tell the men to cease fire. Strauss is a friend who can help."

"You know this fascist?"

"He's not a fascist. He's saved my life in the past. He's a man we can trust."

Anna sprinted toward Strauss. A surge of adrenaline quickened her pace. She beamed.

She nearly tackled Strauss when she reached him, squeezing him with all her strength. "It's so good to see you," she sobbed, "I never thought I'd see you again."

"They told me you were dead," Strauss said before tightening his embrace. "I refused to believe them."

The eerie call of the whippoorwill echoed from the blackness. "We have to go," Strauss said as he started jogging toward a tree line. "They're coming for me."

"Who's coming for you?" Anna said, trailing him.

"The *Schwartzwald* entities."

"They're actually here?"

"Yes."

"How many?"

"Two."

"Why?" Anna said.

Strauss pulled the antigravity device from his pocket. "Because they want this, and I'm not gonna let 'em have it."

The barking grew louder.

"Are the Germans chasing you, too?" Strauss asked.

"Yes," Anna said.

"Perhaps we can use it to our advantage. Are those your friends in the woods?" Strauss said.

"They are."

"Are they armed?"

"Yes."

"Tell them to take up positions along this tree line. Maybe a little hot lead will slow these things down."

"How did you survive this long without a weapon?"

Strauss held out the lighter. "I did the same thing Heisenberg did to us back in the Ukraine: I pressed the red button. I must've hurled those things five hundred meters. It may have bought me some time, but it didn't kill 'em."

"Well, do it again!" Anna said.

"I wish I could. When I tried to use it a second time, it didn't work. It needs to be recharged."

When Anna and Strauss reached the tree line, she explained the situation and the plan to her comrades in both Ukrainian and Russian. They nodded and occupied positions along the tree line moments before two hulking black cephalopods emerged from the far tree line and into the open field.

Men cried and prayed. Some screamed. The horrors they'd endured at Sobibór had been hard enough, but the waking nightmares lumbering toward them were enough to drive most men insane. But Anna wasn't like most men.

The men along the tree line aimed their rifles at the squid-things as the ink-colored creatures crept forward.

"Now!" Anna yelled. With their rifles and pistols, the men unleashed a wall of steel on the two interlopers. The creatures howled, but redoubled their advance.

An alien extended a tentacle, its tendrils flexing a semicircular device, firing a green beam of light. A camp escapee disintegrated near Anna.

"This isn't working," Anna said, exasperated.

With the encroaching entities to her front, Anna heard the barking dogs drawing closer from behind. She was certain the animals were hot on her band's scent. Ahead, the entities were closing in, seemingly undeterred by rifle and pistol fire. Anna concluded that small arms wouldn't stop these creatures. Only tanks and machine guns could put these cephalopods down.

"We need to get out of here," Strauss said as if reading her thoughts.

"But there's nowhere to go," she said, "We're trapped between a hammer and an anvil."

"Not if we use the hammer to smash the anvil," Strauss quipped. "Tell your men to disperse and hide. The entities aren't after them. They want the antigravity device.

"I'll run toward the dogs. That should lead the entities right into 'em. All you need to do is get your men out of the way. With the Germans fighting the creatures, your men should have enough time to make it to safety."

Another shimmering ray uprooted and then pulverized an oak tree.

"Sounds like a plan," Anna said, antsy to get moving, "But I'll only do it on one condition."

"Name it."

"I'll give the order if I can stay with you."

"Why'd you want to do that? The last time you surrendered to my countrymen, you almost died. They promised me your safety. Did they lie to me? What happened after they took you in? Was there an accident at Sobibór?"

Tears welled up in Anna's eyes. She wiped her tears away with the back of her hand, suppressing her emotions. She didn't want to show Strauss any weakness. Not here. Not now. She knew Strauss would blame himself and agonize over his decision to surrender to the Germans. No. She needed him to focus on the present, to survive the next minute, the next hour, the next day.

"Don't worry about it. I'll tell you some other time. But understand this: I'm coming with you. No matter what."

Strauss nodded, and Anna ordered her men to spread out.

Soon, the strange beings had advanced to within fifty meters of Anna's defensive line. She saw the entities up close for the first time: coal-black cephalopods dripping with tar black ooze. The inky substance stretched from one end of the open field to the other, soaking and fouling the ground like an oil spill. The creatures' penetrating red eyes unnerved Anna, as if they could stare into the depths of her soul. Their tentacles writhed and sputtered along, corded muscle and sinew propelling the space demons forward in a seemingly unnatural method of locomotion. Their vertical maws wheezed and trilled the songs of the whippoorwill, haunting the night with their menacing and ethereal resonances.

Anna grabbed Strauss's hand and raced toward the approaching Germans. Conical searchlights scanned the forest, and dogs barked frantically, hot on the scent of their quarry. Men growled orders in crisp and efficient German.

Anna prayed that Strauss's plan would work.

Behind Anna, men screamed, and she worried she'd lost more of her comrades, men who'd entrusted their lives to her. *So many deaths, so many lives wasted*, she thought, *And it's all my fault.*

"*Nicht schießen! Ich bin ein deutscher Soldat!*" Strauss announced when a German patrol blundered into him. Anna dove behind a nearby tree, listening.

The Germans stopped dead in their tracks, apparently confused by Strauss's ruse. Regaining their senses, they raised their weapons toward Strauss, demanding his name, rank, and serial number. But it was too late. The twin horrors entered the woods, their tentacles and tendrils leveraging the trees to propel themselves forward faster. Eyes wide, the soldiers holding Strauss hostage panicked. Some of them turned tail and fled for their lives, while others froze. In the confusion, Strauss called Anna, and the pair sprinted past the indecisive patrol.

As they sped through the woods, Anna and Strauss heard more screams from the Germans behind them. Anna and Strauss kept running, never stopping to rest or hide. Anna could barely keep up with Strauss's pace. At first, she blamed her weakness and exhaustion on her time at the camp. But Strauss's endurance seemed almost superhuman. Then Anna's heart sank with a gut-wrenching realization: Strauss was still on Pervitin.

While Anna struggled to keep pace with Strauss, she realized they had no plan. They were running back toward the death camp with no rhyme or reasons. Exhausted and nauseated, she slowed to a jog. Strauss looked back at Anna, then he ran to her, putting his hand on her shoulder. "You all right?" he said.

Anna nodded, catching her breath, and then said, "Strauss, what's your plan?"

"We need to find Heisenberg. He's the only one who knows what this thing is truly capable of," Strauss said, clutching the anti-gravity device.

"No," Anna said in anger, as if no explanation were required.

"I know you don't trust him, Anna, but he's the only person who can help us."

"No. There must be another way. The Americans."

"Anna, we'll never make it to the United States without Heisenberg's help. Showing the Americans the full range of what this device can do is the only way they'll ever agree to take us in."

Anna didn't respond. She couldn't. After what she'd been through, Strauss would never understand.

The silence stretched for a minute or so. Strauss seemed uncertain, as if he didn't know what to say. "Well, either way," Strauss said, "we need to get moving. We can talk about this again after we put some distance between us and the *Schwartzwald* entities."

Anna nodded and said, "Slower this time. You're still taking Pervitin, aren't you?"

Strauss glanced away and then nodded. "I am. I'm sorry. When all this ends, and we are safe in America, I swear to you, I'll quit."

Anna didn't believe him. Saying he'd beat his addiction was one thing. Actually conquering it was another.

"All right," she said. "Let's go."

Strauss and Anna jogged through the woods for another hour or so, until Anna had reached the point of utter exhaustion. "Strauss, we need to stop and find a place to rest and hide. I can't run any longer."

"C'mon!" he said, "You can do it. Just push a little harder."

"No," she said with finality, "I don't have the chemical enhancements you do."

That silenced Strauss. Whether it was from guilt, shame, or both, he stopped dead in his tracks and said, "All right."

They uncovered a small culvert under an unpaved country road. There, they lay in wait as suffering men howled in the distant darkness. Soon, the chaos had given way to a deep and menacing silence. As Anna drifted off to sleep, several unsettling questions haunted her: Where did the entities go? Where were her men? Had they survived?

A deafening explosion rattled Strauss and Anna from their slumber. Strauss's best bet was that the aliens had destroyed the crashed saucer to prevent it from falling into German hands. Straus and Anna emerged from the culvert. More fires blazed on the horizon. Then, two disks accelerated into the sky, zipping toward infinity.

∞

2255 Hours Local Time, 15 October 1943, Royal Air Force Station Watton, England

The Douglas C-53B Skytrooper's propellers hummed, as the pilot conducted his inspection of the aircraft. D'Alessio triple-checked his parachute harness and inspected those of the three German agents. The London Free Germans were a curmudgeonly lot, willing to trade their lives for the chance to stick it to Hitler. The OSS's London office of its Secret Intelligence Branch had sent these men to D'Alessio so he could supervise their insertion into Nazi Germany. While they weren't part of D'Alessio's mission, the OSS thought it'd be a good idea to insert D'Alessio and the agents on the same jump to increase their likelihood of success.

Trade unionists all, the men had good reasons to loathe the Nazi regime, so much so that they were willing to parachute into their own country's war-torn occupied territory without reception committees, safe houses, or substantial material support. And they were willing to do it alone. If the Nazis discovered them, they'd torture and then hang or shoot the captured agents. D'Alessio thought the men were crazy bastards, but he admired their bravery.

Max Klug, codename WEDGE, was a coal miner from the Ruhr Valley. A bear of a man with dirty blonde hair and fierce blue eyes, he'd fled to the Saarland in 1934 to escape the Nazi Regime. He'd had to flee again to France and then to England in early 1935 after the League of Nations had approved the Saarland's reintegration with Nazi Germany, and the Nazis had begun imprisoning opponents of the regime.

Where Klug was the brawn, Hans Ruh was the brain. Physically, Ruh, codename LEVER, was the antithesis of Klug. Short and wiry with dark hair and eyes, Ruh had strapped his bifocals with a band around his head to keep them attached during the upcoming jump. D'Alessio had never been comfortable with the machine tuner and avowed Communist from Berlin, but Ruh's quiet determination and thoughtful character made him a useful organizer. When the Nazis had occupied his trade union's offices back in May 1933, a Nazi storm trooper had beaten Ruh so savagely that he'd lost his right eye and spoke with a stutter.

Johann Götz, codename AXLE, was a tank turret mechanic from Nuremberg noted for his ability to fix anything. But he wasn't a grease monkey by any measure; he was more of a grease pig judging by his slightly overweight bulk and porcine features. After the Nazis seized control of his trade union in early 1933, his maltreatment at the hands of the Nazi Party faithful had occurred with regularity at their annual NSDAP rallies beginning in September 1933, as various storm troopers and military officers had exploited his skills fixing equipment, while frequently refusing payment. More often than not, they told him it was his patriotic duty. After one well-timed turret fire when a Panzer I he'd rigged passed Hitler's review stand, Johann became a hunted man, who understandably fled the country for greener pastures in London.

Among the three, Johann was a ray of sunshine in contrast to Klug's raging temper and Ruh's fits of depression. His can-do attitude and boundless optimism were a huge relief to D'Alessio. Yet, underlying that contagious sense of optimism was a hidden well of fury threatening to boil over into action. D'Alessio just hoped it happened at the right time.

After triple-checking the men's parachute riggings, D'Alessio visually inspected their gear, which the trio had laid on tarps in the hangar bay. Each man carried a rucksack containing C rations, a lensatic compass, maps, grenades, and a battery-powered Joan-Eleanor (J/E) transmitter-receiver. The last device had a collapsible antenna, weighed three pounds and was six inches long. It transmitted at high frequencies so German shortwave radio operators couldn't intercept transmissions to Allied headquarters.

The men were issued German Lugers, so if the Germans captured them, their firearms wouldn't compromise their affiliation with Allied governments. D'Alessio also added a Browning thirty-caliber machine gun with tripod to the mix, stacking several cases of ammunition on the aircraft. He never knew when he might need heavy firepower.

As far as D'Alessio was concerned, these men were just along for the ride. Once they landed, they had separate missions and objectives. But until they landed safely, D'Alessio was in charge.

The men had all spent the last two weeks infiltrating a German POW camp on London's outskirts gathering intelligence about conditions on the Eastern Front. They'd also used their time at the camp to hone their cover identities. But the call had come earlier than many of them had expected. Either way, they would be jumping into the hot zone imminently.

Before boarding the aircraft, D'Alessio addressed men whom he barely knew. "All right gents, off we go to the land of the Huns. Our mission is to parachute over Eastern Poland. Our aircraft will travel at close to its maximum speed to avoid daylight. Until we all land securely, I'm in charge. That means when you land, you head toward the designated grid coordinates for a headcount. Once everyone reports in safely and we cross-load any supplies we may have lost in the jump, you'll be free to conduct your primary missions. Are there any questions at this time?"

Klug raised his hand. "Go ahead, stud," D'Alessio said.

"When do I get to kill Nazis?" Klug said.

"Sooner than you think."

The men then boarded the aircraft, as D'Alessio cracked a smile. He was looking forward to this.

Chapter 23
Hunted

0535 Hours, 16 October 1943, Outside Sobibór, Poland

Strauss awoke to the distant call of the whippoorwill. As he peered outside the culvert, the light of the sun began to break over the horizon. Somehow, he and Anna had been able to catch a few hours of restless sleep after the disks had vanished.

But the memory of that sound, that eerie whippoorwill trill, haunted him, so ghostly in its essence and so malevolent in its manifestation. Strauss had been naïve to think the entities had left. He sensed they were still here, somehow. But what had piloted their craft? Why did their craft leave, and what, if anything, did they leave behind?

Then, he imagined the worst: what if the *Schwartzwald* entities had spent the night converting the guards and camp survivors into their own parasite-infested minions.

Strauss shook Anna. "Wake up!" he said.

"Huh," she said.

"They're coming!" he warned.

"Who's coming?"

"I don't know exactly, just listen."

As if on cue, the spectral trill of the whippoorwill echoed through the forest, getting closer.

"But they left," Anna said, "I saw them."

"Maybe they can remotely pilot their machines. Or worse, maybe they left something. I don't know. But we need to get out of here and fast."

Anna struggled to her feet, checked her weapon, and prepared to move out.

Again, the call of the whippoorwill echoed through the early morning twilight. The two hustled out of the protective shelter of the culvert and raced toward Sobibór.

Strauss had wondered what had happened to Anna at the camp, but she'd refused to speak of it. But ever since then, her confidence seemed shaken. He desperately wanted to know, but dared not ask. He didn't want to be an obstacle to her recovery. So he waited, biding his time, and focused his thoughts on finding a way out, on surviving. After all, that's what Strauss did best.

Strauss wrestled with his desire for Anna. Having almost lost her made his yearning for her more intense. But his feelings for Anna ran much deeper than that. They had an instinctual trust for one another, the kind that can only be forged and tempered through the deprivation and chaos of war.

But Strauss also struggled with the knowledge that his son was somewhere out in the world. He longed to see the boy the Reich had given away. Giving his son away was so diabolical in its method and so callous in its means. How could he tell Anna about a son he'd never known? How could he explain his mixed feelings about the woman who had borne him his only son? How could he reconcile his love for two distinctly different women?

The questions made his head hurt, so he popped another Pervitin tablet to make the pain go away.

Anna frowned, but said nothing.

Strauss and Anna wended through the ravines and gullies of Poland's swampy hinterland to mask their movement, leveraging their experiences from the harsh Russian landscape. But avoiding open fields and hills entirely would be impossible.

The pair emerged from a tree line and into an open field. Shots rang out, seemingly from nowhere, narrowly missing Strauss and Anna by less than a meter. Tufts of smoke heralded the bullets' impacts.

Instinctively, the pair broke out into an all-out sprint toward the nearest covered and concealed position. A bullet grazed Strauss's rib, searing him with its heat and forcing him and Anna to dive to the ground, making themselves smaller targets.

They crawled desperately toward a gully about fifty meters ahead of them and covered with bushes. More bullets impacted the ground, originating from a distance and range Strauss couldn't determine. If he looked up, he was certain he'd be hit.

After they reached the gully, Anna and Strauss collapsed, exhausted and dripping with sweat. Strauss ducked down, and using the cover of the bushes, scanned across the field. Against the rising sun, all Strauss could see was roughly a dozen human silhouettes moving in an unnaturally cadenced gait.

Now it all made sense.

Far to the east and several hundred meters above the walking corpses, two disks hovered, silhouetted against the rising sun. The *Schwartzwald* entities watched from above, probably waiting for their confederates to wear down Anna and Strauss.

But the cadavers were coming, advancing inexorably toward Strauss and Anna's position, and neither Strauss nor Anna had the firepower or wherewithal to stop them.

Just when Strauss thought all hope was lost, and he was ready to quit, he heard a rumble from the west. As he raised his eyes toward the sky, he spotted an aircraft, gliding overhead. The insignia on the aircraft was not the Germanic black-and-white iron cross Strauss had expected to see, but the white star one might find on an American plane. Strauss had to check twice to believe it. It just didn't make any sense for the Americans to send an aircraft this deep into German territory.

A green ray enveloped the aircraft, batting it aside like a child smacking away a toy airplane.

Then Strauss saw four dots eject out of the aircraft. The dots slowly expanded to tiny fabric cones drifting toward the earth like dandelions on the wind.

Parachutes.

Strauss glanced at Anna. "We need to chase those parachutes. I think the Americans are coming to us."

Before Anna could get up to move, Strauss cupped her face in his hands and tried to kiss her, but she pulled back, suddenly cold. But Strauss ignored her reaction. What he had to say was too important. "I missed you and worried you were dead. I'm glad to see you're not."

Anna blushed. A first. Strauss couldn't tell if she was flattered by his words or if she was embarrassed by her lukewarm reaction to the attempted kiss. "I missed you as well," she admitted, awkwardly.

"But there's something I need to tell you, that I've been struggling with for a long time," Strauss said, grasping for the right words.

Anna's eyes stared into his as if she was expecting him to express his love for her. Blushing, she looked away. "Now is not the time for such things."

Strauss felt awkward and embarrassed. He still hadn't had time to process his feelings for Anna, and the way she'd second-guessed his next words only made telling her the truth that much harder.

He did what he had to do. "Anna, Inge and I have a son."

The expression on Anna's face contorted from an expression of tenderness to a look that Strauss guessed was one of shock and anger. She turned her head, and said, "Now you tell me this?"

"I'm sorry, I only learned of it after we were separated."

A bullet whizzed over his head.

"We need to get moving," Anna said.

Chapter 24
Airborne

"Sir," the pilot said over the closed loop intercom system, "there are dozens of brushfires just beyond the drop zone. Your men should do the jump now before we get too close to the fires and overshoot our LZ."

"Let's do it!" D'Alessio ordered. D'Alessio figured there'd be some margin of error, but they were close enough to Sobibór's coordinates that jumping here was probably the best they could hope for.

The preparation lights began flashing. The men double-checked each other's harnesses one last time. Seconds later, D'Alessio opened the aircraft's cargo door, and began his count, "One one thousand, two one thousand…"

D'Alessio tapped Ruh on the shoulder first. The man stepped off from the aircraft, his static line rippling backward and his chute expanding on its way to the surface. D'Alessio started his count again and then signaled Götz to jump. Then Klug shuffled to the front of the queue. When the ursine man watched his comrades falling toward the surface, his eyes widened and he made as if to turn back, but D'Alessio shoved his boot into the man's backside, forcing a screaming Klug out of the aircraft.

From the cargo door, D'Alessio observed two black disks zoom out of the sun's morning glare. An instant later, a disk fired a green energy beam at his aircraft as it flew over the drop zone. The aircraft vibrated with intense energy, making it hum like the inside of a bell.

D'Alessio repeated his count, a routine that was more suited to calming one's nerves than for avoiding accidents. When the aircraft began to spin out of control, he abandoned his count, and leapt out of the aircraft. His ripcord nearly decapitated him as it pitched and yawed in the frenetic dance of the spiraling aircraft.

Seconds later D'Alessio's chute opened, whipping him into sudden deceleration. As D'Alessio glanced up to inspect his parachute's canopy for holes, the aircraft above spun end over end, as if a giant had swatted it out of the sky. It careened out of control until it crashed somewhere over the horizon in a towering fire of jet fuel, smoke, and debris.

D'Alessio nervously steered the risers on his parachute toward the drop zone, while he surveyed the ground below. And it was utter chaos. Dozens of brush fires peppered the field below.

As the ground rushed up to meet him, D'Alessio saw dozens of armed soldiers and men in striped uniforms ambling through the field. D'Alessio braced himself for a hail of bullets as he descended helplessly toward the surface.

Scores of muzzle flashes beneath him underscored his concern. But as D'Alessio drew closer toward the ground, he noticed that the advancing soldiers pointed their weapons at something ahead, and they didn't seem interested in firing at the targets above them.

D'Alessio yanked his risers, shifting his chute toward the west, steering toward a ravine that bisected the field. The last thing he wanted was to land in the middle of a firefight.

What the hell are they shooting at? he wondered.

Soon, the ground rose up to meet D'Alessio, so he shifted his attention from the firefight and toward his landing. D'Alessio's combat load landed on the surface with a thud.

Feet and knees together, he kept repeating to himself while making a conscious effort not to lock his knees. Breaking his legs because he tensed up on the drop zone would be an embarrassing and fatal way to end the mission.

Instinct took over, and D'Alessio executed his parachute-landing fall, landing feet first. He then used his stomach muscles to roll, dissipating the energy of the fall.

D'Alessio landed hard, but not hard enough to twist an ankle or break a leg. He was a bit bruised up, but nothing that would hamper his mission. After he had a chance to breathe and to establish his bearings, he rose to his feet, collected his parachute and equipment, slung his rifle on his shoulder, and focused on gathering his team.

About a hundred meters east, across from the ravine and on the field's edge, a parachute was tangled in a maple tree. The tree's branches wobbled as the trapped parachutist struggled to cut himself loose.

Ruh.

D'Alessio unslung his rifle and advanced on Ruh's position by way of the ravine. As he meandered through the terrain, he turned a corner and stumbled into a German soldier and a woman wearing a striped uniform racing in his direction. D'Alessio swung back behind the corner, readying his rifle. His heart thumped in his chest.

"*Wer ist da?*" D'Alessio asked in stunted German.

"*Ich bin Georg Strauss, und sie ist Anna Ivanova. Bitte nicht schießen.*"

"*Sprechen Sie Englisch?*" D'Alessio asked, giddy that he'd discovered two of the people he'd been reading dispatches about for the last few weeks.

Now, came the hard part. How would D'Alessio capture Strauss and Ivanova without killing either one?

"Yes, a little," Strauss answered.

"Good," D'Alessio said, "I'm going to come around the corner with my rifle trained on you. I don't intend to shoot, but I will if you make any sudden movements."

"Go ahead."

D'Alessio rounded the corner slowly. Both Strauss and Anna looked haggard, each with deep black rings around their bloodshot eyes.

"Please," Strauss said, his hands raised palms facing outward. "We've been trying to reach the Americans. Please, get us out of Poland. We need to get to the United States. Your Soviet Allies have made a pact with the devil, and the devil is coming. Right. Now." Strauss nodded toward the soldiers and prisoners marching toward the ravine.

"Why are they after you?" D'Alessio asked.

"They want this," Strauss said, holding out a cigarette lighter.

"They're gonna kill you for a fucking cigarette lighter?" D'Alessio said, incredulous. "What kinda bullshit is that?"

"No bullshit," Strauss said. "It's an antigravity device. I can't prove it, because it's out of power. But if you and your men can get me and Anna safely to Dr. Werner Heisenberg, he can show you how to use it. Then we can all take it back to your leaders."

D'Alessio was beginning to doubt this man's sanity. But then again, two foo fighters had just knocked his aircraft out of the sky.

"Who are those people?" D'Alessio said, nodding toward the soldiers and civilians.

"They're no longer people."

"Wah?"

Strauss pointed through the bushes. "See for yourself. Look at their eyes."

D'Alessio peeked through the bushes. Barely over a football field away, he saw the men walking stiffly toward them. When he glanced at their eyes, they had an eerie green glow.

D'Alessio turned his head back toward Strauss. "I've still got men out there. What the hell are those things?"

"Honestly, I'm still not sure," Strauss answered, "But I do know there's some sort of parasite inside them, and the people the parasites have infested are no longer in control of their own bodies."

"Well, fuck," D'Alessio said in the most eloquent and succinct manner he could frame his dilemma.

D'Alessio scanned the field ahead. Ruh kicked and wriggled his body in a futile struggle to free himself from the maple tree. D'Alessio spotted Klug on the field's northern fringes, fleeing the parasite-men. The ursine man lumbered toward the tree line, slowed by the weight of both his rucksack and a thirty-caliber machine gun and its tripod.

Jesus H. Christ, D'Alessio thought. *We need that fucking weapon.*

But D'Alessio could find no sign of Götz. D'Alessio placed his hand on Strauss's shoulder. "If you help me, chief, I promise you I'll take you to England with me. But America. I can't promise you that."

Strauss translated D'Alessio's offer to Anna in German. She nodded, and Strauss extended his open hand toward D'Alessio. "You can count on our cooperation."

The two shook hands.

"Great. First thing's first. How do we kill those things?" D'Alessio said.

"Grenades, machine guns, tanks, heavy artillery, anything that can quickly separate or incinerate limbs. Otherwise, they will keep coming," Strauss said.

"Shit," D'Alessio said, then he pointed at Klug. "You see that man over there."

"Yes."

"He's lugging around a thirty-caliber machine gun. If we can get to him, or if he can get to us, we can take those things down."

"Impossible," Strauss said. "Those things are the best shots I've ever faced. Better than the best of human snipers. If we expose ourselves, they'll kill us."

"Can they see through smoke?"

"I don't know. Why?"

"I've got two smoke grenades. We can use them to mask our path to my friend. If we survive, we can set up a strongpoint with that thirty, and then go to town on these things with the machine gun."

"Which town?" Strauss asked.

D'Alessio rolled his eyes: idioms. "It's just an expression," D'Alessio said, "It means we take out the automatons with the machine gun."

"I see," Strauss said, "Since I am not sure if this will work, I volunteer to go first."

"It's your funeral," D'Alessio said.

"But I'm not dead yet."

D'Alessio laughed. "Never mind. Sounds like a plan. You ready?"

Strauss nodded. D'Alessio pulled the pin on a green smoke grenade. He tossed it about fifty yards between Klug and the automatons. At that point, Klug was already on his stomach setting up the machine gun. About a dozen dead things advanced on his position.

"Klug!" D'Alessio yelled, "I'm sending over a friend. He's dressed in a German uniform. Don't shoot him. He's here to help."

Klug signaled D'Alessio with a thumbs-up. D'Alessio glanced at Strauss and said, "You're good to go."

Strauss waited for the smoke to billow. Apparently satisfied, Strauss sprinted across the field parallel to the smokescreen. He rolled into a somersault when he reached Klug.

D'Alessio breathed a sigh of relief. Then he watched Strauss and Klug work together to set up the thirty cal.

Thank Jesus, D'Alessio thought.

D'Alessio pulled out the second grenade and glanced over at Anna. He had butterflies in his stomach. He'd been so focused on his men and making a deal with Strauss that he hadn't noticed what a voluptuous treasure this broad was. "Well, look at you," he said, fully aware she had no idea what he was saying. "*Sind Sie fertig?*" he said.

"*Ja,*" she said.

D'Alessio tossed the smoke grenade and waited a few seconds for the smoke to build. Then he and Anna tore across the field toward Klug and Strauss. Seconds later, Klug opened up with his machine gun on the parasite-men. And it was beautiful. A wall of steel tore through the grass at the attackers like a hundred tiny scythes cutting through a wheatfield. The man handled the weapon like it was his brush and the automatons, his canvas.

The steady THUNK THUNK THUNK hummed like a symphony. Three beats presaged each crumbling corpse-man. Three bullets to tear limb from torso and muscle from bone. Each successive strike birthed a floundering and sputtering carcass. It was if Klug had been born to kill these abominations.

But D'Alessio knew better. This Strauss character knew what the hell he was doing. He'd likely coached Klug on exactly what to do to put these bastards down.

Soon, D'Alessio and Anna joined Strauss and Klug in their fight. While Strauss spotted targets for Klug, D'Alessio fed the thirty-caliber machine gun with belt after belt of ammunition.

"Strauss," D'Alessio said, after loading another ammo belt into the thirty. "Can you ask Anna to keep her eyes out for one of my men? He's a bit heavy set and probably carrying a rucksack."

Strauss nodded and shared D'Alessio's description of Götz with Anna. D'Alessio stared across the field at Ruh and despaired as the man flailed helplessly in the maple tree. D'Alessio desperately wanted to rescue his companion, but the automatons blocked his path. D'Alessio just prayed that Ruh didn't draw too much attention to himself.

But Ruh was a magnet for attention. As the German flailed and rocked the tree's branches, an automaton separated from the pack and marched toward Ruh.

"Stupid motherfucker!" D'Alessio yelled, pounding his fist into the dirt. Klug and Strauss stopped firing the thirty and glanced back at D'Alessio.

"Ah, sorry guys, I didn't mean you," D'Alessio said, embarrassed. He pointed at the tree. "Klug, you see how that dumb fuck Ruh has his parachute stuck in that maple tree?"

Klug nodded.

D'Alessio continued, "Can you shoot his merry little ass down."

"Why would I shoot his ass?" Klug said.

D'Alessio wanted to kick himself. Like Strauss, Klug seemed to have trouble understanding D'Alessio's frequent and colorful use of American idioms.

"Fuck! Not you too," D'Alessio said, exasperated, "What I meant is, can you shoot that branch so that he and his fucking parachute fall to the ground?"

"Couldn't that kill him?"

"It might," D'Alessio shrugged. He pointed at the automaton shambling toward Ruh, "But I guarantee that if you don't shoot Ruh down, that thing <u>will</u> tear him apart. He might hit the ground hard, but at least he'll have a chance at survival."

"I see your point," Klug said. The massive German angled the thirty cal's barrel about thirty degrees from the horizontal, locked the tripod into position, and fired several three-round bursts at the branch from which Ruh's parachute dangled.

D'Alessio could hear Ruh cursing in German from all the way across the field. Ruh's griping was so loud that D'Alessio could understand every one of Ruh's curses, despite the ear splitting hammering of machine gun fire. Bullets from Klug's machine gun had set fire to several of the tree's branches, shrouding the maple tree in smoke. But a sudden crack and thump told D'Alessio that Klug had hit his mark. D'Alessio just hoped Ruh survived the fall.

The lone automaton continued to advance toward Ruh's position. Frustrated, D'Alessio jumped to his feet. He began to run toward Ruh. But Strauss tackled D'Alessio a split second before a round whizzed over D'Alessio's head.

"Not smart," Strauss said.

D'Alessio struggled to regain his composure. "Jesus. You weren't joking about their aim."

"No, I wasn't," a dour Strauss said.

D'Alessio wracked his brain for a plan to save Ruh, but he kept coming up empty-handed. But failure was not an option.

The sharp sound of pistol fire cracked in the distance. "That sounds like a Luger," Strauss said.

D'Alessio nodded. "That's Ruh. And that fool has no idea that a Luger is about as effective against these things as a spitball is against a starving tiger."

More pistol shots reverberated through the valley, but the thing kept charging toward the smoky maple tree.

"Ruh! Use your grenades, you dumb shit!" D'Alessio yelled from across the field. Seconds later, the automaton exploded in a shower of bone fragments and guts.

Crisis averted, D'Alessio redoubled his efforts in feeding the machine gun with belts of ammunition. Klug continued to spray the remaining automatons with withering fire until the field was littered with writhing and twitching human limbs.

As D'Alessio tried to catch his breath, someone tapped him on the shoulder. "What did I miss?" a rosy-faced Götz said.

D'Alessio smiled. "I could kiss you, you stupid motherfucker." Then the American glanced up into the sky and watched as the twin disks spun and inexplicably retreated over the horizon.

Chapter 25
Uranverein

Professor Werner Heisenberg woke up to a firefight.

Lying on a hospital bed, his ears were ringing from the cacophony of small arms fire. Bullets zipped overhead on a diagonal path toward something behind him and to his right.

There was a dull pain in his chest, and he felt a bit numb and wheezy, as if high on morphine. Wait. He *was* high on morphine. He'd vaguely remembered boarding an aircraft, and then losing consciousness. Now, he had no idea where he was, when it was, or what was happening.

A smoky haze filled the room as two SS officers fired round after round from their submachine guns. Everything appeared to be in slow motion. Their faces contorted into grimaces, the men wore full battle gear, including their helmets. And they seemed scared, really scared.

Heisenberg looked left, and watched in terror as the officers' bullets peppered a nurse from across the room, her eyes glowing dull green. She kept moving forward into their gunfire.

The room's only door sprung open, and a man wearing a stethoscope entered, walking steadily toward the two officers. One officer swung his submachine gun around and riddled the doctor with bullets. Each hit registered with a thud, splattering bloody viscera on the walls and jerking the doctor backwards. But the doctor kept stumbling forward, fighting against the bullets' momentum.

It took several seconds for Heisenberg's morphine-addled mind to put things together, but when he did, his mind raced, seeking solutions.

He had no idea where he was or how long he'd been unconscious, but he had to assume the worst. Unless someone told him otherwise, he was witnessing an alien infestation. And there was only one solution for that.

And then he finally understood why it had been so easy for him to escape that NKVD camp. The guards' laxity was no accident; it was by design. The Soviets had used him as a vector.

Heisenberg glanced casually behind him, and saw an albino multi-tentacled thing the size of a small dog. It flailed its tentacles, wrapping them around the SS officers' necks. Choking, the men emptied their clips into the creature. Using the two men as anchors, the pale squid-thing catapulted itself forward and out a window, glass shattering onto the floor. The officers' bodies followed as the creature's corded tentacles ripped them through the window.

The two bleeding corpses shifted their attention to Heisenberg. He rolled left and onto the floor. He stumbled to his feet. If Heisenberg hadn't been so high on morphine, his tumble would've been agonizing. But he had no time to dwell on hypotheticals. He had to stem the infestation.

The doctor's bloody hands reached for Heisenberg with a surgeon's precision and locked onto Heisenberg's neck. Rather than choking the life out of Heisenberg as the physicist had feared, the doctor held Heisenberg in place.

Terrified, Heisenberg glanced over his shoulder to find the nurse shambling across the room, wielding a bloody scalpel.

No, it cannot end like this, Heisenberg despaired.

Small arms fire reverberated outside. "I'm still in here!" Heisenberg screamed, terrified no one would reach him before the walking corpses lobotomized him. "Help!"

Then the nurse was on him, her hand grasping the scalpel and calmly directing it toward his forehead.

Then, two more SS troops entered the room and emptied their submachine guns into the nurse and the doctor. Heisenberg sank to the floor to avoid being hit, the bullets' searing casings burning him as he crawled toward the exit.

Passing through the room's threshold, he staggered to his feet. More soldiers rushed toward the room, ignoring him as he ambled down the corridor.

Heisenberg shuffled forward, stopping twice to vomit blood before he reached a reception area. There, he found an empty desk with a black rotary telephone resting on top of it. From under the desk, someone whimpered. Heisenberg walked behind the counter, and found a pretty blonde woman hiding and crying. The expression on her face was a mixture of confusion and sheer terror.

"Do you mind if I use your telephone?" Heisenberg asked matter-of-factly, his request punctuated by the sound of continuous small arms fire further down the hall.

The woman sobbed.

"Well, I'm sure you won't mind if I use it then," Heisenberg said as he grabbed the phone and dialed Heydrich's headquarters. While he waited for an answer, he glanced at the woman and said, "Excuse me miss, could you kindly tell me where we are and what day it is?"

"What?" she said, tears rolling down her face.

"Where are we? What day is it?" Heisenberg repeated.

A man picked up the phone on the line before the woman could answer Heisenberg's question. "Ah, yes," Heisenberg said, "This is Quantum Knight, please patch me in to Heydrich."

While Heisenberg waited for the transfer, he yelled, "Where are we?"

The woman cried, but finally said, "At the University of Lublin military hospital. It's the sixteenth of October."

"Thank you, Fräulein," Heisenberg said.

Three weeks. Heisenberg had been out for three weeks. He shuddered at the thought. Then, he heard Heydrich's firm voice on the other end of the line. "Hallo?"

"Sir, this is Quantum Knight."

"Excellent. It sounds like you're in good health," Heydrich said.

"Sir, I don't have a lot of time, but I wanted to let you know that we have a situation here."

"How bad is it?"

"Bad enough that I recommend deploying the Donner Device."

"Has Lublin been infested by a *Schwartzwald* entity?"

"Yes," Heisenberg said.

"Given what the Donner Device will do to every living thing within two kilometers of the blast zone, are you absolutely sure this is what needs to be done?"

"I am," Heisenberg said.

"You do realize that once we deploy this weapon, we'll no longer have the element of surprise if and when we use it against the Soviets?"

"I do. An alien infestation within our territory is a much greater threat to us than the Soviets are."

"Fine. I'll send in a bomber. In the interim, I need you to report to the Lublin airfield. You have a follow-on mission in Eastern Poland. We've located your friend Strauss and the Soviet Jewess," Heydrich said.

"Yes, Sir," Heisenberg said. He hung up the phone and left the hospital.

ဆ

0900 Hours, 16 October 1943, Lenino, Byelorussia

General Valentin Kravchenko strolled down the trench line, chomping on his pipe. He smiled at the skeletal and haggard men tearing into the cold, hard earth with their charcoal-black spades. There was nothing more efficient than having men digging their own graves.

Today would be a good day. The general was probably the only Soviet officer who stood to benefit from a Soviet battlefield loss. Of course that's not what the propagandists were saying. After all, while the Germans still controlled Hill 217.6, the Soviets did seize and successfully retain the Lenino bridgehead. Moreover, the Poles had indeed fought with bravery, but the Germans had slaughtered them nonetheless because of General Gordov's stubbornness and incompetence. Stalin was infuriated by the man's lackluster performance, especially since Gordov was a Russian, not a Pole. And then there was the idiot whose brilliant idea was to adulterate the Polish force with Poles who'd been shipped in from Siberian concentration camps. Kravchenko couldn't wait to get his hands on that genius.

Kravchenko laughed, and then nearly choked on the thin smoke that still lingered over the battlefield like death's ghost. The comforting smell of rot began to settle in. It was all routine now for Kravchenko. He often wondered what he'd do with himself after the war. Certain men had a knack for violence. In it, they found the most creative ways for self-expression using the human body as a canvass.

Soon, the recriminations over the battle would come, and Kravchenko would be there to carry out Stalin's orders to the letter. And if Kravchenko was lucky, his orders would allow some room for creative interpretation. There was nothing sweeter than executing a once powerful man accustomed to sending other men to their deaths. It was an art that few men had the stomach for. But Kravchenko manipulated the instruments of death and torture like Vincent van Gogh wielded a paintbrush.

Today's work would be more mundane. A few deserters here, a few cowards there. Not glamorous work, but honorable work. Culling the weak and irresolute from the Revolution made Kravchenko swell with pride.

The trench the men were digging was now neck deep. It was good enough for government work. He turned away from the trench and walked toward the machine gunners. He raised his right arm and then swung it down. The NKVD gunmen methodically walked their machine gun fire from the edges of the trench toward the middle, riddling the gravediggers with smoking lead.

After several more seconds, he gave the gunmen the signal for a ceasefire. He turned and walked to the lip of the trench. He gazed down on his work. There was nothing like watching the twitching bodies of the newborn dead, their blood slowly pooling and rising upward from the newly churned dirt. Then there was the curious hope that one of them still survived. The poor soul would be drowning in blood by now, biding his time, praying to God no one would notice. The thought made Kravchenko giggle. God wouldn't save them. He never had. No one had ever escaped one of Kravchenko's firing squads.

At night, the *Keldrahdi* would come to make superior soldiers of men who in life had amounted to nothing, but in death would help realize Lenin's dream of a global Revolution. He was just happy to be a part of it, turning one traitor at a time.

"Sir!" someone yelled from behind, ripping Kravchenko out of his contemplative mood. He turned and then scowled when he saw Colonel Nimerov approaching the trenches.

Kravchenko raised a bushy black eyebrow. "This better be important."

Nimerov smiled. "It is, Sir. I have excellent news to report."

"Well, good news certainly doesn't get better with age. Out with it, man!"

The colonel nodded. "Sir, the *Keldrahdi* have informed me that Heisenberg is no longer a host. The infestation of Nazi Germany has officially begun."

For a day that had already begun with such an auspicious start, Kravchenko couldn't have imagined that it would have continued to take such a positive turn. Kravchenko slapped Nimerov on the shoulder. "That's excellent news! Where is ground zero?"

"Lublin."

Kravchenko glowered at Nimerov. Lublin hadn't been part of the plan. "Lublin? As in Lublin, Poland?" Kravchenko said, his temper on the verge of erupting into an all-out rage.

"Yes, sir," Nimerov said, his blank expression failing to mask his obvious confusion.

"You incompetent twit!" Kravchenko yelled, "The infestation was supposed to start in Berlin. The plan was for it to strike at the heart of the Third Reich. What the hell happened?"

"Reich doctors extracted the parasite before Heisenberg reached the capital."

Kravchenko crossed his arms over this chest and fumed silently. How would he explain this screw-up to Stalin? How could Kravchenko spin it so would look like a deliberate tactic designed to increase the probability of success?

"Well, I suppose it is probably better that the infestation began in an area where the Germans have fewer resources to contain it. Had we unleashed it in Berlin, the Germans would have been in a better position to bring the full weight of the Third Reich to bear in ending the plague. Not so in Lublin," Kravchenko said, more to convince himself than to sway Colonel Nimerov.

A sudden flash of light illuminated the horizon. A mushroom cloud billowed in the western sky.

"What on earth was that?" Nimerov said, his voice trembling.

Kravchenko lowered his head in shame. "That, Colonel, is in the same direction as Lublin. And, therefore, it is likely the end of our operation. It seems the Germans have some wonder weapons of their own."

"What's next, Sir?" Nimerov said.

"You should pray to that God you believe so much in. But remember," Kravchenko said as he nodded his head toward the trenches, "they had prayed to God too."

❧

0900 Hours, 16 October 1943, Sobibór, Poland

Heisenberg watched the growing mushroom cloud roil over Lublin. He wished the Germans hadn't had to deploy the enhanced radiation weapon over a city of tens of thousands of innocents. But the Reich had no choice. Heisenberg prayed that God would forgive him.

His stomach and chest still ached. He put his hand under his shirt, tracing the deep scar down his chest. Something had cracked his ribs open and somehow had extracted the entity inside him. He hadn't thought it was possible. He'd have time to ask Heydrich who'd saved him later. For now, he had to suffer the consequences of his actions.

Heisenberg convinced himself that deploying the radiological wonder weapon was the most efficient means of wiping out the contagion while minimizing structural damage to the city. The Soviets would call it a capitalist's weapon, but Heisenberg saw it as a pragmatist's tool. But the more he tried to rationalize his actions, the more he felt like a heartless butcher.

God help me, he thought.

Chapter 26
Decisions

"Where do you think they went?" D'Alessio asked, his heel pinning down a German's severed head, its eyes blinking and its tongue wagging.

"I don't know," Strauss answered, "but I suspect they'll be back. My best guess is that they've left to gather reinforcements. Now that we have a heavy weapon, they don't have the manpower to take the device from us right now."

D'Alessio nodded. It seemed like a reasonable expectation, but D'Alessio didn't feel like hanging around too long for those things to return. "We should un-ass the area after we take some samples."

"Un-ass?" Strauss said, "I am not familiar with this term."

D'Alessio rolled his eyes. "It means we need to get the hell out of here before your countrymen show up."

"Ah, yes. Agreed." Strauss pulled out a knife and looked at D'Alessio. The German then shifted his eyes toward the severed head. "Pardon me."

D'Alessio lifted his boot, and Strauss cut open the dead German's skullcap. Even D'Alessio had to glance away when he saw the licelike parasites writhing in the man's hollow skull. But glancing away wasn't so bad when he got another chance to take a look at that exotic redhead. *Man*, he thought, *she was a real hot ticket*. D'Alessio winked at Anna, but she just turned her head and looked away.

Klug pulled out a tin container from his rucksack, emptied the peanuts inside, and handed it to Strauss. "*Danke*," Strauss said as he scooped the parasites into the tin and sealed it.

"*Gleichfalls*," Klug replied.

Strauss stabbed tiny holes into the container's cover. "Do they also need oxygen?" D'Alessio asked.

"I have no idea, but your people would prefer live samples, no?"

D'Alessio nodded.

Now that D'Alessio had his biological sample and the team that controlled the antigravity device, he had to make a critical decision. Should he quit while he was ahead and return to England—the proverbial bird in hand? Or should he continue the mission to find Heisenberg, maximizing the value of his intelligence haul—the proverbial two in the bush?

On the one hand and by most measures, D'Alessio was in possession of perhaps the greatest intelligence coup in American history. All he'd have to do now was radio headquarters and coordinate an exfiltration mission.

On the other hand, this approach had its drawbacks. Without Heisenberg, American scientists and military officers might never figure out how to recharge the antigravity device. If that happened, D'Alessio would invariably have to risk his neck in yet another harrowing mission behind German lines. Either way, D'Alessio had to cancel the three initial TOOL missions—AXLE, LEVER, and WEDGE. He needed the Free Germans' skills and firepower to either track down Heisenberg or to get the device, the sample, and Anna and Strauss back to Britain. Breaking the bad news to the Free Germans wasn't something he looked forward to.

"What's next?" Ruh said, shining a figurative light on the one question D'Alessio had hoped to avoid for as long as possible.

D'Alessio took a deep breath and said, "Fragmentary order. We're canceling the TOOL missions and heading for a safe house in Danzig. I'm going to coordinate an exfil mission. We need to transport these biological samples, Strauss, Anna, and the antigravity device back to England as soon as possible."

"But that's not our mission," Ruh said, "and it's not what I signed up for. I'm here to provide critical intelligence on the Reich, not to escort a man and a woman back to England."

D'Alessio grabbed Ruh by both collars, and got into the Free German's face. "It's your fucking mission now because I say so. Just because you didn't choose the mission doesn't mean that the mission didn't choose you."

Then D'Alessio scowled at the other two Free Germans, his hands still gripping Ruh's collars, and said, "Are you two with the fucking program?"

Klug, smiling, glanced at Götz, and Götz chuckled. Both men nodded.

"I don't think your plan's a good one," Strauss said.

D'Alessio released Ruh, brushed off his field jacket and swaggered toward Strauss. Strauss extended his right arm, palm facing outward. "Stop right there. If you touch me, I will kill you."

D'Alessio smiled. When Strauss didn't, D'Alessio knew the man was serious.

The American decided to back off. After all, he reasoned, the other three men were under orders. Strauss was not.

"What's your recommendation then?" D'Alessio said in a challenging tone.

"I agree with everything you said with the exception of Heisenberg. Without him, the device is worthless. We need to find him first before you return to England."

D'Alessio fumed, then chuckled. He needed to resolve this impasse quickly. Finding Heisenberg somewhere in the heart of enemy territory was madness.

The American decided to appeal to Strauss with logic. "Do you even know where Heisenberg is?"

Strauss looked annoyed. "No."

"So you're willing to risk this device falling back into the hands of your countrymen, and you fully accept the possibility that these samples may never make it back to England on the off chance that we'll find Werner Heisenberg somewhere deep in Nazi-occupied Europe? Are you insane?"

But Strauss wouldn't back down. "No. I'm just hopeful."

"Hope and a penny couldn't buy you a pack of cigarettes. What does Anna think?" D'Alessio said touching Anna playfully on the small of her back.

Anna bristled.

Strauss frowned.

"What? She doesn't have a vote?" D'Alessio said, forcing the issue.

"Fine," Strauss said, "I'll ask her for her opinion." He turned to Anna and asked her in German.

Anna shot D'Alessio a calculating look, and all D'Alessio could think about was bedding this voluptuous redheaded broad. Then she replied in German, "The American is right. We can't risk these gains on the unlikely prospect of finding Heisenberg in occupied Europe."

The way Anna sneered when she said "Heisenberg" was not lost on D'Alessio. He wondered what history Anna and the physicist had to have generated so much ill will.

D'Alessio glanced back at Strauss. "So it's settled then? We go to Danzig without the physicist?"

Strauss shot Anna a wounded look, and then turned back toward D'Alessio and nodded.

"Great. Let's consolidate our gear and get the hell out of…" A blinding flash of light cut D'Alessio off. "What the fuck was that?"

To the west, a smoky funnel expanded in the air, sucking up dust and debris from the surface, and billowed into a mushroom cloud that towered over the horizon.

"Jesus H. Christ," D'Alessio said, staring down at his watch to mark time. Nearly five minutes later, the delayed and sustained roar of the blast accompanied by fierce gusts of wind, swept through the area. D'Alessio shook his head and said, "My God, what on Earth was that?"

Strauss shrugged. "I wish I knew, but it can't be good,"

"Well," D'Alessio said, "Whatever it was, it happened about fifty-five to sixty miles from here. I don't like the look of it. We need to get the fuck out of here, and fast."

D'Alessio addressed the group in German, "All right folks, gather your gear. We're off to Danzig."

Chapter 27
Point Alamo

1030 Hours, 16 October 1943, Outside Sobibór, Poland

Soldiers!

Anna and the others raced away from the rugged unpaved road across an open field and toward a copse of oak, pine, and maple trees. The sky was overcast. Gray and bloated nimbus clouds gathered on the horizon.

Scores of German infantry spilled out of lorries. The men fired their rifles at the spies and fugitives in their midst.

Anna reached the grove first, setting up a sniper platform. Anna wasn't optimistic about the team's chances of survival. Using her rifle, she laid suppressive fire, so that Strauss and the others could make it to safety. After Anna took out the first German officers, the Germans either dropped to the ground or huddled behind their trucks for cover.

Strauss and D'Alessio arrived next. Strauss planted the thirty cal's tripod. Soon, Ruh and Götz joined the others, shooting their Lugers at the enemy.

"Move your ass!" D'Alessio called out to Klug. "We need that thirty cal!"

Dripping with sweat, Klug nodded and lumbered toward the copse, the thirty cal slumped over his shoulder. Tufts of dirt landed all around his feet as bullets zipped by him.

Klug collapsed behind a tree, hyperventilating. Strauss grabbed the thirty cal and mounted it on the tripod. Klug crawled over to Strauss and took aim at the infantry across the field.

Klug aimed his thirty at the trucks' engine blocks, taking out the Germans' mobility. Then, he blasted away at the infantry, shredding their formations.

Anna watched nervously as the German soldiers attempted to set up several machine gun emplacements. After taking out all the trucks within range, Klug directed his firepower against these machine gun teams, the barrel of the thirty cal glowing red hot as it churned out slags of metal.

Strauss and D'Alessio saved their rounds for German officers, taking out several in well-aimed shots. Ruh and Götz were taking pot shots at the enemy with their Lugers. Given their pistols' limited range, the two Free Germans didn't hit many targets, but they still earned Anna's respect for their gumption. She admired them even more because they still risked their lives despite knowing what the Germans did to traitors.

D'Alessio handed Anna his M1 Garand rifle.

"But I already have a rifle," Anna said in German.

"I'm just curious. I want to see what you can do with this," D'Alessio said, nudging the rifle into her hands."

I wonder what this is all about, Anna thought. *Maybe D'Alessio's just testing me to see if I'm as good a sniper as Strauss claims.* But she sensed that he wanted something else from her as well.

"Fine," Anna said, taking the M1 Garand.

Anna didn't disappoint, killing five officers in five minutes from a distance of over three hundred meters. D'Alessio watched, his mouth agape.

"That was impressive," he said, stroking her back. Anna flinched.

Sex was the last thing on her mind, especially given what she'd had to endure at Sobibór. No. It would be a long time before she'd get over that. Either way, it probably wouldn't matter anyway. She'd probably be dead soon.

"*Fick!*" Klug howled in German.

D'Alessio asked Klug a question in English. Klug answered in the American's native tongue. D'Alessio slammed the butt of his rifle into the dirt, and yelled, "Fuck!"

Anna didn't speak English, but she understood D'Alessio's sentiment. "What's wrong, Klug?" Anna asked in German.

"The barrel's running too hot, and we don't have a replacement. From here on out, we're going to have to rely on small arms fire to get the job done," Klug replied.

Fuck, indeed. Or more like fucked. Once the thirty cal stopped firing, the Germans began maneuvering their forces toward them.

The ground rumbled.

Tanks!

Four hulking armored behemoths rumbled across the field. Their turrets traversed and converged on the grove.

D'Alessio's eyes widened, his rifle slackening in his arms. Strauss seemed unshaken. "Panthers," he said in a monotone.

Scores of soldiers huddled behind the tanks, using the armor as protection from small arms fire, as the steel panzers lumbered forward.

D'Alessio started punching a nearby oak tree, spouting what Anna could only guess were colorful obscenities in his native tongue.

Ruh sobbed.

Götz fumbled to cool off the thirty's barrel, pouring canteen water on it.

Stunned, Klug watched Götz.

But Strauss did something else entirely: something that made no sense to Anna. Still, Anna knew by this point, that Strauss had better survival instincts than anyone she'd ever known.

Anna watched in utter confusion as Strauss pulled out his entrenching tool and yelled, "Dig!" in German.

D'Alessio threw up his hands and said three words, the last of which was "fuck." Then he opened his rucksack and pulled out something that looked like a radio transmitter. Strauss ignored the American and thrust his spade into the dirt. Trusting Strauss, Anna followed the German's example.

As Anna dug, she heard a voice on the other end of the transmitter speaking in English. She couldn't understand much, but heard one word over and over again: Alamo. She thought back to her days as a Ukrainian schoolgirl studying world history. The name sounded significant, but she couldn't remember why.

A tank round cleaved through a nearby maple tree, shattering it into a hail of splinters, and veiling the grove in a haze of smoke and fire.

"Fuck!" D'Alessio said as he grabbed his own spade and started digging.

The tank engines grew louder as they approached. Anna heard the Germans barking orders. She could even smell the bratwurst on their breath.

No. Never again.

Anna pulled out her Luger and pressed it to her temple, finger on the trigger. Strauss's eyes widened. "Anna, please! No!"

Anna summoned her courage. Killing herself wasn't as easy as she'd thought.

"Anna, please. I promise you I won't allow them to separate us again. Just give me a chance. Please!" Strauss pled, tears in his eyes.

"I can't fall into German hands again, Georg. You just don't understand. What they did to the Jews at Sobibór—what they were going to do to me. What they did to me. I won't let it happen again."

Strauss held his hands out in a calming gesture. "Please, Anna. Don't do this. First I lost Heinz, then I lost a son I never knew. You're the only one left. The only one I care for."

Anna lowered her weapon. "What about Inge?" she asked.

Strauss hesitated, but before he could answer, the German soldiers started closing in.

D'Alessio whispered in Anna's ear in German, "Extraction Point Alamo. Danzig. Three weeks. Before morning nautical twilight. Pass it on."

D'Alessio then buried his transmitter. Strauss did the same with the antigravity device and the biological samples. Even if the biological samples perished from lack of oxygen, Anna knew that dead samples were better than none.

Seconds later, the soldiers swarmed them, pointing their rifles in everyone's faces and yelling, "*Hände hoch!*"

The fugitives and spies all raised their hands.

Then a familiar voice spoke. "Whatever you do, don't shoot them. We need them alive. Understand?"

Heisenberg.

Chapter 28
Leverage

"You're alive," Strauss said as he looked out from the grove at Heisenberg. "What happened? Why did you abandon us?"

Heisenberg frowned. "The parasite took control. When I woke, I had marched deep behind Soviet lines. NKVD agents had escorted me to someone named General Valentin Kravchenko. He claimed to head the NKVD's Special Technical Bureau."

"Then, why are you still breathing?" Anna said, scowling.

"That's actually a mystery to me, Anna," Heisenberg said, scratching his head. "When I attempted an escape, I was actually surprised at the relative lack of security."

Anna smiled. "For a Nobel Prize winning physicist, you are an incredibly stupid strategist."

Heisenberg blushed and then frowned. Strauss supposed Heisenberg wasn't accustomed to someone calling him stupid.

"How so?" Heisenberg said.

"Well, let's see," Anna said, her voice boiling with contempt, "You'd been infested with an alien organism whose species had made a pact with the Soviets. That alien organism apparently reproduces using humans as hosts.

While that species had agreed not to infest living Soviet citizens, it hadn't made any similar arrangement with the Nazis. So, in theory, you were a vector. The Soviets were obviously using you to infest the citizens of the Third Reich."

"Well, I'm pretty sure they won't succeed," Heisenberg said confidently, pointing to the dissipating mushroom cloud.

"Why not?" Anna said gesturing behind her at the field. "There are likely scores of the parasites strewn about that city, and I doubt even the most meticulous of Germans will find them all. And since no one seems to know much, if anything, about their biology, you have no way of knowing if your bomb succeeded, do you?"

Heisenberg frowned again. Strauss guessed that the physicist hadn't considered that possibility.

"Thank you for the warning," Heisenberg said. "We'll quarantine the area, and likely bleach it with white phosphorous. That should kill everything within several hundred meters or so."

Strauss still wondered how Heisenberg had managed to survive. "Is the parasite still inside you?" Strauss asked.

"Fortunately, no. Your field expedient Pervitin solution was quite successful, if temporary. I owe you my life for that. In return for your quick thinking, I promise you I'll do my best to ensure you get a relatively light prison sentence."

"Prison sentence," Anna yelled. "For all Strauss knew, he was shooting at more infected soldiers. You cannot hold him accountable for his actions here. Your men attacked us first. He was simply defending himself."

"I'm sure he will have his day in court," Heisenberg said.

Anna glared at Heisenberg as if she were poised to attack the physicist, so Strauss rested his hand on her shoulder and mouthed the words,

"Not now." Strauss swiveled his head back to Heisenberg. "Why are you out here with all these soldiers?"

"Heydrich knows about the disk. He also knows you stole it and crashed it here. I'm here to recover both the craft and the antigravity device," Heisenberg explained.

"Well, it looks like you'll fail on both counts because we have neither," Anna said.

Strauss swung back toward Anna, flaring his nostrils, widening his eyes, and clenched his jaw to signal to Anna that if she said anything more, the Germans would probably kill her.

She nodded, fuming.

"The craft's about a kilometer or so in that direction," Strauss said, pointing east. "Though I doubt you'll find much left of it. Two alien disks chased me there and shot it down. They also probably destroyed the craft after I'd scuttled it. You'll be lucky if you find anything more than fragments at the crash site."

"What about the antigravity device?" Heisenberg asked.

"What's it to you?" Strauss said, knowing that the device's location was the only leverage he had to keep his companions alive.

"While most of the details are classified, I can tell you that that device is the only thing preventing human extinction," an animated Heisenberg said.

Strauss took a chance. "Well, we have it."

"Motherfucker! You dumb motherfucker!" D'Alessio swore in English. One of the soldiers pulled back the bolt on his rifle in a spine-tingling click.

Strauss continued. "But I'm not gonna tell you where it is, until I have certain guarantees about the care and safety of my comrades."

"You know I can't promise you anything, Strauss, but I'll do my best to protect you and your people."

"That's not good enough," Strauss said.

"I don't think you're seeing the big picture here," Heisenberg said, "We're talking about the survival of the human race. Stop being so selfish."

Now Strauss was pissed. "Fuck you, then. We're done here. Shoot us and be done with it. I'm never telling you where that device is."

Heisenberg stood silent for several seconds, and then said, "Men, take these prisoners to the trucks. We'll interrogate them when we get back to headquarters."

The German soldiers marched the prisoners out of the grove and into the field.

Boom! The ground shook with a deafening thunderclap. Struggling to regain his hearing, Strauss saw swirling smoke and twisted metal where one of the Panthers once stood. A beam of green light struck another Panther, destroying it in a riot of metal shards and flame. Strauss glanced at the sky; the two alien craft had returned.

They probably never left, Strauss thought. *They'd probably been waiting, biding their time until they could gather more hosts. The large concentration of German soldiers was exactly what they'd need.*

Heisenberg froze.

"You gonna do something, chief?" D'Alessio said to Heisenberg in English, "Because if you don't we're all gonna die."

Then, Heisenberg found his nerve. "We're not going anywhere without the device. Without it, we're all dead anyway."

Another Panther dissolved, and Heisenberg's men looked ready to bolt.

Duty weighing on him, Strauss dug up the device and handed it to Heisenberg. "For humanity."

D'Alessio balled his fists, and nearly punched Strauss, but a soldier tapped D'Alessio with the muzzle of a rifle, stopping D'Alessio dead in his tracks.

"What the fuck are you doing?" D'Alessio yelled in English, seething.

"You're a good, man, Strauss," Heisenberg said, "I promise I'll do everything in my power to see you're rewarded for this."

Heisenberg opened the cigarette lighter and attempted to activate it. When it failed, his eyes widened. "It's out of power?" he said. Heisenberg hesitated, and then said, "Strauss, I want you and your people to come with me. I'm the only one who can protect them now. We need to recharge the device. There's a power source at Sobibór. Follow me!"

At the mention of Sobibór, Anna's hand grabbed Strauss's arm, her nails digging into the skin beneath his sleeve. He turned to regard her and saw her eyes wide with animal-like fear. He wished she'd tell him what had happened there, but without that knowledge, he could do nothing but follow Heisenberg. "I'm sorry, Anna, we have to go. If we stay here, we die. It's as simple as that."

Anna nodded, her eyes welling with tears. Strauss turned toward the group, "C'mon! Let's go!"

The entire group—prisoners and soldiers—sprinted back toward the lorries that Klug hadn't had a chance to ruin.

A German eighty-eight millimeter FlaK gun fired at the hovering saucers, hammering at the craft with remarkable accuracy, but to little effect. The rounds might as well have been water balloons or rubber bands.

The disks methodically destroyed the German equipment, so long as no humans stood near the vehicles. Once soldiers occupied the trucks, the disks ceased their fire and went after vacant vehicles. Strauss knew why the aliens wanted him and his comrades alive—they probably saw humans as walking cocoons, ripe for infestation.

In moments, Heisenberg and Strauss reached the cab of one of the undamaged lorries. D'Alessio, Anna, and the Free Germans piled in the lorry's bed, along with several of their German captors. When Heisenberg took a seat behind the wheel, Strauss stopped him. "I'm a better driver than you. Just give me directions and I'll get us there."

Heisenberg hesitated, but then agreed.

Strauss hopped into the cab and slammed his foot on the gas. From his side view mirror, Strauss watched the disks hovering over them, trailing his lorry as he trundled down the unpaved road. The other remaining trucks followed.

Strauss had no idea how long his good fortune would last, but he knew deep down it wouldn't be for long. So, he drove to Sobibór as fast as he could. He'd figure out what to do once he got there.

Chapter 29
A Pocket in Time

1130 Hours, 16 October 1943, Outside Sobibór, Poland

Strauss reached a camp in chaos. Soldiers were tearing down fences and bulldozing wide swaths of the camp. Their activity was frenetic, as though they were trying to hide something. An armed SS guard approached Heisenberg's lorry from the front, walking toward Strauss. Strauss pointed to Heisenberg.

Heisenberg leaned across Strauss's lap and said, "We need immediate access to the monoliths."

The guard nodded and waved the trucks through the checkpoint. As Strauss drove forward, he observed the guard through the truck's side view mirror. It didn't take long for the man to react to the mysterious obsidian disks hovering overhead. The soldier turned and ran back to the lorry, signaling for it to stop. Strauss complied, and stopped the vehicle, waiting for the soldier to return.

Frantic, the man gestured toward the sky and said, "What the hell is that?"

Heisenberg rolled his eyes and said, "Don't worry about it. It's classified. However, it will become your concern if we don't get to those monoliths soon."

Shaking, the man nodded absently. Strauss pressed his foot on the gas pedal, and the truck shuffled forward toward the camp. Heisenberg directed him around several meters of fencing until ordering Strauss to halt several hundred meters away from three towering black monoliths. Heisenberg jumped out of the lorry before Strauss hit the brakes.

Strauss stopped the vehicle and got out. D'Alessio, Anna, and the Free Germans emerged from the lorry's canvas-covered bed. Anna trembled so much that she could barely stay on her feet, so Strauss walked over to offer her some support. To Strauss's chagrin, D'Alessio had already done the honors.

Heisenberg huddled next to a monolith, a dark blue film shimmering around the structure's sharp black edges.

The others edged toward Strauss. When Anna saw Heisenberg crouching by the monoliths, she stopped trembling, her hands balled into fists and she rushed toward the physicist.

Sudden movement was death around armed men. Strauss had learned that lesson the hard way, but so should've Anna. On her way to Heisenberg, Strauss grabbed her. She tried to free her arms, kicking and screaming. The raw animalistic intensity of her outburst troubled Strauss. He'd never seen Anna so unhinged.

"Anna, please, calm down. If the soldiers see you this way, they might shoot you. Please."

Anna sobbed. Strauss wanted to comfort her, but he had no idea how. He wanted to scream. But he knew it wouldn't help. Nothing would. So he embraced Anna until her rage began to fade.

"I'm fine now," she said, "Take me to Heisenberg. I need to tell him something."

Strauss's gut told him something wasn't quite right, but he decided to trust Anna anyway. His arm over her shoulder, Strauss escorted her to Heisenberg.

"I'm nearly finished charging the device," Heisenberg said. "I should be able to activate the device in a few seconds."

Then Anna struck, choking Heisenberg before Strauss could react.

"You bastard!" she shrieked, "You knew all along what was happening here!"

"Please!" Heisenberg said, in between gurgles, "Stop!"

Dozens of soldiers trained their rifles on Anna. Strauss raised his hand and shouted, "Don't shoot! I'll handle this!"

Strauss struggled to wrest Anna's arms from Heisenberg, but her grip on Heisenberg's neck was strong. After a herculean effort, Strauss managed to separate Anna from the physicist.

She railed at the scientist as Strauss pulled her away, kicking and screaming. "You knew, you fucking bastard! You knew!"

Anna crawled into a ball, rocking back and forth, seemingly inconsolable.

"Anna, what did Heisenberg know? Tell me," Strauss said, squeezing Anna tightly. But she didn't answer; she probably couldn't. Whatever had happened at this camp, it had shattered her psyche. Strauss wasn't sure if she'd ever be the same.

Strauss cast his eyes toward Heisenberg. The physicist seemed rattled by Anna's outburst. "Why is she so upset at you?" Strauss asked Heisenberg, "What happened at this camp?"

Heisenberg shrugged, shaking his head. "I swear to you I don't know," he said.

"Why are those monoliths glowing? What's powering them?"

"Dark matter."

"Where does this dark matter come from?"

"I'm not exactly sure. According to Heydrich, an unnamed German scientist had discovered a way to harness it. When I'd asked how, Heydrich told me it was classified. But he did say that if I ever needed to recharge the antigravity device, I should come here."

"Liar!" Anna shouted.

"Anna, why do you think Heisenberg's lying?" Strauss said.

Before she could answer, the green beams emanated from the two disks. Soldiers fell, stunned.

Why had the disks waited to attack until now? Strauss wondered.

The instant the disks attacked, Heisenberg opened the faux cigarette lighter and tapped the red button three times. The wind swirled with increasing intensity, sucked inward toward an expanding vortex that appeared out of thin air. The vortex was like a window, a looking glass into another world. On the other side, Strauss glimpsed a world immersed in gloom, a twilight realm enthralled to a black sun. Dark spires wrought from black masonry curled toward the murky sky.

In an instant, the vortex swirled to a close like a constricting pupil. The disks plummeted like stones. Clouds of dust billowed in their wake. Coughing and covered in dust, Strauss could barely see a meter ahead of him.

While the others stumbled, groping about in the confusion, Strauss had already known what would come next. He grabbed a submachine gun out of a dazed soldier's hands and sprinted toward where the disks had crashed.

Strauss tripped and stumbled along the way, losing his momentum, but not his determination.

"Strauss!" Anna's voice called from behind, "Where are you going?"

"I'm taking the fight to the enemy!"

"Wait! We're coming to help!" D'Alessio shouted in German. But Strauss kept running.

In minutes, Strauss had scaled one of the dusty disks, and headed toward its central cone. Eerie whippoorwill trills echoed from the disk. A riot of tentacles exploded from the structure. Strauss dropped to his stomach and fired his submachine gun in measured three-round bursts. RAT-TAT-TAT. RAT-TAT-TAT.

The whippoorwill trills intensified, becoming so extreme that Strauss had to cover his ears.

A lumbering beast slithered out of its disk and plodded toward Strauss, screaming and flailing its tentacles. Strauss took two deep breaths. He aimed for the creature's blood-red eyes, then popped off eight well-aimed shots before rolling toward the disk's edge.

The cephalopod thrashed its tentacles, reaching blindly for Strauss. Its trills reverberated through the fog. Strauss climbed off the first disk and searched for the second one.

Strauss spotted a green shimmer in the debris cloud. He heard a man's muffled yell.

D'Alessio.

Strauss sprinted toward the beam's source, only to find that the second alien had emerged from its craft. Its tendrils grasped a black semicircular device. Aiming the weapon at Strauss, the creature fired. The green beam narrowly missed him as he hurried toward the alien.

Strauss aimed at the tendrils flexing the device. He squeezed out three more rounds. Anna emerged from the haze, stumbling into the alien's line of sight. It pointed its weapon at her and fired. Anna went limp, then collapsed.

"No!" Strauss shouted. He unloaded his clip at the creature. Out of ammunition, Strauss dove to the ground. He rolled for cover.

The creature pointed its device at Strauss. Desperate, he scrambled for cover.

Out of nowhere, a blue beam struck the alien. The creature went limp. Strauss watched in awe as the alien calcified before his eyes. He couldn't believe his good fortune, though he decided not to stick around to thank whoever was responsible.

The second alien disk rested ten meters away, ripe for the taking. Strauss saw an opportunity and acted. He didn't have much time. He could only take one person with him to England.

In the chaos, he'd lost sight of Heisenberg and the man's antigravity device. Strauss didn't have time to search for the physicist amid all the smoke and dust. He supposed an honest-to-God flying saucer would have to do. Which begged the question: whom would he take to England? Anna or D'Alessio? Love or Duty?

More than anything, Strauss yearned to be with Anna. He tried to rationalize why taking her to England would be the most logical choice. If he made a convincing enough argument, he thought, the Americans and the British would trust him. They'd believe his story.

Who was he fooling?

Strauss made his decision. He rushed to Anna and kissed her on her cheek. "I love you, and I promise I'll come back for you or die trying. Forgive me for abandoning you again." A tear rolled down his cheek. "I hope you understand."

Anna lay on the ground frozen. Her features were locked in an expression of shock. But Strauss knew she was there, kicking and screaming inside. Yet he could do nothing. The onus of duty weighed heavier than the love in his heart. Humanity had to come first.

Strauss hugged Anna. Then he left, racing toward the last place he'd seen D'Alessio. He discovered the American's limp body lying in the grass not far from the craft. Strauss bent down, and hoisted D'Alessio over his shoulder, carrying the American like a sack of potatoes toward the disk. He loaded D'Alessio onto the disk's platform, activated it and descended into the craft.

In minutes, Strauss and D'Alessio were airborne. With a heavy heart, Strauss piloted the craft toward England.

Chapter 30
Landfall

1005 Hours GMT, 16 October 1943, Royal Air Force Station Watton, England

"Holy shit!" D'Alessio screamed.

Restrained in a strange metal platform, he struggled to escape. His heart raced. He looked down. Gray clouds and miles of empty air stood between him and the Earth's craggy surface. Whatever was carrying him, it was traveling at an extreme rate of speed.

D'Alessio looked ahead. Strauss was manipulating a series of multi-hued buttons floating on a cushion of air. D'Alessio could only describe them as three-dimensional projections of light. Strauss looked forward, then down, and then forward again.

No, it couldn't be.

Taking a deep breath, D'Alessio tried to calm himself. It wasn't easy. One minute, he'd been fighting aliens; the next moment, he found himself zipping through the sky on God knows what.

"Where the hell are we?" D'Alessio said, his voice cracking at the last breath, betraying his nervousness.

Strauss glanced up for half a second, and then looked back down at the strange runic control system. "Sorry, can't talk. Need to concentrate."

As the surface raced by at an unimaginable speed, D'Alessio decided not to push Strauss. The German could've killed D'Alessio half a dozen times by now. But Strauss didn't. Hell, for all D'Alessio knew, the man had saved D'Alessio's life from whatever they'd encountered at Sobibór.

That he could trust Strauss was about the only thing of which D'Alessio was certain.

As incredible as it seemed, D'Alessio was convinced Strauss had somehow figured out a way to fly this craft. And D'Alessio didn't want to distract Strauss from that.

A glimpse below revealed what D'Alessio judged was the French coast. Half a heartbeat later, they'd crossed the English Channel.

Strauss, you slick motherfucker. You weren't bullshitting after all.

Now that he knew Strauss had things well in hand, D'Alessio began to worry about Anna and the Free Germans. What had happened to them? Had they survived?

The craft decelerated to a hover, then began its descent. Below, D'Alessio spotted the familiar airfield at Royal Air Force Station Watton, England. Spitfires had lined the airstrip. One of the aircraft had already begun its ascent toward Strauss's craft.

The craft shook. Seconds later, two dots on the horizon resolved into the two Spitfire silhouettes. Sparks flashed against the invisible hull. If the attack had rattled Strauss, he didn't show it. He continued to operate the ship's ethereal controls.

More sparks peppered the craft. D'Alessio's stomach roiled. It took every ounce of his will not to vomit. The craft pitched and yawed with each impact. Still, Strauss had somehow managed to control its descent.

Dozens of soldiers and airmen raced toward the runway. Others were setting up makeshift roadblocks with their trucks.

D'Alessio racked his brain to formulate a plan that would prevent them from getting shot. He had to explain why a German soldier was landing an alien foo fighter on English territory. Strauss had done his part. Now it was up to D'Alessio to do his.

The craft landed quietly in the center of the runway. Strauss manipulated more controls until the ship's transparent walls became opaque. The harness restraining D'Alessio retracted into the wall. He stood up. His seating platform merged into the floor.

Strauss's bloodshot eyes marred the face of an exhausted man. For the first time since D'Alessio had been awake, Strauss spoke to him. "I got the craft to England. Can you get them to give me some Pervitin?"

D'Alessio hadn't expected that. He thought the German would have been more concerned about Anna. D'Alessio had heard much about this German wonder drug, but he'd heard nothing of its side effects.

"Shouldn't their first priority be to find Anna?" D'Alessio said.

"Of course," Strauss said, as if it were an afterthought. "I just need something to give me some energy. I don't know if I can make it without another dose."

Strauss rippled with heat. He was lathered in sweat. The man was strung out, and D'Alessio worried that the man might lose it when they reached the ground. Even worse, if Strauss told anyone about his craving for Pervitin, the scientists would take him away to learn more about the German wonder drug. No. D'Alessio had to keep Strauss's addiction a secret.

"I'll do what I can to get you some Pervitin. Just promise me you won't ask anyone else for it. If my side learns you're a user, they'll pick and prod at you until the end of the war or your death. You understand?"

Strauss nodded.

"Good. Now I have to convince these Brits to commit forces to find Anna," D'Alessio said. If they hadn't left the antigravity device and extraterrestrial biological samples in Poland, the British would never waste men and resources on Anna. Fortunately, he had leverage. D'Alessio nodded. "You have my word that we'll eventually save Anna."

Strauss nodded as if the matter had been resolved. *Why did the man never smile?* The German motioned for D'Alessio to step on a platform at the center of the craft. D'Alessio obliged. Strauss activated a floor panel with his boot. The platform rose toward the ceiling.

In seconds, the platform lifted D'Alessio and Strauss up into a hollow conical structure. A door opened to the outside. A cold and wet gale swept into the craft's hermetically sealed vacuum. D'Alessio shivered. Dozens of British soldiers aimed their rifles at the two men from the tarmac below. Many of them shook with what D'Alessio sensed was fear. It wasn't every day that a flying saucer landed in your homeland.

D'Alessio raised his hands. He motioned for Strauss to do the same. Strauss obeyed. D'Alessio knew he had to tread carefully. One sudden move and some Tommy's nervous trigger finger could end them both.

The sky overhead was a dull gray. A soupy mist choked the morning air. It was uncomfortably cold. Realizing that Strauss still wore a German uniform, D'Alessio put himself between the soldiers and his companion, shielding Strauss with his body. Slowly, he and Strauss climbed off the saucer. The instant D'Alessio's feet hit the asphalt the Brits were on top of him and Strauss.

They forced D'Alessio onto his stomach and into an icy puddle. They patted him down with the tenderness and care of a bulldog. He watched them do the same to Strauss.

"On your feet!" a man with an aristocratic British accent shouted. D'Alessio and Strauss stood up. A British colonel approached. He stopped abruptly, six inches from D'Alessio. D'Alessio detected a glint of malice in the man's eyes. "Who the bloody hell are you and what in the Queen's name is that?" the colonel said pointing at the alien craft.

"I'm Captain Jimmy D'Alessio. I'm returning from a series of classified missions under codename TOOL."

"Tool? I know of no such operation," the colonel said, sneering.

Unruffled, D'Alessio said, "Pass that name up the chain, Colonel. I'll wait."

The Brit scrunched up his freckled and red mustachioed face as if D'Alessio had crushed his puppy's throat. "And what of him?" the colonel said, gesturing toward Strauss.

"He's with me. Without his help, we wouldn't have secured this disk. And before you get any crazy ideas, he's the only man or woman on earth who knows how to fly it."

The colonel stared at D'Alessio. After several seconds, he said, "Right then. Can your friend pilot or hover that thing into one our hangars? Right now, it makes a rather attractive target for the Luftwaffe."

D'Alessio glanced at Strauss. "Can you help the good colonel out?"

Strauss nodded.

"Excellent," the colonel said. "I'm sure you won't mind if I and several of my men accompany you and your friend. After all, we still haven't confirmed who you both are."

D'Alessio smiled. "Why, Colonel, I'd expect nothing less from a member of the British Army."

Chapter 31

Wrath

Anna lay frozen, unable to twitch even her muscles. The two portal-spawned alabaster demons crouched over the petrified hulk of a *Schwartzwald* entity. Their stone blue eyes stared out intently from angular, elongated skulls, as they searched the stone alien husk. One removed the mysterious energy weapon from a stone tendril. The entity's digit crumbled. The white demons prowled forward, their half-human, half-wolf legs whirling toward the disk Strauss had left behind. Their speed was both unnatural and terrifying.

The Soviet major felt trapped inside her own body, unable to fight back and completely at the mercy of these strange beings. She worried that at any moment one of the guards would carry her limp body back through the gates of that human hell called Sobibór and feed her to the ovens.

No. She wasn't going to let that happen. She concentrated on her fingers and toes, willing them back to life. At first, she focused on the heat of her body. Then she used that warmth to ignite a fire in her extremities, focusing on one finger and one toe at a time.

The ground quaked. Gusts of dust and debris billowed out from the disk and enshrouded everyone with more dirt. And then, the disk rose to the heavens and zoomed off toward the horizon at some unfathomable velocity.

The facts that Strauss had abandoned her a second time, and had left her in the hands of Heisenberg fueled her rage, an ember of fear erupting into an inferno of wrath.

If Heisenberg emerged from his paralysis first, Anna convinced herself, *She was dead.*

She concentrated. Her index finger twitched, then she wiggled a toe. Soon, she pivoted her ankle and rolled her eyes. Glancing to her right, she found Heisenberg, frozen like a stone. His right hand clutched the antigravity device. His presence fueled her desire to break free. Within seconds she was shaking her right arm.

But the physicist was also slowly coming to life, his arms quivering as he struggled to lift his half-frozen body from the ground.

Heisenberg's trembling forced Anna to redouble her efforts, and within less than a minute, she was on her feet and armed with a rifle. She snatched the antigravity device from his still frozen hands and tossed it out of his reach, several meters behind her. Then, she raised her rifle and aimed it at Heisenberg. "Make one move and I'll shoot your face off," she said.

"Pleas… don," Heisenberg said, his mouth still numb.

Anna craved to kill Heisenberg. And with all the dust and smoke, she'd probably get away with it. But she also wanted to make the man suffer, so she waited until he could speak.

"Please, don't shoot me," he said.

"Give me a good reason why you deserve to live."

"Anna, we suffered through a lot. I have nothing but respect for you."

"You're just saying that because I have a gun in your face. When I wasn't armed, you were perfectly willing to draw energy from those abominations," Anna said, pointing at the monoliths.

"I… I don't understand. Why do the monoliths upset you?" Heisenberg said.

"Because you know very well what powers them," Anna said, ominously.

"Well, of course I do," Heisenberg said.

Anna flinched at the brazenness of his admission.

Heisenberg continued. "The stones are conduits for dark matter. Why is that so objectionable to you?"

"Where did this dark matter come from?" Anna asked like a teacher shaming an insolent student caught in a lie.

Heisenberg panicked. "I swear, I have no idea. Heydrich told me it was classified. I swear."

Anna bucked him in the chest with her rifle butt. "You wanna play stupid? Fine. I'll tell you what the source is you sick and twisted bastard: human souls. Human souls that Nazis like you transferred to this camp like sheep and gassed to death in cold blood. For what? Science?"

Heisenberg squirmed, raising his hands and arms above his head, his eyes widening as if glimpsing the horrific truth for the very first time. "Please!" he cried, "I swear I didn't know!" He crawled to Anna on his knees and grasped at her pant leg, tears in his eyes.

Anna pressed the rifle to his forehead and pulled the trigger.

Chapter 32
Broken Tools

Klug's head was spinning. There was a haze of dust everywhere. His ears rang and his head ached. Covered in debris, Klug surveyed his surroundings. When he looked up, he saw three German soldiers aiming their submachine guns at him. They were yelling, but he could barely hear them. The scowls on their faces told him everything.

Klug looked around. He saw nothing but debris and smoke. The Germans yelled again, jerking their rifles at him.

What the hell were they saying?

"I can't hear you," Klug said.

One of the Germans kicked him in the leg. If the bastard thought that would motivate Klug, he had another thing coming.

Klug slowly stood up, hands raised in the air. Another German swung around from behind and jabbed Klug with the muzzle of his rifle.

"Motherfucker," Klug said. He couldn't help himself.

Another soldier tried to jam his rifle butt in Klug's face. Klug caught it. He used the momentum of the thrust to jam the German behind him in the nose. The man dropped his rifle. Klug swung the muzzle forward firing.

The third German tried to take a shot and missed. Klug turned his rifle, fired, and hit. The German behind Klug scrambled to recover his dropped rifle. Klug was on top of him in an instant, bashing the man's head in with his rifle butt.

Three dead Germans littered the ground.

Klug looked around, swiveling his head back and forth looking for all comers. The sound of the rifle shot would draw attention to his position. Sure enough, a mob of German soldiers began converging on him.

I need to get the hell out of here. Where are Ruh and Götz? I gotta find them. I gotta get out of here? Where's Strauss? Where are D'Alessio and Anna? What the hell?

Klug ran in the opposite direction looking frantically for Ruh and Götz. By the sounds of their voices, the Germans were getting closer.

Shit! I've gotta get out of here.

As he ran forward, Klug heard a man howling in pain. "My leg! My leg!"

By the whiny sound of the man's voice, Klug knew he'd found his man. Covered in crates and shattered wood, Ruh's leg didn't look too good. In fact, it looked downright terrible.

"Ruh, is that you?"

"Klug?"

"Yeah!"

"Aw, help me. My leg's jammed."

"Oh, you're leg's more than jammed."

"What? What do ya mean?" Ruh said.

"Don't worry about it."

Klug worked to get the boxes off his friend's legs. The Germans drew closer.

"Just leave me here," Ruh said. "If you stay and help me, they'll kill us both. Better you survive to fight another day than die here with me."

"Shut up," Klug said.

After getting all the debris off Ruh, Klug slung his rifle over his left shoulder, and then threw Ruh over his right shoulder. He looked at the man's leg, trying not to register alarm. It looked real bad. Klug was almost certain that Ruh would have to amputate it. Otherwise, the man would die of gangrene.

The Germans were almost on top of them. If not for the smoke, Klug and Ruh would be dead by now.

Klug started running. Ruh was howling in pain.

"We gotta get out of here, man. We've gotta get out of here," Klug said.

As they ran forward, Klug heard more voices. More German soldiers were advancing on them from the front. Klug looked in both directions. He couldn't go forward. He couldn't go backward. He tried to go right. Again, more Germans. He turned around. More Germans.

"Shit!"

As Klug continued running toward another group of Germans, he saw rippling electrical activity.

"What the hell is that?" Klug said.

As Klug moved forward into the smoke, he felt a vacuum as if something was tugging him toward it. He saw electrical activity surging in the background like lightning.

As Klug continued to push forward, he saw what looked like a black hole or a whirlpool swirling in the air perpendicular to the Earth.

"What the hell?" Klug said.

"C'mon guys, let's go!"

Götz!

"Götz, what are you doing? There's Germans all around us!"

"I know," Götz said. "It's the only way out, man!"

"What do you mean it's the only way out?" Klug said

"I don't know, man. Either we jump through this thing or we die here."

Klug inclined his head back toward Ruh. "What do you think?"

"Halt!" a German soldier yelled. The crack of a rifle shot forced a decision.

Klug felt a stab of pain on his torso. He looked down. Blood was pooling on his chest. He could barely breathe. He felt a shove as Götz pushed him through the portal.

Chapter 33

Excavation

Anna clawed at the loamy soil until her hands bled. Rain inundated the muddy ground. Beyond the rain's rapid-fire pitter-patter, baying dogs closed in.

Digging one mud pit after another, Anna had come up short. *One way or another*, she convinced herself, *she was going to find that damn transmitter.*

The barking grew louder. Soon, she could hear men issuing orders. There was no time. She had to be ready for Plan B.

Before Anna had fled Sobibór, she'd covered herself with two bandoliers of seven point six two millimeter for her stolen Karabiner rifle, along with three potato masher grenades.

She picked up a broken branch as thick as her thumb and tossed it forward and to her left. Sporadic submachine gun fire fell for her feint, while she watched her pursuers and selected her targets.

Anna aimed her rifle at the highest-ranking officer she spotted and pressed the trigger.

Bedlam.

Frantic screams and a barrage of withering fire pinned her down, while torrential rain pelted her from above. She crawled through the muddy slush to locate her next firing position. Once she put her rifle into place, she found another stick and tossed it. A hail of small arms fire followed. Anna picked another target: a young cocky-looking little bastard huddling next to a radio operator. She aimed and fired, the man's head exploding in a scarlet riot.

Anna ducked, taking cover behind a maple tree. She giggled as the Germans responded by laying down a wall of steel. Anna had always enjoyed being a crack shot, but had never relished taking human lives. But after Sobibór, murdering Germans made her euphoric. She especially loved dispatching German officers, particularly when they did stupid things that made them stand out. The dumb ones always kept close to their radio operator. And from what she'd seen thus far today, it was a target-rich environment for stupid officers.

As the bullets zipped and popped over her head, Anna steeled herself for the coming assault. The Germans nearly always used one squad to lay suppressive fire, while another squad maneuvered toward their target.

Anna waited for the soldiers to draw closer. After several minutes, the suppressive fire stopped, signaling to Anna that the Germans were readying their assault. Again, she tossed a stick, but only two rounds answered. Nearby, an officer admonished a soldier.

Now, Anna had a bead on them. She activated her potato masher grenade, yanking the porcelain ball at the base of its wooden handle, and counted to three. Then she tossed it in the direction of the German voices.

An explosion roared, spattering Anna with clumps of mud, bone fragments, and blood. Seconds later, she heard wailing—intermittent, insufferable wailing.

Anna smiled. *Good*, she thought, *I hope you suffer.*

Indiscriminate gunfire answered Anna's carnage. Anna judged the chaos she'd sown had bought her some time to find the transmitter and escape. But the darkness inside her beckoned her to stay—to bask in the killing of every last German.

But no, she had to be smart, deliberate. She had the swine right where she wanted them.

She peered around her tree and saw a scattered wreck of humanity. Disembodied arms, severed heads, and limbless torsos were strewn across the field. Anna worried she wouldn't find what she was looking for. Then, she spied a survivor, writhing in pain.

Anna aimed and took a shot, hitting the man's arm as if she were tearing the legs off a spider. He screamed. Death was not Anna's goal; forcing the other side to make emotional decisions was.

The stalemate lasted for several minutes, her opponents wavering. Should they send someone to rescue him, or should they eliminate her first?

Smoke billowed.

Anna swore. Sometimes killing the dumb officers left the smart ones to do the thinking. She just hoped they'd use their smoke grenades to cover the man's rescue rather than masking their assault on her. But smoke could also work as a two-way veil. Anna could use it to mask her own withdrawal.

Anna scoured the ground one last time, finally uncovering both the biological sample and the transmitter. Securing both in her rucksack, she slung it over her back, scrambled out of the grove, and sprinted across a second field, heading toward a tree line in the distance.

Dogs!

Three German shepherds loped toward Anna. No matter what happened, she had to make it to the tree line. If she stopped to deal with the dogs, they'd fix her in place so the Germans could swarm her, closing in for the kill.

Meters from the forest's edge, a dog clamped its jaws on her ankle, pulling her down. A sharp pain rippled up her leg. Anna twisted her hips, lowered her rifle, and fired. A puddle of blood pooled under the dog's carcass.

The dog had made a mess of Anna's ankle. Dizzy from blood loss, she struggled to move fast. From the sound of their voices, the soldiers would soon bridge the distance between her and them.

Anna pulled back the bolt of her rifle, reloading an instant before another dog leapt at her throat. She fired, killing the dog in midair.

The last dog was on her before she'd had a chance to reload. Its jaws snapped at her. She used her rifle to block its maws from clamping down on her throat. The animal savaged her arm, ripping chunks of flesh with each vicious bite.

She jammed the butt of her rifle at the dog's head, landing it with a loud crack. Dazed, the dog stumbled back. She staggered to her feet and bashed the animal's skull into a gooey crimson pulp.

A bullet whizzed past. Anna turned and sprinted for the tree line. An adrenaline surge helped her push past the throbbing in her ankle. More bullets savaged the maple and oak trees all around her.

Once she found cover in the forest, she checked her rucksack to ensure the transmitter, biological sample, and antigravity device were still intact. Satisfied, she ran for her life with the Germans in hot pursuit.

Anna staggered through at least a kilometer of dense, old growth forest. Her pursuers inched closer with each passing breath. So close, she could hear their heavy breathing.

Stumbling at the edge of the forest, she nearly tumbled into a river blocking her path. She glanced back and heard the sound of German hobnailed boots crunching leaves. She could smell the cheap Schnapps and cigarettes on their breath. In a minute, they'd be on top of her.

She turned back toward the river. Opening the breech on her rifle, she plunged into the stream. She tensed when her body was submerged into the frigid water, nearly losing her weapon to the current she hoped would carry her north to safety.

Seconds later, two soldiers emerged from the woods. Spotting her, they aimed their rifles. Anna put her rifle's muzzle in her mouth and submerged, careful to keep the open breech above the surface.

A hail of bullets tore through the water, seeking her warm flesh. But Anna knew the danger had passed. The river swept her broken body toward salvation.

And so she floated onward, struggling to stay awake. Her raw hatred of the Nazi regime kept her going. But so did thoughts of Strauss. She struggled with the paradox of loving a man who'd abandoned her twice. Logic told her that he must've had his reasons. Yet his abandonment had inflicted a deep emotional scar. She couldn't decide whether she wanted to kill the man or love him.

Chapter 34
Extraction

Anna shivered under the pier's pylons, huddling in the cold darkness. The waves had receded into the icy Baltic Sea. She took a moment to empty her stomach into the churning waves. Over the past several days, she must've picked up a stomach virus. She was feeling more tired than normal.

She checked a watch she'd acquired from the Polish resistance. It was two minutes before half past the hour: before morning nautical twilight or BMNT in military parlance. It was an odd term to describe the point just before the sun pierced the morning horizon.

If the partisans hadn't recovered her from the Bug River, she would have never made it this far. Smuggling her from safe house to safe house through Nazi-occupied Poland and then into the eastern Reich had been harrowing. But Anna had survived long enough to send a transmission to the British. She just hoped they'd live up to their part of the bargain.

The last vestige of night yielded to the early morning sun's red-yellow glow. The light shimmered on icy gray waves. A black dot crested the horizon, bobbing in tune with the sea's roiling waves. As it drew closer, Anna spotted two human forms, paddling the zodiac with two wooden oars. The first sliver of the sun pierced the veil separating night from day. Anna reflected the sun's light with her compact to signal her position.

The silhouettes on the zodiac signaled back and quickened their pace. Five minutes later, Anna could make out Strauss's and D'Alessio's faces. She very nearly shouted for joy. Strauss had promised he'd return for her and he had delivered on that promise.

Anna waded into the frigid sea as the zodiac neared the shore. She climbed into the raft, wrapped her arms around Strauss and kissed him for as long as he let her.

Strauss leaned into her embrace, matching her passion with lusty enthusiasm. Pressed up against her, she felt his excitement. But then he abruptly pulled away from her, no doubt compelled by some notion of misplaced loyalty. First it was the Reich, and now it was probably that damnable woman.

"I'm sorry," he said, "I can't. Inge. And the child."

Anna drew back and shrugged. D'Alessio suddenly looked hopeful, making Anna feel even more awkward and uncomfortable.

She could sympathize with Strauss. The man needed some space and perspective. Come to think of it, so did she. It would take her a while before she could be intimate with another man. She needed time to heal.

They all did.

D'Alessio grabbed her arm. By instinct, she yanked it away. He raised his hands in the air in surrender. "Anna, I'm sorry. I didn't mean to startle you, but I need to ask you something extremely important."

Anna braced herself for what she expected would be a not-so-subtle solicitation. But then D'Alessio's face took on a more serious expression.

"Go on," she said.

"Have you heard anything from Klug, Ruh, or Götz?" he said. "We haven't heard a thing about them since Sobibór. And we're really worried about them."

For the first time, Anna saw a sense of vulnerability in this man. He really seemed to be concerned about these so-called Free Germans. It only made her answer that much harder to deliver. "I'm sorry. I've heard nothing from any of them since Sobibór."

He lowered his head for a moment, and then nodded. "I see. Well, I suppose I'll have to settle for one good thing today." Then he smiled. "It's good to see you again, Anna."

She smiled back and clasped his arm. "Don't worry, D'Alessio. You'll find them. I know you will."

He nodded, and then the trio rowed out into the sea and toward the American submarine waiting in the distance.

Soon the Americans and British would have the German antigravity device and the *Schwartzwald* entity's biological samples. But the war wasn't over yet—far from it. This was only the end of the beginning. But it was an auspicious start. And at least now, humanity had a fighting chance.

&

Date and Time Unknown, Somewhere Inside the Vortex

The light overhead nearly blinded Klug when he opened his eyes. "He's awake" a voice said from across the nondescript white tiled room he found himself in. He lay on what appeared to be a hospital bed. When he tried to sit up, something forced him back down as if he were pinned to the bed by invisible restraints.

His chest tingled. It felt as if millions of insects were crawling on it. When he looked down at his torso, he screamed.

His skin *was* crawling.

"Calm down, Klug," a familiar voice said. An instant later, Götz ran up to Klug's bed. "Relax. You're gonna be all right. The smartest thing we all did was jump through that portal. If we hadn't, we'd all be dead by now."

But Götz's words did little to settle Klug while Klug's chest boiled with activity. "Help me! Help me! What the hell is happening to my body?"

"You're gonna be all right, Klug. The nanites are knitting your chest back together. You'll see. You'll be good as new, just like Ruh is."

"Ruh's... alive?"

"Yeah, he sure is. You saved both him and his leg."

Klug was beginning to calm down. While his chest tingled, it didn't hurt. And it was comforting to hear that Ruh had survived. But something didn't seem right. Klug had been certain that Ruh's leg had to be amputated.

"Wait. I saw Ruh's leg. It was a ruined mash of flesh, muscle, and bone. There's no way any doctor could have saved it." And then other questions begged for an answer. "What are nanites? And why the hell am I being restrained?"

Götz put his hand on Klug's shoulder. "All in good time, old friend. You need to heal first. I promise you you're in good hands."

Something was off about Götz. The man's words still didn't convince Klug that everything was all right. Götz's words somehow seemed forced. "Fine. I'll wait a bit. Where's Ruh?"

Götz's hand tensed. Then he pulled it off Klug's shoulder. Something was definitely wrong. Götz dropped to one knee and whispered in Klug's ear, "Still your mind. They can hear your thoughts."

Klug could feel his own heartbeat quickening. "What do you mean?" Klug said in a panic. "What does that mean?"

"We are in a bubble within a bubble," Götz said.

The room began to vibrate.

"What do you mean? A bubble within a bubble? What the hell does that mean?" Klug yelled.

Götz had a hunted look in his eyes. He pointed to a wall and then put a single finger to his lips. "Shhh!"

The center of the wall spiraled into an open corridor. Three smooth, pale tentacles corded with veins shot out of the portal. The first tentacle was twisted around Ruh's limp body. The tentacle unfurled and Ruh fell to the floor with a dull thud.

"Ruh!" Klug yelled. He tried to struggle against his invisible bonds, frantic to help his friend.

"Calm down, Klug. Please!" Götz pleaded, his eyes wide like a frightened animal. "Surrender yourself to them. It only hurts more if you resist."

Klug only screamed louder as if the mere act of defiance would convince his captors to retreat.

Four tendrils from the other two tentacles clamped down on both Götz's and Klug's skulls. Klug could feel it sucking the memories from his mind.

Götz collapsed. His body shook as if Götz were in the thrall of some sort of seizure. The strain on Klug's mind was exhausting. He found it harder and harder to breathe. Klug struggled against the intrusion, but he wasn't strong enough to stop it. His will paled before the intelligence that was violating his mind. His breathing grew shallower, more labored. Then darkness.

Chapter 35
Revelation

1045 Hours GMT, 17 November 1943, Royal Air Force Station Watton, England

The portly and bespectacled doctor entered the lily-white hospital room with a bounce in his step. His stethoscope swayed over his rotund belly. A wispy red fringe stretching around the back of his skull from temple to temple was all that remained of his disheveled hair. His ruddy cheeks and bloated jowls radiated with joviality.

Anna hated him the instant she saw him.

The hospital room was clean, almost too clean for Anna. It had an antiseptic quality that masked the grim reality outside its falsely comforting walls. In their supreme arrogance, these Brits seemed to believe that a tiny channel of water would protect them from the coming cosmic horror.

The corpulent doctor gleefully extended his bloated hand and sausage fingers toward Anna. Reluctantly, she shook it.

"I'm Doctor Wilbur Childs," he said in passable German. "I apologize for my poor German. My understanding is that you only speak Russian and German. I'm the only doctor in this hospital who speaks German, and unfortunately, no one here speaks Russian."

Glaring at Childs, Anna said, "And Ukrainian."

"Excuse me?" Childs said, raising his eyebrow.

"I speak Russian, German, *and Ukrainian.*"

Childs shot Anna the dejected look of a wounded puppy. "Ah, I'm, ah, sorry. I didn't mean to offend."

She shrugged. "What do you want?"

The fat Brit smiled, exposing a thin gap between his top two incisors. "I wanted to give you some fantastic news."

Anna rolled her eyes. "Tell me this 'fantastic' news."

Childs pressed his glasses against the bridge of his nose. "Well, your body has suffered through more trauma than most women suffer in a lifetime. Yet somehow you made it through. I'm very happy to say that you have an excellent prognosis."

Anna scowled at Childs's "most women" comment. "Interesting," she said, "I doubt many men have been through what I've been through either."

Childs blushed. "No, I suppose not. And I'm certain no man in history will have gone through what you're about to experience about seven months from now."

Now he had Anna's attention. "What do you mean?"

He flashed Anna that infuriating gap-toothed smile of his, and clasped her hands. "Well, that's why I'm here. Despite all the punishment your body has suffered, I'm very excited to tell you that your baby has survived."

"My what?" Anna said in a stupor.

Childs grinned. "Why, Miss Ivanova, you're pregnant."

No. It can't be. Please don't let this be true.

"Impossible," Anna said as she glowered at Childs.

"Oh no. I'm fairly certain you're about two months pregnant." He frowned. "I really thought you'd be more excited by this news, Miss Ivanova."

"Leave me alone," Anna said, scowling.

Childs's touchy feely approach was really starting to irritate Anna. Combined with his cluelessness and inability to sense her disappointment, she was uncertain if she'd be able to contain her overwhelming desire to slug him.

Footsteps echoed in the hallway.

A man's shadow crossed the room's threshold.

Strauss.

Childs pivoted toward the German. "Ah, Herr Strauss." He grabbed the German's forearm with both hands. "I also wanted to congratulate you. You're going to be a father."

Moments ago, Anna had been mortified. Now, Childs had just turned a very private crisis into a public shaming, and he seemed to be utterly clueless about what he'd done.

Strauss looked at Anna as if confused. She could imagine him wondering why she chose to be with some other man and not him. She was terrified he'd see her pregnancy as some sort of a betrayal.

Her German companion reacted with silence. His eyes lingered on Anna as if he were searching for an answer or begging her to explain the inexplicable.

But for Anna, this matter was a personal one. She owed no man an explanation, even if it was Strauss. She still was struggling to get over her violation at Sobibór.

Childs broke the awkward silence. "I'm really sorry, but I thought you'd both be a little bit more enthusiastic about this news."

Glaring at Anna, Strauss turned toward Childs. "I'm not the father." Strauss glanced at Anna one last time. Tears formed in his eyes. "I'm sorry, I have to go." He spun on his heels and left.

Anna did nothing. She could do nothing. Paralyzed by a volatile stew of emotions ranging from terror to loss to regret, she didn't have the will to explain what had happened to her to the only man in the world she truly trusted, and perhaps even loved. She really wished she could, but she wasn't ready yet. She didn't know if she'd ever be.

Epilogue
Götterdämmerung

1930 Hours, 18 November 1943, Dark Side, Moon

The species' hibernation cycle would have to end earlier than planned. Soon, the Earth would be in full bloom. The queens woke their children to prepare for the harvesting. And so the cycle of retreat and resurgence would begin anew, as the species deposited its seed on the rich blue world across the cold black chasm of space between the Earth and its moon.

On the dark side of the moon, the hives gathered their drones and warriors in teeming formations. Thousands of black disks hovered behind the moon, waiting for their queens' telepathic signals to swarm.

The Race would end this conflict once and for all so that it could eliminate the only threat to its harvest. While access to the wormhole still seemed limited, the *homosapiens* beyond it were evolving at a rate multiples faster than those on Earth. So much so that they were evolving into a breed apart. Soon, these trans-humans would have the technology to challenge or even destroy the hives' carefully laid plans.

The Race had been roaming vast stellar expanses for millions of years, desperately searching for a suitable host species to provide the raw material for rebirth. And they'd found the humans, a species still in the cradle, but also one with much potential.

Better to crush the eggs in the hatchery than to face the wrath of an adult swarm. The time to strike was now.

℘

2011 Hours, 18 November 1943, Flakturm Tiergarten, Berlin, Germany

Obergefreiter Karl Schneider was enjoying a good book when the air raid sirens sounded. He grabbed his rifle and *Stahlhelm*, jumped to his feet, and raced up the stairs toward the Zoo Tower's roof. Scores of other soldiers scrambled to their stations. Crewing one of four twin mounts of the one-hundred-twenty eight-millimeter FlaK forty guns, Schneider held one of the most important posts in Berlin's air defense system. From there, he protected the government center of Germany's capital from enemy bombers.

He was one of three hundred and fifty anti-aircraft personnel manning the anti-aircraft artillery on the Main G building, not including a number of Hitler Youth auxiliaries who assisted the crews. The reinforced concrete tower with its five-meter thick roof and eight-meter thick walls was nearly impervious to Allied attack.

By the time Schneider was in position, the boys at the L building, which held the critical radar and detection equipment, had already radioed his crew the critical altitude and velocity data on the lead bomber, which had just passed into the zone of preparation. Schneider scrambled to get his gun into position. When the boys at Building L and personnel working at a number of local offices triangulated the lead bomber's position with three searchlights, Schneider prepared to put up a wall of fire on the incoming aircraft.

He prayed to God that he would send every last one of these bastards to Hell. Both the Brits and the Americans had taken the bombing of innocents to new levels in this horrific war. Anyone who deliberately firebombed innocent women and children deserved to suffer a nasty death.

Before his promotion to manning a FlaK gun, he had manned an eighty-eight. Back then he'd despised the cowardly bombers so much, that he'd fired at the downed pilots as they descended to earth in their parachutes.

When Building L sent the signal that the lead bomber had passed into the engagement zone, the FlaK guns opened up, each barrel launching a shell that weighed as much as a teenage boy, at a rate of up to twelve rounds a minute.

Building L was reporting hundreds of incoming Avro Lancaster aircraft. Schneider was thrilled to have the opportunity to shoot down as many of them as possible. Soon, the incendiaries he'd launched into the night sky hit their targets, forcing several pilots to abandon their Lancasters.

Preliminary reports from the ground suggested that the damage wrought by the British bombs had been minimal. The fact that the skies were cloudy had likely been a factor, but he knew his contribution had been decisive. Tonight would be a glorious night for the Reich.

Then he heard radio traffic suggesting that the radar crews spotted new bogeys coming in from the East. Had the Soviets coordinated an air raid with the Brits? No, the aircraft were coming in at speeds that were too fast for the radar crews to get data that made any sense. At max speed, the Lancasters could only fly a shade faster than four hundred fifty kilometers per hour. These craft apparently traveled at over one million kilometers per hour. At that rate a craft could travel the distance between London and Berlin in just over three seconds. No, the readings must have been faulty. Nothing man had constructed could travel that fast.

At first, Schneider didn't believe the data, but the crews on L Building repeated their radar readings. Given his gun's design, by the time his crew entered the altitude and speed of the incoming bogeys, the aircraft would be gone. Still, he followed his orders, preparing for the next wave of bombers. In half a second, a black swarm of disk-shaped craft swept over the city. Then, without warning, they stopped in mid-flight, hovering over Berlin.

Most of the men on the tower were dumbstruck by the disks' presence, but not Schneider. Whatever they were, they came from the East, and therefore likely originated from Soviet Russia. He contacted his spotters at Building L, and asked for the proper coordinates. Training his gun on the strange disks, he put his finger on the trigger and prepared to fire. But the strange craft fired first, raining a swath of destruction throughout Berlin.

He squeezed off a volley of shells, hitting one of the hovering craft's center of mass. When the smoke cleared, the craft was still airborne and firing blue rays of plasma into the city, seemingly unscathed by his shells.

He watched in horror as the shells from other batteries seemed to bounce off the attacking disks that were annihilating Berlin.

Then, another black craft emerged from nowhere and began attacking the other craft, downing two of them in quick succession. The invaders reacted by swarming the maverick craft like iron filling to a lodestone, and blasted it out of the sky. Schneider watched in despair as the solitary craft hurtled from the night sky and landed somewhere in the distance, marked by a thunderous roar and the flash of a mushroom cloud over the horizon.

The encroaching disks then resumed their attack on Berlin until not one building remained standing, and fire raged in the city for the next three days.

₭

2312 Hours, 18 November 1943, Wolfsschanze, near Rastenburg in Eastern Prussia, Germany

The instant Adolf Hitler entered the conference room, the General Staff stood at attention. From their careworn faces and bags under their eyes, Hitler could tell that the men were ill-prepared for a late evening briefing.

Good. Apparently, Hitler wasn't the only person this unscheduled meeting had disturbed from his sleep.

Maps depicting every critical sector on the Eastern Front papered the room's walls. Gray and red icons depicted numerous Wehrmacht and Soviet divisions. And at the moment, there were far more red than gray icons.

Hitler shuffled toward an empty seat between Keitel and Jodl. He waved his right hand and said, "At ease."

As one, everyone in the room took their seats.

Hitler faced Keitel and said with some venom, "Field Marshal Keitel, what's happened that is so important you felt compelled to disturb my sleep?" A creature of habit, Hitler did not appreciate interruptions to his schedule.

Keitel seemed to do his best to remain calm, but Hitler could sense an air of unease about him. The Führer hadn't seen Keitel this shaky since Stalingrad. "Mein Führer, Berlin was bombed this evening."

That was odd. Since when did German military officers speak using the passive voice? From his experience as a corporal in the First World War, even Hitler knew that German officers stressed the use of active voice in all communications. After all, no one would take a hill if the orders weren't explicitly clear as to whose responsibility the mission was. The fact that Keitel, a throwback of Prussian stock, framed the attack without explicitly identifying the perpetrator was a bad omen. If there had been an attack on Berlin, it had likely been a very dire one.

After Keitel spoke, everyone was silent. The officers in the room seemed to be hanging on Hitler's next words. Hitler worried that if he reacted too harshly to the news, he might discourage his people from sharing essential information with him, a common problem for leaders in elevated positions like his. So he attempted levity. "Keitel, I hope you're not still trying to apologize for cancelling my inspection of our newest winter uniforms," Hitler said with a smile.

No one laughed.

Hitler assumed a more serious tone. "All right then, out with it Keitel. Was it the Americans or the British? And what's the damage assessment?"

Keitel glanced at Jodl. Keitel swallowed a lump in his throat and said, "Mein Führer, I'd like to dismiss the rest of the staff aside from myself and Jodl. What we need to tell you is something of the most sensitive nature."

"Fine," Hitler said, "Everyone out!" With one imperious wave of Hitler's hand, the High Command staff scurried out of the room like rats fleeing a fire.

"Go on," Hitler said.

"Well, *Mein* Führer, there's one more person I've invited to this conference. He will be able to provide you with a level of operational and technical detail that I cannot. Do you mind if this individual joins us?" Keitel said.

"No. I do not mind. Send him in," Hitler said.

Keitel nodded and then shouted, "Heydrich! Enter!"

The very archetype of the Aryan superman, Heydrich strode into the room. Hitler's sour mood brightened when he saw one of his favorite officers. His lips even curled into a smile. Hitler was proud to have so perfect and faithful a servant as Heydrich. He also felt grateful to the Progeny for saving this indispensable man's life.

Hitler stood to greet Heydrich. Heydrich clicked his heels together and held out his right hand in the customary Nazi salute. Hitler returned the salute and his eyes welled up after seeing Heydrich for the first time since the man's presumed death.

Hitler quickly rubbed his hands over his eyes, feigning tiredness in a clumsy attempt to hide weakness. He walked over to Heydrich and hugged the man. "My friend, I was so worried I had lost you. But competent men like you don't die. They set things in place long before their mortality is put at risk. And because of your forward thinking in developing the *Lebensborn* program and harnessing the ideas of our leading physicists, you bought yourself and Germany salvation. What would I do without you, my dear friend?"

Heydrich blushed. "*Mein* Führer, I do nothing but my duty. I serve only you and the Fatherland."

Hitler relaxed his embrace of Heydrich and looked over at his two generals. "You see, my friends, this man is a true servant of the German people. I wish we had more men like him under our banner."

Both men nodded with apparent discomfort.

Good, Hitler thought, *Let that notion sink in. Maybe it will drive them to further victory on the Eastern Front.*

Hitler turned back toward Heydrich, "Now, my dear friend, what news do you have for me?"

Heydrich's jaw tightened. "Well, *mein* Führer, the news is not good, so I'll give it to you straight."

"You always do, and I've always appreciated your forthrightness. Tell me what happened."

"The *Schwartzwald* entities have finally come out into the open. They leveled the government section of Berlin in what I believe was an attempt to draw out the disk we and the Progeny captured from them."

"And did they succeed?"

"Unfortunately, yes, *mein* Führer. While the Progeny were able to improve on the alien design, their improvements were only moderately successful. The Progeny downed three *Schwartzwald* craft, but the aliens outnumbered them by over a hundred to one. They never had a chance."

Hitler struggled to rein in his temper. "I see. And what of Berlin?"

"Well, *mein* Führer, the good news is that the *Schwartzwald* entities ended their attack after destroying the captured disk."

"What's the bad news?"

"The government district is a twisted wreck. Preliminary estimates indicate that over one hundred thousand people are either missing or dead."

Hitler lowered his head, forcing himself to modulate his emotions in a way that wouldn't demoralize his leaders. "Did the Soviets take part in the raid?"

Heydrich shook his head. "No, *mein* Führer, but the British apparently did."

"So the British are also working with the entities?"

Heydrich again shook his head. "I don't believe so, *mein* Führer. The attacks didn't seem to be well coordinated or even connected. In fact, our anti-aircraft artillery batteries successfully repelled the British attack. The entities launched their raid several minutes later."

Hitler thought about the political implications. Sure, the Brits had likely failed. But from a propaganda perspective, the reports of widespread destruction would indicate otherwise. If the British were strategically astute, which they certainly sometimes could be, they'd claim victory. This was not good, not good at all.

"What's your recommendation?" Hitler asked.

Heydrich nodded. "*Mein* Führer, I've been thinking about that during my ride here. The good news is that the Progeny have all the schematics they need to manufacture these devices from scratch, though they've advised me that they still don't quite have the metallurgical know-how to replicate the hulls. However, that was yesterday. An entire year has passed for them. They assured me that they expect to make many new technological advances in materials science over the next thirty years. Given how their technological prowess has grown exponentially with each day that passes, I don't doubt their prediction."

"Is that thirty years for us or thirty years for them?"

"It's only a month for us."

"Excellent. Please do go on. What's your recommended course of action?"

Heydrich paused and then said, "I think we need to lift the veil and execute Operation Ragnarök."

"I see," Hitler said. It was a gamble. But at this point in the war and against an enemy that would likely turn on the Soviets if it defeated the Germans, a gamble was all he had. "How soon?"

"Two months, tops. Seven weeks to develop the necessary technological sophistication to produce comparable or superior wonder weapons, and one week to mass produce them and genetically engineer more warriors."

Hitler nodded. He contemplated the decision. He worried that sooner or later the Progeny would reach a level of technological sophistication where they wouldn't need German manpower to defeat the Soviets. If that happened, they might well decide to conquer Earth with or without the help of their so-called ancestors. The only thing Hitler could do now was win the war long before that happened. "Do it."

Heydrich nodded and began to render Hitler the Nazi salute half a second before Hitler stopped him. "One last thing. What's your plan for keeping us in the war for the next two months?" Hitler asked.

"We've been experimenting on a drug formulation called D-IX. The drug is five parts oxycodone, five parts cocaine and three parts Pervitin. Initial tests have been very encouraging. With one tablet, the average human male can march ninety kilometers carrying a twenty-kilogram basic combat load for twenty-four hours without rest. We can mass-produce this Nazi cocktail within the month. We can then supply it to all our forces on the Eastern Front shortly thereafter. That should buy us sufficient time to hold off both the Red Army and the *Schwartzwald* entities until the Progeny can return to our dimension and reinforce our dwindling numbers."

Hitler nodded. "Do it."

৪১

0830 Hours, 19 November 2204 (1943 Concurrent Time), New Berlin, Dark Sun

SS-*Standartenführer* Percival Strauss checked the nanosensors on his advanced laminate armor as he stood before the battalion he would lead into the outer realm. The panels reflected the everlasting gloom of this twilight dimension. His electromagnetic camouflage panels made his arm disappear and then reappear with a single thought.

In the midst of a lichen-encrusted rock garden, his men readied their molecular destabilizers, inspected their equipment, and tested their armor. Hardcore warriors, all, they still betrayed some of the tentative behaviors all soldiers did before going into battle the first time. *Oberscharführer* Fischer cleaned his weapon incessantly. *Hauptsturmführer* Brunner stalked along the parade field, unnecessarily memorizing his own operations order.

The fact that none of these men would ever see their families again given the time differential between the two dimensions likely made many of them even more tense than they probably already were. That his men were nervous didn't bother Percival. In fact, it inspired him. He could use their fear of the unknown to motivate them in combat.

The jagged, slate peaks of the Barbarossa Mountains towered above the massive neoclassical architecture of old New Berlin. The stark monolithic structures were about as subtle as the lash in conveying the primacy of the state over the individual. But in over two and a half centuries, Nazi architecture had evolved past that into doubled-helix structures that twisted toward the murky heavens and shimmered with energy efficient photonic diodes. They stretched toward a black sun that would one day swallow them all.

Percival was looking forward to seeing and actually touching green trees and plants once he reached the other side. Aside from the humans that lived here and the black hydroponic weeds that the scientist caste cultivated below the surface, Percival's realm was lifeless. The proto-humans on the far side of the veil didn't know how good they had it.

After twenty generations, his family had acquitted itself well in the outer realm's forever war. But those contributions were becoming more and more marginalized as the techniques for manufacturing super soldiers became more mechanized and efficient. The latest techniques in neural information transference now made it possible to grow a genetically engineered human adult in a vat and provide him or her with a lifetime worth of memories and experiences in less than seven years.

As time passed, achieving victory became more urgent. With each passing day, humanity lost a little bit more of itself in service to the progenitors. If only they could keep the portal open for more than mere minutes. Without that constraint, this war would have been over a hundred years prior.

In the next phase of the war, Percival worried that the cerebrals wouldn't be able to hold the wormhole open long enough. Those bastards were impossible to communicate with. After two hundred and sixty-one years, the genetic engineering of the scientist caste had nearly bred out its humanity. More mind than man or woman, their brains made up more than seventy percent of their body mass. And each one of them was already as big as a tank. The cerebrals were all connected to one another in a massive network of shared consciousness. Their neurons fired so rapidly that simple voice communication no longer sufficed. And opening one's mind to someone with twice the cranial capacity of an average Dark Sun human and with four times as many neurons, let alone a network of thousands of them, would invite certain death. The stories about what the cerebrals' interrogations had done to proto-humans were horrifying enough.

The leader caste left all the computationally intensive details up to the cerebrals. Manipulating the complexities of n-dimensional manifolds in space-time using topological quantum field theory and plotting nondeterministic waypoints with fractal probability distribution functions were things only a network of cerebrals could accomplish. Yet the details of trans-temporal travel somehow still eluded them at times. Specifically, the scientist caste couldn't figure out a way to keep the vortex open long enough to get a battalion of men through, let alone a division.

Yet Percival's battalion was ready, ready to bring honor to ten generations of warriors. Sometimes he wondered why his people still served these Neanderthals. They should be ruling the savages outside the temporal bubble. The average Dark Sun human was twice as smart, three times as fast, twice as strong, and genetically engineered to perfection in their caste's chosen specialization.

Technically, the people outside were more human than those in Dark Sun. After all, their genes were one hundred percent human. And the Progeny, well, you could barely call them human anymore. Hell, you could barely call them one race. The warrior caste was almost more animal than man, which, depending on the function, had some admixture of bear, wolf, fox, eagle, and various other predatory genetic material. Their sight was more eagle than man; their strength, more bear; their speed, more wolf. In fact, they would probably look so alien to modern humans that if the greater mass of humanity knew of their existence, they wouldn't believe that the Progeny had descended from modern humanity.

Percival was ready for the coming war. Humanity wasn't the problem. The *Schwartzwald* entities had to be stopped. And the Race had to take the fight to them. Now the Race had a fleet of advanced astrocraft, far more advanced than what the *Schwartzwald* entities had brought with them to Earth. He just hoped he could push enough of them through the vortex before it collapsed.

The scientists had been unable to provide him with any certainty about the portal. They could only give him a range of potential outcomes. In one parallel universe, Earth would be sucked into space-time, collapsing in on itself and vanishing forever. In another, the portal would remain permanently open, and they would be able to move forces through at will. In yet another, the portal would be unstable, collapsing before they could get everyone through. In the most likely outcome – the seventy-eight percent outcome – they'd have twelve hours. Twelve hours seemed like a lot of time, but when you're pushing through large forces, it isn't all that much. They planned to send ten advanced disks through first, the finest aircraft that humanity had ever fielded. Each craft had the capability to engage and defeat a hundred or more of the *Schwartzwald* disks.

After the craft went through, they'd push through as many *Fuchs* scouts and *Jäger* divisions as they could before the portal closed. In the end, Percival was more motivated to find his ancestor, Georg Strauss, than anything else. He couldn't understand why the man had turned against the Fatherland. He wondered what could have driven the man to betray his country.

Percival had dozens of other questions he wanted to ask Georg. Fortunately, he would meet the man in the flesh soon enough.

END

About the Author

Sean is a technology and finance professional, and nationally bestselling award-winning author who writes science fiction and horror as well as nonfiction. Over fifty of his short stories in publications such as *The Year's Best Military and Adventure SF*, *Year's Best Hardcore Horror*, *Terraform*, *Galaxy's Edge*, and *Vastarien*, among others. He is the editor of the *Weird World War III*, *Weird World War IV*, and *Weird World War: China* anthologies. He is also the host of the YouTube channel, *Through A Glass Darkly*, where the paranormal meets military science fiction and fact.

Sean was a research associate at the Harvard-Stanford Preventive Defense Project where he worked on energy security issues. He won the 2006 Policy Analysis Exercise Award at the Harvard Kennedy School of Government for his work on policy solutions to Iran's nuclear weapons program. Sean also spent time at Booz Allen Hamilton as an intelligence analyst focusing on strategic war games and simulations for the Pentagon. Before graduate school, Sean was a cavalry officer in the United States Army where he trained American forces for combat operations in Iraq and Afghanistan at the National Training Center.

Sean holds a Master of Business Administration from Harvard Business School, a Master in Public Policy from the Harvard Kennedy School of Government, and bachelor's degrees in History and Electrical Engineering from Stanford.